"Sue Browning," Josh c
 The ghost turned
was gone. The whole half was a skull grinning with missing teeth. Holes pockmarked the facial bones, left by shotgun pellets.

"Can you understand me?" Josh asked.

"What are you doing?" Peanut asked.

The ghost nodded. She moved closer. The movements looked like she skated. Josh took a step back. His heel hit the edge of the pavement, and he stopped.

"Can you talk back to me?"

She stared him head on, one eye completely normal, the other a hollow socket in bone.

"Why have you been coming back more frequently?" he forced the words out of his mouth. "Is it related to Hazel's curse and the Homecoming dance?"

Biggie suddenly quit singing. The song became an old 50's tune Charlotte played on her bad days. The chorus said sha boom or ka boom. It had been a long time since he'd listened to it.

"I ain't got time for this," Peanut said.

He tried to walk off, but the ghost of Sue Browning turned and stared at him. He sat back down and took a long puff off his blunt.

"Charlotte," a voice crackled over the speakers in heavy interference as the singers definitely sang sha boom, sha boom. "Tobias. Baby blue crepe paper. Mercury Monterey. Corey Aaron."

A Macabre Ink Production —Macabre Ink is an imprint of Crossroad Press.

Copyright © 2020 by Vic Kerry
ISBN 978-1-951510-49-7
All rights reserved. No part of this book may be used or reproduced in any manner whatsoever without written permission except in the case of brief quotations embodied in critical articles and reviews
For information address Crossroad Press at 141 Brayden Dr., Hertford, NC 27944
www.crossroadpress.com

First Edition

AS AN OLD MEMORY

by VIC KERRY

Dedication

This book if for all those kids who came of age and lost their innocence in the 1990s, especially a group of fifty-odd adolescents that made up the Oakman High School class of 1997. Also, this is for Aunt Dale, who came of age in the 1950s. Finally, I dedicated this book to the memory of Uncle Al. He never got to read any of my books, but I think he would have liked them.

Acknowledgements

There is a book in this story that is an essential plot point. It's called *Jeffrey Presents Thirteen More Modern Southern Ghosts*, which is written by Kathryn Tucker Windham. There really isn't a book called this, although Mrs. Windham was a very real person who wrote several "real" ghost story books set throughout the South, with two volumes about Alabama ghosts in particular. Anyone of a certain age who grew up in Alabama has read those volumes numerous times and slept with the lights on after every single reading. I never met Mrs. Windham. She had passed away by the time I wrote this book, but there was no way a ghost story set in Alabama with kids that grew up with her books as characters couldn't feature her or her resident ghost Jeffrey. Thank you, Mrs. Windham, for all the chills and thrills you've given me and every other Alabama child since *Thirteen Alabama Ghosts and Jeffrey* was published.

I need to thank some other people. Firstly, thanks to the people at Crossroad Press and all its imprints, especially including the editors and publishers. I'd also like to thank Don D'Auria, who bought this book for Samhain Publishing, even though it got caught up in the shutting down of the publishing house.

Much of the psychiatric information used in this story came from Dr. Syed Aftab. I give him a lot of thanks. Additional psychiatric information came from other staff psychiatrists and long-time nursing staff of the Behavioral Medicine Unit. Some people let me kill them in this story, which was nice of them to do. Here's to Debbie L., Sue P., Sheila C., and Connie I. I thoroughly enjoyed killing some of you (You know who you are *cough* Sheila.)

As always, a big thanks to my wife Lauren, who reads everything first to tell me if it sucks or not. *Merci*, to Laura who beta reads and edits for me. Thanks to my other family members who express interest in my work and encourage me to keep going. Thanks to the readers. I hope you like(d) this one.

Lastly, a huge thank you to all the awesome alternative rock bands from the 1990s. Your songs were the soundtrack of writing this book. Without them, I would have never gotten through this.

Darkly,
Vic Kerry

Prologue

1956
The evening before Homecoming

Charlotte fumbled an armful of crepe paper rolls as she walked into the gymnasium. The dance committee had run out of streamers and sent her to the five-and-ten to get some more. She hoped they wouldn't be angry because the store was out of the school colors. Apparently lots of people had put a run on the place making floats for the parade. The closest that old man Shannon, the five-and-ten owner, had to the school colors were baby blue and gray. They'd work. There wasn't that much left to decorate anyway. If they put those streamers near the back of the basketball court, no one would notice.

The heavy metal door into the lobby was hard to open with her hands full. She negotiated it using her feet and elbows. A few of the rolls of gray paper nearly spilled from her arms. She juggled them and kept everything in place as she made it into the lobby. The door closed hard, leaving the lobby dim. The only light was what streamed in from the diamond-shaped windows in the swinging wooden doors leading to the basketball court. Charlotte hollered for help. One of the guys would help her. Boys always bent over backward to help her. She'd coerced several of the guys to join the dance committee.

No one came. She huffed and headed into the basketball court, blaming the lack of help on the fact that music blasted over the loudspeaker. Tommy Jones had hooked that up for them. He was savvy when it came to hi-fis.

Charlotte gave the swinging doors a push with her hips,

and they swung open. She stared up at the rafters as she turned around, searching for the best place to hang the new off-colored streamers.

"Don't jump all over me, but this is all old man Shannon had. We can hang them in the dark corners," she said, spying those corners. When no one answered her, she shouted to drown out "Sh-Boom" by the Crew Cuts playing on the record player. "Guys?"

When she looked down, all she saw was red. Blood covered every square inch of the polished wooden floor. She had waded into it without realizing it. The baby blue and gray rolls of paper toppled out of her hands and hit the floor. The rolls soaked up the horrible red flood. A overload of sensation overtook her, starting as a tingle at the base of her neck, turning bitter in her mouth, roaring through ears like heavy static and engulfing her vision in a velvet blackness. Charlotte crumpled to the ground. Her hair soaked up blood like the crepe paper as the Crew Cuts song faded out into a hiss of empty vinyl grooves.

Chapter One

1996

Alan McAdams studied the changes that the head coach had made to the football team's playbook over the weekend. He looked up after someone tapped on his office's doorjamb. His son, Joshua, stood framed in the doorway, one strap of his backpack resting on his shoulder. Alan had harped on his son many times to wear both straps or he'd injure his shoulder, but the boy had too much of his old man in him. He'd never listened about those kinds of things, so why would his son? You pay for your raising, as they said.

"What'cha need?" Josh asked.

"Coach called an extra-long emergency practice today," Alan said.

"Emergency practice?"

"I know, but apparently he got a hold of some new film of the team we're playing for Homecoming. Apparently, they aren't as bad as we thought when the school booked them. According to him, they're actually pretty awesome. I'm letting you know because we rode together."

"Correction, you rode with me. Do you want me to pick you up after the practice?"

"No, I want you to leave me your keys. I've got no idea how long this will take, and I don't want to wait for you to answer the phone and drive back here. I'm already hungry."

"Come on; it's my car, and I was going to give Jessica a ride home," Josh whined.

"It may be *your* car, but *I'm* paying for it, so keys." Alan held out his hand.

Josh dug into the pocket of his jeans and pulled out his keys. He tossed them to Alan.

"I guess I'll tell Jessica we're walking."

Alan put the keys in his desk drawer and brought out a white paper sack with a gold pestle and mortar logo on it. The top was folded and stapled closed. He tossed it to his son, who fumbled the catch but secured the prescriptions. Josh should've played football; he would've been a decent receiver.

"Those are for your Aunt Charlotte. Drop them off on your way home."

"It's out of the way," Josh said.

"Only a couple of blocks. The exercise will do you good. It won't be that long until baseball season starts, and you're looking a little out of shape."

His son gave him the most sarcastic look that any teenager had ever given him. Without another word, Josh turned and walked away.

The final bell rang, echoing through the weight room. Alan got up from behind his desk and grabbed his clipboard with the new plays the team would practice. Coach Turnbuckle wanted everyone in the screening room by 3:15. The boys would be coming in from the field. He could already hear the first ones entering. It wouldn't be long until he'd smelled the first one. They were in the middle of an Indian summer, and it was particularly hot and humid today.

The telephone rang as he rounded the corner into the locker area. He stopped and looked over his shoulder. Only three people would call him at that time of day. He'd just talked to Josh, and his wife would be in her car on the way home by now. It had to be his dad. Alan hurried back and grabbed the receiver on the fourth ring. If the fifth had echoed out, he would've been too late. His father always hung up after the fifth ring.

"Hello," he said.

"Son, it's your dad."

"What do you need? I've got to get to practice."

"I think I need to go back to that doctor."

"What doctor, Dad? You've got several of them."

"The one that handles my *problem*."

His dad whispered the last word like someone would hear. For a few months, his dad had been under treatment for Parkinson's disease. Things weren't going the best, and his dad was embarrassed about it.

"He's a specialist. I don't know if you can get an appointment. Plus, I can't miss tomorrow. I'm giving a test in every class."

"You teach health and history. No one is going to care," his dad said. "I need to see that doc."

"Dad, if you're shaking too much, he told you to get more rest. You're probably too tired."

"That ain't it."

"What is it? I don't have time for a game of twenty questions," Alan watched the clock on the wall tick closer to 3:15. Coach Turnbuckle would jump him hard if he walked in a second late. He'd done it before.

"I don't want to talk about this over the phone. Come by when you're done with practice. We can talk then."

"It might be late."

"That's fine, swing by Hardee's and get us something to eat."

"All right. I'll be there when I can get there."

His dad hung up the phone without saying another word. Alan looked at the wall clock. He had enough time to leave a message on his home answering machine to tell Diane he wouldn't be eating supper at home. He hated that too, because it was pork chop night. It would be another week before he'd get them again. His two boys would assure that he wouldn't have any leftovers for lunch tomorrow.

"Come on, Dad." Thomas, his younger son, poked his curly auburn head into the office. "You're going to be late."

Alan got up from his desk and followed his son through the locker room into the cramped film room. The whole team sat there, waiting for the show to start. The smell of the place overwhelmed him. He'd been helping coach the football team for a while now, but that many sweaty boys in one room could be overwhelming. It was bad enough when he had to haul Thomas home after practice when he hadn't showered in the field house.

"When we finish this evening, you'll need to walk home or catch a ride with one of your friends," Alan whispered to his son.

"How come? You kept the car, right?" Thomas whispered back.

"Yeah, but I've to go check on your grandfather after this. I might not get home until late."

"Can I have your pork chop?" Thomas asked.

"I assumed I didn't have a choice in that decision, but thanks for asking."

He turned his attention to the film playing on the television at the front of the room. Their Homecoming opponents looked like a college team. They ran plays Alan didn't think high school students were capable of doing. He imagined the Blue Raiders would get massacred.

"They're going to kill us," Jonathan Smith said to Garret Miller, who sat beside him.

"Good thing we're having a massacre dance instead of a Homecoming dance," Garret said back.

"You two want to stop the chitchat?" Coach Turnbuckle said. "Watch this film without any more commentary, Statler and Waldorf, or you'll be running bleachers until you Gonzo yourself."

The two players turned back to the video. Alan wanted to grab them both and grill them about their comment. The school had shot down the student proposal to have a Homecoming dance themed around the massacre. Apparently, some students were still planning one.

"What do you know about the Homecoming dance?" he whispered to Thomas.

"It's going to be at the old gym," his son answered back.

"Is it going to be themed about the massacre?"

"I don't know." Thomas pushed on Alan. "Be quiet. I'm already going to have to walk home. I don't want have to run bleachers too."

The sack of medicines rattled as Josh walked. He was glad that he wasn't trying to sneak up on someone, because he'd already have given away his position. Jessica walked beside him. She hadn't been upset that they had to walk home, although she did insist this meant he would have to drive her home twice more to make up for it. Josh didn't mind in the least. Since she transferred at the beginning of the school year, all Josh wanted to do was drive her home every day, and maybe a few other things.

They turned the corner of Second Avenue and Cherry Street. His Aunt Charlotte's house was a block away.

"There are a few things I need to tell you about Aunt Charlotte before we get there," Josh said, a little quicker than he'd wanted.

Jessica laughed at his blurted statement. "I think we've got time. You don't have to rush it."

He composed himself. One of the things he worried about was people meeting his aunt and his grandfather. Fortunately, he and Jessica could cross the grandfather bridge at another time.

"My aunt is... different," Josh didn't want to call her crazy, but that would be the most appropriate word.

"Everyone's a little different."

"No, I mean very different. These medicines are for mental stuff."

"You mean she's crazy," Jessica said.

"We usually don't call her that, but, yeah."

"What do you mean? Does she hear voices, or does she go over the edge like Bette Davis in *What Ever Happened to Baby Jane?*"

"She doesn't hear things, and I have no idea who Bette Davis is. I can't describe her. You'll have to see."

Jessica gave him a strange look as they crossed Third Avenue. "You don't know who Bette Davis is? We'll have to change that. I've got her movies on tape. You'll love it."

"Are they in black and white?" Josh asked as they stopped in front of a small white house with a green and yellow striped metal awning over a screened in porch.

"Some of them, but they're creepy, at least the ones I've watched."

"Good." Josh hated creepy movies, but if Jessica liked creepy stuff, she was about to see it in person.

He walked up the sidewalk and rang the bell beside the screen door. The hook and eye loop latch was in place. His Aunt Charlotte always kept the doors locked even though Pinehurst had very little crime, and she terrified almost everyone.

The door to the house opened, and Charlotte bounced out onto the porch. A smile beamed on her face when she recognized Josh. He held up the bag of medications. She hurried across the porch and opened the screen door.

"Come on in," she said.

"I can't. We've got to keep going. Dad asked me to drop off your meds. He got caught at work," Josh said.

"Homecoming is coming up," Charlotte took the sack of medicines. "Are they having a dance?"

Josh swallowed hard to avoid answering the question. His aunt seemed to be having a lucid day today, but she was still dressed in bobby socks and an outfit that would fit right in on *Happy Days*. She waited with quiet anticipation.

"I think they are," he said, "but I'm not going."

Charlotte looked past him to Jessica. "You telling me you're going to let that girl go by herself. What kind of gentleman would that make you?"

"Aunt Charlotte, that's Jessica. She moved here at the beginning of school. We're friends."

"How are you, sweetie?" Charlotte waved at her.

"I'm okay. How are you?"

"I'm feeling pretty good. Been thinking about heading down to old man Shannon's store before he closes for the day."

"Okay," Jessica said with a sweet tone.

"Aunt Charlotte, that store closed before I was born," Josh corrected. His dad told him to always orient his aunt to reality if she slipped into the past. "Remember, it's 1996, not 1956. You are still in Pinehurst, Alabama, but you aren't in high school anymore."

"Don't treat me like a fool, Joshua McAdams. I meant the dollar store. Old Man Shannon used to own one. Old habits die hard."

"Just making sure," Josh fidgeted. "We need to go."

Charlotte gave him a passing look before waving and letting the screen door slam shut. She hooked the lock. Josh turned and headed down the sidewalk. He pulled on Jessica's arm as he passed.

They headed for her house a few streets over. He kept waiting for the questions to start, but they walked in silence until arriving at her house, painted bright red with pink shutters.

"So, what was up with your aunt?" she finally asked.

"What's up with your red house and pink shutters?" Josh came back.

Jessica looked at her house. "We've not had time to change that."

"Aunt Charlotte hasn't had time to change either."

"That doesn't make sense. I wasn't being mean. Something very serious had to happen for her to dress like that. I'm not going to make fun of her, and I wasn't doing that when I asked the question."

"You know how some of the kids at school wanted to have a massacre-themed Homecoming dance?"

"Yeah."

"Do you know why they wanted to have that?"

"We're going to massacre the other team," Jessica made a motion with her arms like a cheerleader.

"No, that's not it at all."

"I really thought it was because Halloween was coming up. I think a costume ball would have been a better idea, but the principal and teachers shot down that massacre idea anyway."

"It had nothing to do with Halloween either, and the teachers shot down the idea because of the real reason for that theme. Forty years ago, a bunch of students at our school were murdered while decorating for Homecoming. Aunt Charlotte was the one who found them." Josh paused to make sure he wasn't overwhelming Jessica. "Ever since then, she's come back and forth between now and 1956. Sometimes she gets in both times, remembering people from the present but thinking it's 1956 and vice versa. They used to say she was schizophrenic. Now they call it PTSD."

"That's horrible. Did they ever catch who did it?"

"Aunt Charlotte was a suspect, but she couldn't have done it. The brutal nature of the whole thing took the spotlights off of her."

"They never caught the murderer?"

"A black guy, the only one in the whole school, was lynched for it. He never even went to trial."

"That's even worse."

"It *was* 1956. The school wasn't even desegregated yet. He got to go there because the closest all-black school was fifty miles away. His parents were domestics for the richest man in town. Most people think that he didn't do it, but there's no way to prove differently."

"I'm sorry about all that." Jessica touched him on the shoulder. A shock of electricity went through him.

"Well, it's nothing. I've been around the legend my whole life. You get used to it."

"Still, it's a sad story. I'll see you tomorrow."

Jessica walked up the sidewalk and into her house. Joshua turned and started his walk home. The sun began to disappear behind the trees, and he wouldn't make it before the streetlamps flickered on. His backpack weighed heavier. He put the other strap on his shoulder and walked at a brisk pace, deciding to go a little out of his way to avoid Aunt Charlotte's house.

Alan walked into the kitchen of his childhood home. Everything looked as it did the day he moved out to go to college. Even the table and chairs were the same ones he grew up eating at. Only the refrigerator was new, and that was because the old one had finally passed the point of repair. He sat a pizza box on the table and listened for his father. The toilet flushed on the other side of the house. The sound of heavy footsteps came down the hallway.

"Is that you, Alan?" his father asked.

"I'm in the kitchen."

Simeon "Sim" McAdams walked into the kitchen. He stood slightly hunched over but remained formidable, like a retired bareknuckle boxer. His hands were thick and meaty. His age-spotted arms looked like tree trunks. The skin on his face showed the ravages of years of working in the elements and of hitting the bottle way too hard. He looked at the table.

"Pizza? You brought that for supper? I said Hardee's."

"I didn't want a hamburger," Alan said. "Besides, you love pizza. The other day you told the boys that you'd eat it every day if you could afford it."

"I said no such of a thing. I ain't got time for I-ty food. You ought to throw it out."

Alan shook his head and grabbed two plates from the cabinet. He was glad he had come to check on his dad. Apparently, the old man was having a bad day like he'd said. Before Sim could say another word about the meal selection, Alan put two slices on a plate and passed it to him.

"Smells pretty good," Sim said. "Is it a supreme with extra I-talian sausage?"

"Like you like it, Dad." Alan got a couple of slices for himself.

Before sitting down, Sim went to the fridge and pulled out a can of Pabst Blue Ribbon. He held it out to Alan to ask if he wanted one too.

"Do you have a Coke?" Alan asked.

"RC be okay?"

"Fine."

Sim reached in and brought out a can of RC in the same hand that held his can of beer. He passed the soda off to Alan and sat down across from him. They cracked open their cans at the same time. The sound made Alan smile, even though he was concerned about his father's choice in beverage.

"Dr. Sharp said no drinking."

"That's not what he said," Sim sank a gulp. "He told me to cut back. I only drink two beers a day, one at lunch and one at supper."

"I'm pretty sure he said none at all. The alcohol interferes with your medications."

"If I don't drink at least one a day, I get the shakes." Sim bit off a large hunk from his slice of pizza. "Besides, that dope he gives me doesn't work."

"Maybe it's because you're not following his instructions."

"Maybe it's because he's an idiot," Sim sounded unreasonably agitated.

"What's been going on today? Why did you call me and tell me you needed to go back to the doctor, who in your opinion is a quack?"

Sim bit off some more pizza and swallowed it down with another gulp of PBR. "It's getting worse."

"What's getting worse, the shaking? You have Parkinson's. It would eventually happen. That's the nature of the disease."

"Nah, it ain't the tremors unless I ain't drank nothing. It's the other thing."

"Your memory? Quit beating around the bush and tell me. I've not got all night."

"Don't sass me, boy. You ain't so big that I can't still tan your hide."

"Daddy, I've got to work tomorrow. I've missed my favorite supper of the week with my family to sit here and eat greasy pizza with you. I'm not being sassy. Tell me."

"I'm seeing things." Sim looked embarrassed, as if other people could hear him.

"What kinds of things, like dots or shadows?"

The older man shook his head. "Faces, or a face. I see it when I look in a mirror. It's over my shoulder, fuzzy like. I can't make out who it is."

"Dr. Sharp said that sometimes Parkinson's patients see things, especially faces."

"It's been getting closer and clearer." Sim's hands visibly shook. He took a long drink from his can of beer. "At first it was a tiny spot of a thing, I thought it was a smudge on the mirror or a fingerprint on my glasses. It got larger and larger until I recognized it as a face."

"Are you hearing voices? Does it talk to you?" Alan leaned in for what the administrators at school called *active listening*.

"I ain't that gone. It does seem to be getting a body though. I don't know if it's the Parkinson's disease I supposedly have, or if I'm going crazy."

Alan cleared his throat. His father's disbelief in his diagnosis irritated him. They both had looked at all the test results in Dr. Sharp's office. He understood that Sim had a touch of dementia along with Parkinson's. Dr. Sharp said it came from the years of hard drinking.

"Call tomorrow and get an appointment as a soon as you can. In the meantime, make sure you're taking your medications like you're supposed to, and cut down to one beer a day."

Sim looked defeated. "All right."

"I'm going to go, Daddy. Put the extra pizza in some foil. It'll be a good lunch for you tomorrow." Alan stood to go.

"How's Charlotte? I read about those stupid kids over at the school trying to have a massacre anniversary dance or some hog shit like that. I figured if she heard, it might send her off the tracks again."

"I was supposed to take her meds to her today, but I sent Josh instead. He'll tell me tonight, and I'll let you know."

Alan walked out the back door. He looked over his shoulder before stepping off the small porch. His father sat eating a third slice of pizza, finishing off his can of beer and Alan's can of RC.

Josh's car sat lower to the ground than Alan liked. He felt like he rode inches from the street's surface. The boys liked it, and the price was right. The front scraped on the pavement as he pulled out of the driveway. If Josh or Thomas, who had his permit, were in the car with him, a lecture would follow. They forgot that he paid the note on the thing and would have to pay for any damage that happened.

Alan loved the car's power. Twenty-second Street was a long, straight stretch of road, and it was empty. Alan flipped on the high beams and floored the accelerator. The tires squealed, and the smell of rubber filled the air. He never got a lecture from his sons about laying down tracks, because he never did it with his sons in the car. The last thing they needed was for him to give them that bad example.

The car shot down the street. The speed excited Alan like nothing else could. He needed a thrill tonight. He worried about his dad. Although the old man was cantankerous and had been for most of Alan's life, he was still his father, and Alan cared about him.

The houses along the street blurred. The lights from the windows streaked out into lines, or that's how Alan imagined it. Driving that car was like traveling faster than the speed of light. The car started down the sloped street. The old gym was on the left. He glanced over at it like he always did, not knowing what he expected to see but still anticipating something. Tonight, he got his wish.

Lights glowed in the high windows. Alan hit the brakes, and the tires squealed again. That would have definitely gotten him a lecture from his sons. As soon as the car came to halt, he looked back over his shoulder. Sure enough the lights were on. When he'd passed by on the way to his dad's place, it looked as dark and brooding as it always did, like some kind of monster staring down on the town.

"I hope those kids haven't broken in to decorate for that stupid dance," he said aloud while making a U-turn.

Alan drove up the maintained driveway to the gym. He parked in front of the main doors. The headlights illuminated the chain and padlock that secured the doors. He got out to check the two side doors. The grassy area on the side of the building closest to the road was freshly mown. Not a single weed or goldenrod sprang from the ground. For the life of him, Alan could not figure why the school system and city kept up the place. They didn't use it for anything, but the maintenance was better than what was provided for the "new" gym that the school used.

The side door was locked. He shook it twice, hard, to make sure. A glance up found the lights still glowing in the windows. He walked around the building to the door hidden from the street. If students had broken into the place, it would have been there.

That door was sealed tight as well. Now, when he looked up at the high rectangular windows, only the moon reflected in them. Something cold shivered up his spine, raising goose bumps on his skin. Alan listened for any sound of commotion. If the kids had broken in, they might have heard him snooping around. Nothing stirred except a slight wind that rustled a few dead leaves on the sweet gum trees behind him.

Something about the rustling gave him the creeps more than the place itself. It almost sounded like whispers of words he couldn't comprehend. Alan sprinted back to the front of the gym, just like he had when he was ten years old, and almost dove into the car. Without putting on his seat belt or looking behind him, he turned the car around and hauled it back to the street.

He switched on the radio to help calm his nerves. Even if the dial was on the alternative station that Josh and Thomas liked to listen to, Pearl Jam or Bush would be better than his own thoughts with the sound of those rustling leaves that still lingered in his memory. The expectation of "Jeremy" or "Machinehead" slipped away. Alan had picked up the names of those songs through the osmosis of living and working with the teenagers, but it didn't matter—because one he had definitely known for years played from the radio. The Crew Cuts singing "Sh-Boom" blared from the speakers.

He took long enough to look at the radio setting before punching the closest preset button. The boys had put it on the oldies station for some reason.

"This is 105.9, The X. The best station to hear all the alternative hits in the Birmingham area. Here's a great one," said a DJ with a pronounced lisp.

A song started playing that Alan definitely recognized. Josh listened to it all the time because he and most of his friends were born that year. He smiled, because he knew the band name, the Smashing Pumpkins, and the song: "1979". If the boys had been in the car, he'd have gotten a lecture on how lame he was for pointing out his knowledge of *their* music. Even though the tune was melancholy, it helped settle Alan's nerves and definitely cleansed his palate from the Crew Cuts, the rustling leaves, and the lights in the gym window.

Chapter Two

1956
Night of the massacre

Sim sat in an uncomfortable straight-back chair in the sheriff's office. Bud Johnson, dressed in his street clothes, chomped on his cigar and drank a cup of coffee. Sim watched the sheriff probe him with his eyes. A good fifteen minutes passed without a word being spoken while they waited for a transcriptionist to arrive. No one had even offered him a drink. The sheriff's coffee smelled disgusting and looked like old motor oil, but anything would help his dry mouth. All the excitement of the evening had left him parched.

"Could I get something to drink? My mouth is very dry," Sim asked.

Sheriff Johnson rolled the cigar from one side of his mouth to the other. "Spence," he yelled into the larger common area of the department. "Get this fellow something to drink."

Jimmy Spence, the night deputy, who everyone made fun of because of his game leg, stood up. "All the coffee's gone, and the water coming out of the tap is still brown."

"We've got a drink box, don't we?" Sheriff Johnson asked with a strong tinge of sarcasm in his voice.

"Yeah," Spence answered.

"Spend a nickel and get this man a Coca-Cola."

Sim watch Spence fumble in his pocket and disappear into a different part of the building. A few minutes later he limped back, carrying a dripping bottle of Coca-Cola. The cap was already removed. He gave it to Sim. The sweet, syrupy soda burned a little as it went down, not like whisky, but it had good carbonation. Pinehurst's bottling plant had some of the best Coca-Cola around. Sim had gone up to Jasper trying to get a job as a grease monkey after getting out of the Coast Guard before he got married. He'd drunk a dope up there, and it was nothing compared to his hometown's Coke.

The sheriff drummed his fingers on his desk and rolled his cigar to the opposite side of his mouth again. "About time you got here," he said as Mrs. Timmons from the probate office walked in. She looked less prim than she normally did. Sim supposed it was because she'd been called in well after normal business hours. She wore pants, which were unusual to see a woman like her wearing.

The sheriff stood and let her sit behind his green metal desk. He sat in another guest chair that he pulled up next to her. "Miss Timmons," he said, removing the cigar so that his words weren't slurred, "take down everything this gentleman says very carefully."

"I will." She brought out a top spiral notebook and pen from her large purse. "What exactly are we going to be doing? You were very vague on the telephone."

"Miss Timmons, there's been some killings. Sim McAdams here found the bodies. We need to get his statement down. This has to be very official."

She looked at Sim and at the sheriff. Her darting eyes made Sim a little uncomfortable. "Did he do it?"

"I doubt it. Very few mass killers drive like a demon out of hell to tell the sheriff about what they did," Sheriff Johnson said.

"Why aren't you dealing with the investigation?" she asked.

"I have my best men working up at the gymnasium. The city police are there too, along with half a dozen or so ambulances to take those bodies down to the hospital."

"A half dozen or *so*?" Mrs. Timmons became pale.

"Are you going to be able to do this or not?" the sheriff asked. "The last thing I need is you passing out when he starts telling his tale."

"Maybe something cool to drink would help," she said.

"Spence," the sheriff yelled. "Get Miss Timmons a drink out of the box."

"Water will do," she said out the door to the deputy.

"It's coming out of the tap brown," Spence replied.

"I don't like the sound of that. A Grapico will do if you have it. I don't like dark drinks."

Sheriff Johnson turned to Sim. The time had come for him to tell what he knew. Sim sank another burning slug from his bottle of Coke and put it on the desk. He drew a deep breath.

"I had gone to the gym to check on how things were going up there," Sim started. "A bunch of the seniors were decorating for the Homecoming dance. My sister, Charlotte, was one. One of the teachers—my fiancée, Connie Dearborn—was helping too.

"So, I get there and walk into the lobby, but there's not any noise coming from the basketball court. The only sound was a needle of a record player riding the end grooves. Charlotte's car was parked out front, as were a couple of pickups. I recognized Jerry Madison's."

"Couldn't miss that thing. It's fire-engine red and as loud," the sheriff broke in. "No telling how many times I had to pull that speed demon over."

"She's a fast truck. I told Charlotte that she better not ride with him. I always told her that he'd flip that thing over and kill himself one day," Sim stopped and got very quiet. He shouldn't have said it. He had found Jerry murdered with the rest of them.

"Go on," Sheriff Johnson said. "Tell us the rest."

"I walked into the basketball court and that's when I found them. All sprawled out, covered in blood. I could tell they were all dead, except for Charlotte."

"How could you tell?" the sheriff asked.

"They'd all been shot up and a few of them looked like they'd been hacked on with a knife." Sim shook his head and grabbed his Coke for another swig to calm himself down. "It was horrible. I walked through the gore on the floor to my sister. She was breathing. Her chest rose and fell. I figure she got there after it happened and passed out when she found them. When I tried to rouse her, all she'd babble about was the color of the crepe paper and Tobias Abernathy, that Negro boy that was going to the high school."

"When she gets a little bit better, we're going to talk to her," the sheriff said. "Right now, they've taken her on to the hospital. Don't worry, they'll get her better."

Sim nodded. "I hope so. She didn't need to see any of that. It was hard enough for a grown man to stomach, much less a girl. "

"Tell me who all you found there," the sheriff asked, "and how you found them."

"Besides Charlotte, the first person I saw was Connie slumped over a step ladder. The whole of her back was torn up. It looked almost like ground beef. I couldn't see her face, but she'd lost enough blood that her hands were already gray."

Mrs. Timmons whimpered. Sim looked at her. The blood drained from her face.

"Spence," Sheriff Johnson yelled. "Where's that drink?"

Spence rushed in with a bottle of orange soda. "I was trying to find a Grapico, but we must be out. Only fruit drink we had was an Orange Crush. Is that okay, Miss Timmons?"

"Anything's fine," she grabbed the bottle and drank about half of the soda before sitting the bottle down and picking back up her notebook. "I think I can go on now."

"Once I made sure Charlotte was okay, I moved her into the lobby, so she wouldn't have to stay in that horrible place. I turned my attention to who else was there. Sue Browning lay face up on the floor in a big pool of blood. Next to her was Jerry. He'd been cut on. Looked like his throat had been slashed after he was shot. Sheila DeLeon dangled from a ladder. Ben Harris lay at the bottom of that ladder. He'd been cut too. Tommy Jones was in the back of the room. I didn't go over there close enough to see what happened to him. I thought that was everyone there and started back to the lobby to get Charlotte and load her up in my truck to haul her down here. That's when I found Debbie Eva. I won't describe her. Not in mixed company."

Sim stopped and finished off his bottle of Coke. He almost asked Mrs. Timmons for her soda, but she'd finished hers when he stopped the story.

"Anything else?" the sheriff asked.

"Not that I can remember. Am I going to be arrested?" Sim asked.

"Did you do it?" Sheriff Johnson asked.

"Of course not. What kind of idiotic question is that? Connie was my fiancée."

"That being the case, we won't be arresting you today." The sheriff gnawed down on his stogie. "Why don't you go home and get cleaned up. Head over to the hospital to check on your sister after that."

Sim nodded and stood to leave. "What about Connie's folks?"

"My chief deputy is responsible for contacting families. Whatever you want to do with her folks is up to you beyond that."

"Charlotte seemed awfully focused on that colored boy," Sim said. "Kept repeating his name and 'no.' Oh yeah, I seen him tearing up the road away from the gym right before I got there."

"I'll put up roadblocks, and we'll have a talk with him," the sheriff said. "Get on home now before you decide to do something stupid."

Sim left the sheriff's department. He wanted to go home and clean up. Dried blood streaked his hands, and it painted his face as well. The smell of it filled his nostrils.

Everything would have to be done in a hurry. Tobias Abernathy wouldn't make it back to the Harrington Plantation that night. He and the boys had business to attend to.

Chapter Three

1996

Josh looked up from his homework when his dad walked into the house. Thomas did the same from across the room, but he turned back to his math without much more attention paid. Josh wasn't as easily distracted, mainly because he hated trigonometry and barely understood it.

His dad looked different. Something about the loose expression on his face made Josh feel uncomfortable. Rarely did Alan McAdams walk around with a slack jaw and eyes that seemed to focus on nothing in particular.

"Is everything okay?" Josh asked.

"I Iuh? Yeah." His dad said.

"That didn't sound convincing at all." Thomas put down his textbook. "Are you sure?"

Alan look at Josh and then at Thomas. His expression stayed the same. "Your grandfather's fine."

"Did something happen to the car?" Josh almost jumped to his feet to look out the window.

"No, no, the car's fine. I'm fine. Your grandpa's seeing things." Alan sounded much clearer.

"You said he was fine," Thomas said. "Seeing things doesn't sound fine to me."

"It sounds schizophrenic." The words shot out of Josh's mouth before he could stop them.

He never liked his grandfather. As he grew up, he tried to hide that fact to keep from hurting his father's feelings. Sometimes he got the impression that his dad didn't like his grandfather very much either. Although they'd never explicitly talked about it, Josh was sure Thomas didn't like him. That didn't mean he wanted a member of his family to lose his mind. It was bad enough that they all had to deal with Aunt Charlotte. No matter how the thought weighed his mind down with guilt, it was the truth.

On the other hand, he was relieved that it was his grandfather that troubled his father, not any damage to his car. Josh knew how his dad drove the car. One day it would end up smashed while Alan was driving it. To Josh, his car was the most important thing in his life. Without it, he'd have to ride to school with his dad. Worse would be borrowing the family car to have any kind of social life. That would place him squarely in the realm of the nerds, a wasteland of Chewbacca t-shirts and "Live long and prosper" salutes.

"I thought you came in." Josh's mother, Diane, walked in and kissed Alan on the cheek. "What's the matter with you? Is your dad worse?"

Alan tried to change his expression. For the most part it worked fairly well, but that strange, distant look still clung around the corners of his eyes.

"He said that he's seeing faces again, but I think he's exaggerating a bit. The doctor told us that seeing faces was common in Parkinson's disease. His story sounds more like he's trying to get us to pay more attention to him."

"Maybe we should," Diane said. "He is your father."

Alan walked around the sofa and sat down. Josh's mother followed him and took his hand. His dad looked at Thomas and at him. The look of distance changed to embarrassment.

"I hate to say this in front of you boys, but I spend enough time with him. He wasn't a good father, and he's always had a horrible attitude."

"Especially toward black people," Thomas said from behind his book.

"And Mexicans, Italians, Jews, the Japanese," Josh continued.

"And women," Alan added.

"All of you stop. He's your dad and grandfather," Diane said. "You can't talk about him like that."

Thomas peeked slyly over the top of his math textbook. "Come on, Mom. Josh and I heard what you called him under your breath when we told you Dad wasn't going to be home for dinner."

"I didn't say anything."

"I didn't hear *bastard*," Thomas said. "What about you, Josh?"

"I thought you said *mustard*."

Alan snapped his fingers. "Both of you, stop. He's a bad person, but he is still your grandfather, warts and all. Thomas, I better not hear you say anything like that again."

"I was quoting," Thomas protested.

"Paraphrasing is more like it," Diane said.

"You do it again, and you'll be grounded for a week," Alan said.

"Mustard," Thomas said, sticking his nose back into his book.

"If Sim isn't why you're so worried, what is it?" Diane asked.

"Boys, put your books down," Alan said.

Josh and Thomas did so. It was strange for his dad to make that request. Usually he demanded that they pick up their books more often, but he wouldn't make a joke about it. A strange seriousness radiated from his father tonight.

"What is it?" Josh asked.

"Are kids at school planning a massacre anniversary dance?" Alan asked.

"I think some of them have talked about it, but I don't know if they are or not."

"They definitely are," Thomas said. "Martin and Drew have been talking about it for days during practice and after. Apparently, a bunch of the seniors are getting psyched about it."

"How do you know all that when I'm the senior?"

"Because I'm a football player, and you're a nerd."

"I play baseball."

"Ooo, baseball. I hit a ball with a stick and maybe get to run around a field."

"Were they planning to have it at the old gym?" Alan asked.

"I don't know," Thomas said.

"I've not heard anyone say where they planned to do it," Josh said.

"That's horrible," Diane said. "Why would they be so insensitive to have such a ghoulish thing, especially where it happened?"

"Why does the city maintain the place just to keep it locked up? This whole town has a morbid obsession with that place, with that event." Alan paused. "I saw lights in the old gym when I was coming home. When I investigated, thinking it was probably some of those air-for-brains kids messing around, the doors were locked, and the light blinked out."

"Creepy," Thomas said.

A cold chill ran up Josh's spine and froze his mouth before he could agree with his brother. Aunt Charlotte seemed to be slipping back to her adolescence more than usual, and his dad saw lights at the old gym. The fortieth anniversary of the massacre drew closer.

Their mother patted Alan on the shoulder. "I think that your mind was playing tricks on you. The stuff with your dad, the big Homecoming game, and Charlotte are weighing on your nerves. Those lights were the reflection of headlights in the glass. It happens all the time when I'm driving past places at night."

Alan rubbed his face. "Perhaps. Maybe I should think about taking a personal day pretty soon. It's too early in the school year for me to be this stressed."

"Try having trig with Mrs. Shaddix. I can't understand a word the woman says." Josh attempted to change the subject not only for his dad's benefit but his own. The creeps had hold of him.

"Is the class that tough?" Diane asked.

"Math is hard enough for me," Josh said, "but have you ever talked to her? She has a horrible speech impediment. I thought she was Chinese the first time I heard her speak without seeing her."

"That's horrible," his mother said.

"It's true, though," Alan and Thomas said at the same time.

Josh stood up. "I think I'm going to go for a walk."

"This late?" his mother asked.
"I'm feeling antsy. I won't go far." He looked at his brother. "You want to go?"

Thomas shook his head. Josh didn't waste any more time. He squeezed between his chair and the couch and headed out the door.

The cool October air refreshed him. The smell of autumn filled his nostrils, something he hadn't noticed earlier when he was walking home. Too many other things distracted him. Smoke from a smoldering leaf fire somewhere drifted through the neighborhood. Each window in the houses on the cul-de-sac glowed. He walked from his house at the top of the street down toward the last house. He'd loop and walk back home.

His dad's attitude freaked him out. Never had he seen him so upset by something. Normally Josh would have shaken it off and gone about his business, but with the anniversary of the massacre coming up and his fellow students planning such a stupid dance, he felt like someone from the beyond might have taken notice. According to every scary movie he'd ever seen, that wasn't a good thing.

A dog barked in the distance as Josh rounded the end of the cul-de-sac. Its hollow, lonely sound floated on the long autumn night. Another joined in, until a small choir of howling and barking echoed through the trees. It was like in an old Western movie when the coyotes started to howl after the wagon train stopped for the night. The music of it pumped through Josh. It made him want to run with the wild animals. He started to jog up the street.

Without noticing, he'd sprinted out of his neighborhood and headed toward his grandfather's house. Something deep and unconscious kept pushing him forward even after his side split from a stitch of running at full speed for way too long. His chilled breath filled his lungs and pushed through his nostrils scalding hot. He lathered like a racehorse. Everything accelerated faster in his body until he felt himself ripping apart at the seams. Blood roared in his ears. His heart thumped in his chest like Animal beating the drums in the Electric Mayhem. His insides quivered to the point that he felt they would explode.

Then, in the distance, something did.

Josh fell onto his back. The pavement slammed the air out of his lungs. He attempted to gasp, but nothing would come. The echo of the explosion reverberated through him and down the street. It surrounded him. It engulfed him, drowned him. He wasn't certain he hadn't been the thing that exploded. Once his breath returned, his sense of awareness did as well. None of his vital parts lay sprayed across the pavement. He stood, twinging a bit from the hard spill on the sidewalk. The sky looked normal. The expectation of some fireball floating up into the sky faded.

He looked around. Everything was the same. Nothing seemed affected by the explosion. The houses stood on their foundations. The lights still glowed in their windows. No one stood on porches or stoops to see what the commotion had been. The only thing different was that no dogs barked. Josh wasn't even sure how long they had actually barked after the compulsion to run overtook him.

He took another moment to get his bearings. As he'd somehow suspected, he stood at the bottom of the hill the old gymnasium stood on. It loomed in the darkness, looking like it might have in 1956 on the night his aunt and grandfather had found the massacre victims. No lights illuminated the high windows like what his father had seen. Nothing lit the place, not even the moon. Josh wanted the fact that it looked like it always did to give him some sort of comfort, but it didn't. Instead, the place seemed to watch him through its high narrow windows.

He wasted no time. Despite his aching feet and burning legs, Josh started running home. He hoped that the faster he could get away from that place, the better he would feel.

As he got farther and farther from the gym, his pace slowed to a jog, then a trot, a walk, and an amble with a limp. He held his side. Maybe his dad had been right about his needing to shape up. He definitely didn't have to run as much as he did during baseball season, and right now, he wished that wasn't the case.

An hour passed while Josh limped home. The stitch never went away, although he caught his breath halfway there.

The dishwasher ran in the kitchen, making the only noise in the dark house. The time on the VCR flashed 9:30 as he passed through the living room to head up to his bedroom. He couldn't imagine that he had been gone so long, and that his folks had gone to bed without giving him some kind of lecture. They had to be concerned for his safety after the explosion.

The nightlight shoved into a plug halfway up the staircase lit the way to his room. When Josh stepped on the landing, a floorboard beneath the carpet creaked as always. He and Thomas called it the *sneak-in alarm*. One of his parents would be flying out of their bedroom and up the stairs, red-faced and in the midst of giving him a lecture. He walked the few steps to his bedroom without a single parental unit popping up. Great effort was taken to close the door quietly behind him. He didn't think he'd done anything wrong, but he didn't want to tempt fate.

"Where have you been?"

Josh almost screamed but caught it before it slipped out. The strain made his throat feel raw. It took him a moment to answer.

"What are you doing in here, Thomas?" he asked.

"Waiting for you. Do you know it's a school night?"

"Thanks for the reminder, Dad," Josh said back. "I'm glad you're all so concerned about my safety that no one came to check on me."

"Why would we? I told the 'rents you came back ages ago. I figured you'd slipped off to meet Jessica and finally taken the cellophane off your pecker and made a move."

"I was taking a walk around the block."

"Long walk."

"Something took hold of me, like a primal feeling. I started running and ended up at the old gym when the explosion happened."

Thomas turned on the lamp beside Josh's bed. The light showed the curious expression on his face. "What explosion?"

Josh rolled his eyes. He couldn't help it. "Don't give me that. The shock wave knocked the air out of me. It had to shake the windows if nothing else."

"I promise I didn't hear an explosion. I thought you'd snuck off," Thomas said.

"Did you hear all those dogs howling?"

His brother shook his head. "I think you might need to go the doctor with Grandpa Sim. You may have caught his Parkinson's."

"Get out of my room," Josh opened the door. "You can't catch Parkinson's, and I'm not crazy. It happened. You'll see. Folks at school will be talking about it tomorrow."

Thomas walked out of the room with a shrug of his shoulders. The nonchalant, sarcastic gesture made Josh angry, and he punched his brother as hard as he could in the shoulder. Thomas flinched and let out a yelp. Before he could throw a punch, Josh shoved him out the door and locked it behind him.

"That's okay, I'll get you tomorrow, Grandpa Sim," Thomas said through the door.

Josh had it coming tomorrow. His brother might be two years younger than him, but he was twenty pounds of muscle heavier and a good three inches taller. The punch he packed could make a rhino cross-eyed. It was still worth it, though. He took off his clothes and pulled on a pair of faded red basketball shorts with the number twenty-three flaking off the leg and crawled into bed. He left the lamp on.

Sim sat at his kitchen table with the phone book opened and the portable phone beside it. He'd been looking up the number for Dr. Sharp. Before he could dial up the doc, the phone rang. It had been Johnny House. They hadn't spoken in ten years. The sound of his old friend's voice had taken him a minute to recognize. Even though he'd wanted a pleasant conversation about the old days, Johnny had broken some unpleasant news. Marshall Williams had killed himself the night before.

The news had streaked through him like a lightning bolt. It had been even longer since he'd talked to Marshall, but they'd been good friends for most of their early life. Sim never figured he'd be one of those old men prone to suicide.

Johnny hadn't known the details, except that Marshall's son had found him at breakfast time. He was a bit happy he didn't know how his old friend had done it. It might give him ideas. After his diagnosis of Parkinson's, Sim had decided he would end it all when the time was right. There was no reason to lose your mind and act like a child. Plus, he had far too many skeletons locked up in his closet to let out once he went batty.

The phone at Dr. Sharp's office rang twice before the colored receptionist answered. Her thick molasses accent gave her away. Sim almost asked for the white nurse but didn't. The receptionist worked him into a 10:00 a.m. appointment. He'd have enough time to get ready and get over there.

Without finishing his cold coffee, Sim got up and started his morning routine. He walked to his bathroom and started the shower, not giving the hot water time to warm before he climbed in. Eventually, the water started steaming. Sim lathered the bar of soap in his hands and began scrubbing himself. He believed in two things when it came to bathing: Ivory soap was the only soap a man should use, and no real man should ever use a washcloth. The only exceptions were the men in the coal mines and mechanics, who bathed in Joy dish detergent. They were manlier than him, because they didn't care if their skin completely dried out. His hands chapped too easily and cracked open too often to use straight dish detergent.

Alan used Dove, a lady's soap. What was worse, he let his boys use the same thing. They'd all be lucky if those two grandsons didn't end up queers. He didn't worry too much about his youngest grandson, but Josh concerned him. The twerp was scared to ask a girl out and never talked about girls. He buddied around with girls, probably styling their hair.

Sim washed his hair with the same bar of Ivory. The sparse hairs he had on his head didn't need a specific shampoo. He let the concern over his possible queer grandsons wash down the drain with the suds. The room floated with steam when he stepped out onto the cold tile floor. An old towel lay on the floor as a rug. It squished beneath his feet because he never let it dry out. There was no point. He was the only person who showered at his house.

The mirror over the sink looked silver with condensation clinging to it. He cleared enough space with his towel to shave his face. Although Sim dreaded looking into that mirror, he refused to go out of his house with whiskers. Back in his time only beatniks and pinkos wore stubble, or even worse, those stupid goatee things. He noticed some of the younger men wearing those now, boys who came from good families. The one thing he'd give Alan credit for was not letting his boys wear facial hair. The shaving cream cooled his hot skin. He made a few passes with his razor without looking at his reflection. The broad strokes could always be made without staring at your mug. Once that was done, he had to look to get the more sensitive areas.

Sim focused on the reflection of the bit of skin beneath his nose and under his lip. He looked himself over, only staring at his skin to check and make sure he'd left no stubble. As he stood back to wash his razor, he made the mistake of taking in the whole of his reflection. As it had been, a blurry blob floated in the air over his shoulder. Today, the dark places at the eyes were more pronounced. The face even had the beginning outline of a nose. He hoped Dr. Sharp could give him something to stop the hallucinations before he had to take matters into his own hands, which at that moment shook worse than they had in a long while. He didn't want to admit that it was from fear, instead of that stupid palsy disease they said he had, but he couldn't deny it even to himself. That face scared him, because he was starting to recognize it.

Alan and Principal Chapman stood in front of the gymnasium door. They had bus duties in the morning until after Homecoming. Alan couldn't figure out why the principal, who could bow out of any activity that he made the regular teachers do, took bus duty before school. He could think of a million other tasks that were better.

The Hassle twins, both red haired and freckled, walked past. Enoch shook Alan's hand; Amos shook the principal's. Once the freshmen stepped into the gym and the door closed, Chapman wiped his hand on his pants leg.

"I think he licked his hand before he shook mine. That was too moist to be a sweaty palm."

Alan looked at his hand. "I think I came out clean."

Principal Chapman had a disgusted look on his face. "I think that I'll go wash this off."

"Before you go, I've got something I want to talk to you about."

"Can't it wait? I'm getting grossed out."

"I'm afraid the bell will ring, and the chance will slip away." Alan shoved his hands into the pocket of his khaki pants. He brought out a moist towelette from KFC. He got a handful of them every time his family ate there and carried around a few for such an occasion. "Use this."

Principal Chapman took the small packet and tore it open. The alcohol smell wafted out as he rubbed it over his hands. He balled it up and tossed it across the hallway into the garbage can. Leanne Walpole and Garrett Miller walked past and into the gym as he did so.

"Good shot, Principal Chapman," Leanne said.

"Nothing but net," Garrett chimed in.

"Thank you," he said as the door closed behind them. "That will tide me over for a few minutes. What is it that's so important?"

"Are some of the students planning a massacre anniversary dance for Homecoming?" he asked.

Principal Chapman nodded his head. "A small group of them came to me and asked for permission to theme the Homecoming dance that way. I shot it down. It was one of the worst ideas ever proposed to me. It's like the..." he paused to check if any students stood in earshot, "...doofuses haven't ever seen a horror movie."

"I knew you had done that, but a few of them are apparently planning to have their own dance at the old gym."

"That is news to me, but I don't have jurisdiction over the old gym. I'll have to tell the superintendent."

"Could you, please? Because I was driving past there last night, and I'm certain some of the kids had broken in. There were lights in the windows."

"Did you stop by to check?"

"Of course. All the doors were locked, but the lights went out after I started rattling them. It must have spooked them into laying low."

"I'll definitely pass it on to the superintendent. We can't have something like that going on." Principal Chapman looked at his hands in disgust. "That thing from KFC isn't going to get it."

"Thank you for hearing me out," Alan almost shook his hand but caught himself.

"No problem. I know you have a very strong connection with that event. Hold down the fort. I'll only be a minute."

Principal Chapman hurried down the hall. Two more students walked into the gym. Alan didn't know their names and barely recognized them. They were freshmen. Not enough time had passed for him to get acquainted with what the football team called *fresh meat*.

Josh and Thomas walked up. They both looked like they'd jumped out of bed and rushed to school.

"Do we have to go in there? It's only a few minutes until the bell," Thomas asked.

"Rules are rules. Principal Chapman's helping me out. I can't bend them."

Thomas looked around with his hand over his eyes like a sailor in a crow's nest. "Where's he at? I don't see him anywhere."

"He had to go to the bathroom to wash his hands. One of those weird Hassle twins licked his and shook Chapman's."

"That's a good idea," Thomas said. "I'll have to thank the Horrible Hassles."

"You've got better sense than that," Alan said. "Get in there before he gets back."

Thomas licked his palm and held it out to Alan. He popped the back of his son's hand and pushed him through the door. Josh stood there with his too-heavy backpack dangling from his shoulder by one strap.

"Use both straps," Alan said.

"I'll look like a total geek," Josh said.

"Is there something you needed, or are you trying to get me in trouble?"

"Why didn't you and Mom wait up for me last night?"

"You didn't get in late." He was a bit confused because his sons never confessed to breaking the rules.

"Well, I wasn't, but you weren't concerned I was outside when that explosion happened?"

He was confused now. "What explosion?"

"The big one that was strong enough to knock me down while I was running past the old gym."

"You walked all the way there?"

"I ran all the way there, and most of the way back, after that explosion."

"I think you dreamed that, Josh. There was no explosion last night. I don't even think it thundered."

Josh looked confused and a bit downtrodden. "If you say so, but I'm positive it wasn't a dream."

Alan spied the principal walking around the corner. "Go on in. We can talk about this later."

Josh nodded and disappeared into the gym as Principal Chapman came into visual range. Alan smiled at him

"Feeling better?"

"Much. Those Hassle twins are weird," the principal said.

"My son Thomas calls them the Horrible Hassles. My other son, Josh, asked me a strange question."

"Boys will do that. Was it a sex question? Those were always the hardest for me to answer with my sons."

"No, he asked me about a giant explosion last night. I didn't hear anything, not even a loud cricket, but he was so insistent."

"I was grilling out last evening and had to go out several times until bedtime to smoke. My wife has a new policy of no smoking in the house since we renovated. I didn't hear a thing." Principal Chapman shrugged. "Boys his age are weird. It's all those hormones."

"He's seventeen. I think puberty has ended."

"A boy never gets through with puberty. We learn how to hide it."

The bell rang. Alan and the principal moved out of the way as the students burst through the doors. He worried a little about Josh. There was no reason both of them would have been drawn to the old gym on the same night. Certainly, it was too far to run because he felt like it. He needed to visit his Aunt Charlotte after school today. There was no particular reason.

Sim sat on the white paper that covered the vinyl exam table. The gown he wore left him feeling cold. At least the nurse let him wear his pants. He had no idea why he should have to take off his shirt for this examination. Dr. Sharp didn't need to hear his lungs to give him more medicine to stop him from seeing that face.

A polite knock came on the door, but before he could say anything, Dr. Sharp stepped inside. He carried a brown folder with a red sticker tab with *Mc* on it. The doctor pushed the door closed without looking at it or Sim.

"Jill tells me that you are having some hallucinations," he said, finally looking up from the folder.

Sim never liked the look of Dr. Sharp. His head bulged out at the forehead, and his eyes sank too far back into his head. "I'm seeing a face in the mirror. I don't know if that's a hallucination or not."

"Is it your face?"

"If it were my face, I wouldn't be coming to see you. I'm not some kind of idiot." Dr. Sharp looked a bit annoyed, but Sim didn't care. It served him right for asking a stupid question.

"I meant is it an afterimage of your own face, or that of somebody else?"

"I don't think it's an afterimage, but I can't tell who it is. The face is very fuzzy and out of focus."

Dr. Sharp pulled up a short rolling stool with his foot and sat on it. He flipped back in the chart as he scooted closer to Sim. The wheels squeaked on the tile. "According to what I wrote when you were seeing faces before, you could clearly see them everywhere. Are you seeing this face in one particular mirror?"

"No, I see it in every mirror I look in. I reckon it's in every reflection I look at."

"Whereabout is this face?"

"Over my shoulder." Sim pointed over his left shoulder. "It hangs about the level of a man standing two or three feet back."

"What if the wall is closer than that?" the doctor asked.

"I guess it's closer."

"It's only a head, not a neck or shoulders?"

"A head, and it's growing clearer."

Dr. Sharp stood up and took out his stethoscope. He did the normal things with it. Sim followed as instructed, although he thought the whole thing was pointless. Nothing in his heart or his lungs caused that face.

"Your heart is fine. Your lungs sound a little congested, but no more than usual. All your other vitals checked out okay. I don't think you have any kind of oxygen blockage." The doctor sat back down. "I don't think this is part of your Parkinson's either."

"Why did I waste my time coming here?" Sim catapulted off the table and jerked the gown off his torso.

He pushed past the doctor and grabbed his shirt off the hook on the back of the door. Dr. Sharp pivoted around on his stool but never stood. Sim buttoned his shirt and tucked in before the doctor said another word.

"Were you in Vietnam or Korea?" he asked.

"I was in the Coast Guard during Korea. I never had to go over there, and I was too old for 'Nam." Sim shoved his shirttail into his pants. "Why?"

"Have you ever had anything very traumatic happen to you?"

Sim snorted. "Yeah, a lot, but I guess not being from around here, you wouldn't know."

"About what?"

"The massacre."

"Is that when those kids were murdered, and that black boy was lynched for it?" the doctor asked.

"The same. I'm the one who found the bodies. Well, my sister found them first and passed out. I found her and the bodies."

Dr. Sharp nodded his head. "That's traumatic. Sim, I think the face has to do more with something called PTSD or post-traumatic stress disorder. Sometimes when men are in war or see horrible things like you have, it causes damage to their brain. It can cause hallucinations." He jotted down something on a prescription pad. "That's a medication that helps with psychosis. It might make you a little drowsy, but I think it'll work."

Sim took the scrip, folded it, and shoved it into his pocket. "Is that it?"

"Yeah."

Without saying anything, Sim left the room. He walked down the hall and into the lobby. He ignored the colored receptionist yelling about his copay. The idea that he was crazy because of what happened forty years ago enraged him. The fact that the doctor wanted him to take some kind of brain medicine made him madder. Dr. Sharp might as well have blamed seeing the face on his drinking like Alan had. He reached into his shirt pocket as he got to his truck, ready to ball up the prescription, but stopped.

Johnny House always ate lunch at the barbecue joint on the far end of town near the railroad. He had since his wife died of lady cancer eleven years ago. Sim would pay him a visit to talk about Marshall and forty years ago.

He climbed into his truck, started her up, and backed out of the handicap parking space, avoiding using any of his mirrors. It was the only way to keep from seeing that ever clearing face.

It took a little longer than Sim would have liked to get across town. It seemed that every traffic light turned red as he approached it. The few stop signs he came up on required him to wait for two other cars. All the time he avoided looking in any reflective surface. The glare of the sun caused a faint reflective outline of his face on the windshield, so he kept looking forward avoiding any glances over his shoulder where that face floated.

When he pulled up at the pit barbecue place, the sight of Johnny's old Chevette sitting in the parking space near the door relieved Sim. He parked beside it and headed inside. The smell from the pit made his mouth water. There was nothing compared to the smell of barbecue to get the saliva flowing. A sign inside the door told patrons to seat themselves. He looked around the small dining area until he spotted Johnny at a table near the back. His old friend paid no attention to his approach. There were too many ribs on the table for that.

"Mind if I sit down?" Sim asked.

Johnny finally acknowledged him. A smear of sauce covered his face from underneath his nose to his chin. "That's fine. Been a while."

"Wipe your mouth," Sim sat down. "You look like an infant that's been face down in some Gerber. You're sixty-seven years old. Have some respect for yourself."

The other man took his napkin and cleaned his face. A

waitress came over carrying a laminated menu. Sim waved her off. He had no intention of eating in the place. She shrugged and walked away.

"I can't believe you won't get something to eat. These are the best ribs you can get anywhere." Johnny bent closer and whispered. "Can't you put your prejudice aside long enough for lunch?"

"I eat at plenty of places that have colored staff and customers, but ain't nothing in the world going to make me eat in a place owned by one."

"You don't know what you're missing."

"What happened with Marshall?"

Johnny shrugged his shoulder and gnawed on another rib. The sauce smeared his face again. Sim shook his head and pointed to the napkin again.

"All I know is that he killed himself."

"Why?"

"Why does anyone kill himself?" Johnny asked. "I reckon he was depressed or something."

"You talked to him every now and then, right?"

"About twice a month."

"Did ever talk about being depressed?"

Johnny shook his head. "No. But you know how us old men are. We don't talk much about that kind of thing. We're stuck in our ways. Except he'd eat here occasionally and not avoid people for decades."

"That's all fine and dandy, he wasn't me." Sim cut to the chase. He'd been watching his *friend* smack and chew with his mouth full long enough. "Did he ever talk about that night?"

Johnny pushed his plate away from him and wiped his mouth with a clean napkin. He did the same with his hands. Sim watched his playful eyes get hard. The heavy lines in his face got deeper as his brow furrowed and his jowls drooped into a serious frown. The bushy, caterpillar-like eyebrows nearly touched as he squinted and moved so close to Sim that he could smell his sweet, barbecue sauce-laden breath.

"He talked about it all the time. It was an obsession for him. Marshall told me once not that long ago that not an hour went by that he didn't see something that reminded him of that night."

Sim leaned away from Johnny. The proximity of their faces made him uncomfortable. He was a little afraid the coloreds in the joint would think the two of them were two old fairies on a rendezvous.

"Do you think that's why he killed himself?"

Johnny leaned back as well and shrugged his shoulders again. "I've got no idea. I'm not even sure he did himself in."

"What do you mean? You said so."

"I'm not supposed to tell you this because the police are still investigating, but his boy found him hanging from a big sweet gum in his backyard, right at the edge of the woods. Problem is, there was nothing around for him to stand on. The tree limb was too high for him to secure the rope without being on something like a ladder."

"Maybe he'd been planning it for a while and had already set everything up," Sim had his own plans to do himself in when the time came. Hanging wouldn't be his choice, however.

"It still doesn't explain how he hanged himself. From what I've heard, he'd've had to jump off something at least as high as a bar stool to be dangling that far off the ground."

Had Sim been Catholic, he'd have crossed himself. He almost did anyway. The two aging men looked at each other for a few silent moments. The sound of cutlery on the plates echoed through the restaurant, and the enticing smell of the pulled pork from the kitchen made Sim's stomach rumble. One of those pork sandwiches with a tall, cold, bottle of beer would hit the spot, and it wasn't even the summertime.

"Do you ever think about it?" he asked Johnny.

"What? That night? A lot. I wouldn't say all the time like Marshall, but right frequently. Most of the time in here."

Sim looked around at the nearly exclusively black clientele. The town had definitely changed in forty years—he was certain, not for the better.

"Do you ever think of it?" Johnny asked.

"Never," Sim lied. "No reason to. What was done had to be done."

Johnny narrowed his eyes. They looked closed. His face

looked carved in stone. "You think it had to be done. You never have a moment of regret?"

"I don't. What do you think, Johnny? Maybe you've been too influenced by all these niggers these days, but yeah, I don't regret it, not one iota. I'd do it again today." Sim didn't bother to whisper. He yelled it.

Before he could continue his rant, a firm hand caught him on the shoulder. Sim looked up into the face of a very dark, very strong-looking man. Ordinarily a manager would smile at you when they came to ask for compliance. This one looked like he might grab Sim up by the collar and toss him out the door.

"Sir, I'm going to ask you to leave. Right now," the manager said. "I won't tolerate such behavior in *my* restaurant."

In life, Sim had been forced to make a lot of changes to ensure survival. Many of them came about because of age. He couldn't fight his way out of situations like he did in the old days. Now was one of the times to go with the flow. Without another word to Johnny or a look back at the manager, he stood and walked to the door. The manager followed close behind him. He held the door open for Sim.

"You don't think an apology is in order?" the manager asked.

"If you want to be sorry for tossing me out of your establishment, it's your choice. I didn't eat nothing and didn't plan to ever come back."

"I meant to me."

"Nothing to apologize for."

Sim dug his keys out of his pocket and walked to his truck. He backed out, not giving the manager or his establishment another look. If only he could do the same with the face that stared at him in the rearview mirror.

Chapter Four

1956
Sometime around midnight on the night of the massacre

Sim held on as tightly as he could to the old board Marshall had bolted to the back of his cutdown. He hated riding in that stupid car because it bounced around like it had no suspension whatsoever, but it was the fastest car belonging to any of them. Marshall had souped it up to make sure of that. Johnny called shotgun fair and square. Tonight, for the first time he could ever remember, it meant the passenger actually had to carry a shotgun.

The only good thing about bouncing on the makeshift rumble seat was that all the dust from the chase down the long dirt road didn't blow in his face. Marshall and Johnny had the windshield, but most of the roof was gone, and the thing had no doors. Every now and then Johnny would spit mud out of his mouth. Occasionally some of that spittle would land on Sim.

"That boy's got a fast car," Johnny yelled over the noise and the roar of the big V8 engine.

"Ought to, that's a brand new car he's driving. I'm surprised Betsy here can keep this close," Marshall yelled back in his high-pitched voice.

Although Sim had been in the Coast Guard to keep from getting drafted to Korea, Marshall and Johnny had lucked up and failed the draft board. It gave them a few years to get jobs and work around Pinehurst. Unlike Sim, who earned a fair amount serving the country, they hadn't saved any money and had to ride around in cars that were little more than frames. The only good thing about it was they became great shots while hunting squirrel and rabbits to help keep food on their tables. Marshall had even gotten married and divorced during that time. Sim wasn't surprised. He was a little bit of a dimwit, evident in the fact that he couldn't overtake that boy trying to outrun them.

"Can't you take a side road and head him off?" Sim asked. "We've passed two perfect opportunities."

"Betsy can't take sharp or sudden turns going this fast. She'd roll over."

Sim agreed that rolling over in this mess of a car would be bad. He'd certainly bite the dust. As the car went around a big bend in the road, he had to lean into it to keep from flying off the back. Things started to get a little dizzying. In the darkness, it was hard to make heads or tails of anything. The moon was full, but the trees obscured it.

"Get us a little bit closer," Johnny yelled.

"I've got my pedal to the floor."

"Try and I'll get a shot at his tires," Johnny said.

Marshall made a quick move that sent the car into a faster gear. The motor revved. The velocity pulsed through Sim, sinking his stomach to his feet.

"Hold on tight," Marshall said. "If Johnny blows that coon's tires out, we'll stop fast. I don't want you to be slung off."

Sim looked over his shoulder. "Don't worry. I'm hanging on for dear life."

The shotgun blast roared louder than the motor. Johnny let out a war whoop like some injun in a John Wayne movie. Marshall let out a string of profanity no one this side of the military would use. The old cutdown slid in the dirt and flint gravel as it came to a stop. Sim held on with all his strength. His legs lifted up, and he started to flip backwards off the plank. The car halted. He slammed back to the seat.

The three of them bailed out of the car. Its headlights illuminated the fancy sedan stopped in the middle of the road. The dust settled as they passed near it. Sim could see the shredded tire. Johnny had done a good job.

"Hold it right there, boy," Johnny leveled his shotgun toward a black boy climbing out of the car. "Where do you think you're going?"

The boy raised his arms into the air. "I'm trying to get home."

"Ain't nothing out this road except the Harrington Plantation. You don't live there, boy," Marshall said.

"My parents work for Mr. Harrington. I recognize you, Simeon McAdams. Why are you doing this? I've not done anything."

"You've done plenty, boy," Sim walked around to him. "Best to keep your mouth shut now and come along."

"I'll make sure Mr. Harrington knows about this. He'll have the sheriff on you men," Tobias Abernathy said.

"Too late for that," Marshall said. "Sheriff's after you. They know what you did."

"I've not done anything. I tried to warn Charlotte."

Sim didn't wait for another word. He punched Tobias in the stomach. The boy bent over, and Sim pummeled him with blows until Tobias curled up on the ground and begged him for mercy. He stopped. The three angry men picked up the bleeding teenager. They opened the trunk of his car, pulled out his jack and spare tire , and tossed him in.

Marshall changed the tire while Sim drummed a jungle beat on the lid of the trunk as Tobias screamed and begged to be let go.

"Don't you recognize the music of your people, boy?" Johnny yelled in the crack between the fender and the trunk lid. "Or are you too uppity to recognize it?"

The three laughed, and Tobias began to wail for his parents, the sheriff, and finally Jesus Christ, himself, to intervene. Sim switched the beat over to "What a Friend We Have in Jesus". Something deep inside him liked hearing that coon beg. It made him feel powerful. He started singing the hymn that he beat out on the truck lid.

Chapter Five

Alan skipped football practice despite the lecture he would get from Coach Turnbuckle. In his opinion, he'd spent enough time yesterday reviewing film with the team to make up for his absence tonight. Seeing Aunt Charlotte took precedence over everything else. Josh had seemed a little concerned about her after dropping off her medications, and his dad had been curious about her welfare too. That told him that his old man hadn't checked on her in a while.

The drive from school to her house was hardly worth the effort to crank the car, but he intended on heading home after his visit and didn't want to have to walk back to the school, risking getting cornered by Coach Turnbuckle.

Charlotte's car sat in the driveway instead of the garage, so Alan parked on the street. His aunt sat in the metal glider swing on her screened-in porch.

"Come on up," she called out with a wave as he got out of his car. "I'm having a glass of tea. Do you want one?"

Alan hurried up the sidewalk and through the screen door. It slammed hard when he let it go. He'd been meaning to come by and torque down the spring a little. Charlotte held her sweating glass of tea toward him. The ice cubes clinked in the glass as she did so.

"I'll get a glass in a little while," he said as he sat down in a metal rocking chair that matched the glider swing.

"What brings you by?" Charlotte rocked her seat. It creaked and squeaked.

"I came to see how you've been. Since school started and

football practice picked up, I haven't had the chance to come by as often."

Alan looked his aunt over. Josh had probably been right to worry about her. She was wearing one of her outfits from the '50s. She even had a scarf around her neck and horn-rimmed glasses on her nose. He could never quite figure out where she'd found such perfect frames, since she'd only started wearing glasses a few years ago.

"Where have you been today?" he asked.

"I decided to go for a drive. A body gets kind of bored sitting here all day long."

"I've tried to get you to go to those groups at the mental health center," Alan said.

"I'm not like those people, sweetie. You and your daddy would have me put in Bryce Hospital permanently if you had your way."

"We would not. I love you very much and want you to be as happy as possible. That's why I suggested those groups."

"Honey, sitting for five hours a day with a bunch of people drooling and talking to imaginary friends isn't my idea of a fun time." Charlotte took a swig from her tea. "I passed your daddy today while I was driving around. That scoundrel hasn't been by to see me in a while."

"Where was he coming from?"

"That barbecue place at the far end of town. You know the one that's owned by the black folks. I'm surprised the town lets them keep that place open. This place is full of hateful people."

"Aunt Charlotte, it's 1996. There have been black businesses in town since the late 1970s. It's not the old Jim Crow times anymore."

His aunt looked at him very confused. He could tell that the reality orientation that was recommended by her psychiatrist was not sinking in completely.

"Did you want some tea?" she asked again. "I might even have a cold drink in there, probably RC though."

"Don't get up. I can get it myself."

Alan stood and walked into the house. The entryway looked like it had for as long as he could remember. Charlotte had changed nothing since she took over as the sole resident after his grandmother's death ten years ago. Even the black rotary dial telephone still sat on the small table with a lace doily under it. He wandered down the hall, lined with faded portraits of family members, including his high school graduation picture. When he reached the kitchen, the pitcher of tea sat on the counter in a puddle of condensation. He got a glass from the cabinet, where they had always been and would always be, and poured himself some tea. A couple of half melted ice cubes tumbled in as well.

He started back to the porch when he spied his aunt's medications sitting on the small breakfast table. They were in the brown plastic bottles instead of a pill planner like his dad was supposed to keep arranged for her. His old man hadn't been checking on her like he should have. Guilt sank Alan's gut. It probably hadn't been a good idea for him to leave his father with that responsibility after his diagnosis of Parkinson's, but the old man insisted on it, along with keeping her grass mowed. His father loved Charlotte and blamed himself for her state of her mind. He was sure that his aunt might be the only person his dad actually cared anything about at all.

She wasn't doing well, and the usual reason for a decompensation, as the doctor called it, was noncompliance with medication. Alan sat his tea glass on the table and picked up the first bottle. Haldol was in all capital letters. The pill count was thirty. The date told him that it was one of the bottles Josh had delivered yesterday. He started to fumble with the child safety lid so that he could count the pills inside. The particular safety device the local pharmacy used was almost like a Chinese finger trap to open.

"What are you doing?" Sim's voice said from the kitchen doorway.

His father leaned against the entryway. Charlotte stood behind him, peaking over his shoulder.

"Josh delivered these yesterday. I was going to fill her pill planner."

"That's why I came over. I always come the day after she gets her meds filled. I got her a month-long pill planner a few months ago. It cuts down on the hassle."

Charlotte hovered over his left shoulder. "I don't like him coming over often. I might have company, and Sim rubs folks the wrong way sometimes, bless his heart."

Sim glanced at her and flinched a bit. "Don't stand there."

"Sorry." She pushed past him into the kitchen.

"When do you have friends over?" he asked.

"All the time. I'm very popular."

Alan sat the bottle down and took his tea glass. "Aunt Charlotte, you were talking a few minutes ago about how you went for a drive today because you were bored and lonely."

"I thought that was you I passed today out by that colored restaurant," Sim said. "You know you shouldn't be driving that far."

"Neither should you," she snapped back, "and I get lots of visitors. Last night Connie stopped by. We talked for hours."

"Connie who?" Sim asked.

"Like you don't know. Connie Dearborn," she answered.

Alan almost let the glass slip from his hands. His dad's mouth fell slack. Charlotte often lapsed into the past, but she never admitted to seeing or talking to her friends who had been killed that night. Also, anytime anyone mentioned Connie Dearborn, his father looked like the biggest bomb had been dropped. Alan was pretty sure he had never gotten over her. Sim would look through her belongings years after her murder.

"That can't be, Charlotte," Sim said. "It's crazy."

"Why is it crazy? A teacher and a student can be friends. She ain't that much older than me."

"It's crazy because there's no way on God's green earth that woman was here last night," Sim said.

Alan started to get nervous. One of the things that Charlotte's doctor often warned about was causing a jarring epiphany. His daddy was on the way to doing that. It might be the last straw that would make Charlotte snap and never come back.

"Daddy, be careful what you say."

"I will not. She can't be left to believe whatever she wants to because some Kike head shrinker thinks he knows everything."

Alan's ire rose. "He's a doctor and knows his business. The man has worked with Holocaust survivors."

"That makes him the God's truth in bat-shit crazy?" Sim

said. "Charlotte, Connie Dearborn did not come here last night. She hasn't been in this house for forty years."

"I know good and well that she was here last night. She told me that it was okay and that I *had* to buy baby blue crepe paper. She promised me that no one would notice or care."

Sim's face bloomed purple. Alan watched a train wreck in slow motion and could do nothing about it.

"Daddy, let it go," he stressed.

"Charlotte, Connie was murdered by that nigger you were fooling around with forty years ago. You found her and your friends dead in that gymnasium. Every last one of them killed by that Tobias Abernathy for no reason more than you was trying to intermingle the races."

"You son of a bitch," Charlotte screamed.

The two locomotives collided, the bigot express and the crazy train. Charlotte shoved Sim, causing him to hit the floor. Alan grabbed his aunt by the arm before she could throw any more blows. He crossed her arms over her body while standing behind her and held her fast despite her thrashing and cursing. Sim got to his feet, using the table to pull himself up. Alan recognized the look in his old man's eyes. His fearless daddy was about to run off.

"Before you haul it out of here," he said to Sim. "Do something decent and call 911."

Sim narrowed his eyes and nodded. He called for an ambulance and then ran off to his truck like the coward he was. Alan stayed in the kitchen holding his highly agitated aunt in a basket hold, while she cursed and screamed.

He talked calmly to her until the EMTs arrived, using the reassuring phrases Dr. Fein had told him to use if this situation ever happened. They strapped her to a gurney and headed to the emergency room. He chose to let her go alone, thinking his presence might keep her agitated.

Alan made sure that everything was tidy in his aunt's house and that all the lights and dangerous appliances were off before he locked the front door and left. During the drive home, he ruminated over the events, wishing he'd manned up and kicked his dad in the nuts.

Chapter Six

1956
A few weeks after the beginning of school

Charlotte watched in silence as people tossed food at Tobias Abernathy. He sat alone at a table in the far corner of the lunchroom near the door to the kitchen. It was where the school administration made him sit. Unfortunately for him, the garbage cans and slop bins were there, too. Instead of using those bins, her fellow students made him the slop bin. Even her good friends took advantage of him. It was after Barabbas Hassle, with his bright white smile under his flaming orange hair and brown freckles, flung spaghetti on Tobias's head that Charlotte took a stand. The new kid couldn't help it that he was a Negro and forced to go to the all-white school. She knew that he would've preferred to go to a school with his own kind. Dumping food on him for something he couldn't help was no way to treat him. Tobias seemed to take it with ease, knocking the remnants of pasta off of his head and onto the table with a swipe of his hand. He didn't take a stand or show any sign toward retaliation.

She stood and took her tray to the bin. As she passed Tobias, they made eye contact. His dark brown eyes narrowed in anticipation of another barrage of food. After she tossed her refuse and scraps away in the bin, he looked relieved that one person passed without harassing him. Once Charlotte put her plate in the window to be washed by the too-fat lunch lady who was as vicious as the students, she walked back to him, shielding him from the others with her body.

"I'm sorry about all this," she said.

He looked up at her and took another bite of his food, which had been spat in. Something about him eating like that reminded her of Christ as he walked down the Via Dolorosa bearing the cross. Everyone spat at and cursed him too. The Scriptures said so. Why could the others not see that?

"I'm going to stand here so that you can have a moment of relief."

Tobias kept his eyes turned down to the table. "You ought not do that. They'll do worse to you."

"They will do no such of a thing."

"Why are you talking to him?" Suzie Tittle asked as she passed by with her beau Frankie Kemp.

"Because she's a nigger lover," Frankie said, making to toss his leftover milk onto Tobias.

Charlotte slapped his arm, and the bottle flew out of his hand and smashed against the wall. Frankie looked like he would smack her across the face, but the too-fat lunch lady burst from the kitchen.

"What was that noise?" she asked and stepped over the broken bottle on the floor. "Who did that?"

"I did." Charlotte didn't give Frankie time to say a word. "He was going to toss it at Tobias."

The lunch lady snarled at her. "Why would you stop him from that? That uppity colored ain't got no right to eat in here. It ought to be made to eat by the outside garbage cans."

"He's got as much right as anyone else," Charlotte said.

"Please be quiet," Tobias whispered.

"I won't. It's not your fault that your family came here to work for the Harringtons and there isn't a colored school for nearly fifty miles."

"Please, Miss McAdams," Tobias said again. "Let it go. Everyone's got to go back to class."

"He could've dropped out," Frankie said. "Ain't like a colored's got any chance of a good job anyway. He'll be bucking hay or portering a train."

"Better options that what you have," Charlotte said. "How many times have you been a junior now? Twice?"

Suzie pulled on Frankie's arm. "Come on before you get in

trouble. No reason to get suspended over a nigger lover."

The two walked off. The other students started to leave the cafeteria as the bell rang in the hall. Fifth period would be starting very soon. If she didn't leave as soon as the bell rang, she would be late to her home ec class. Her locker was on the other side of the school, but she continued to shield Tobias until every student left. The lunch lady loomed over them the whole time.

"Don't think you're going to waltz out of here, either one of you," she said. "Boy, clean up that table, and around it as well. I ain't slipping on any food."

"You probably wouldn't be able to get back up," Charlotte said. "You're as big as a milk cow."

The lunch lady grinned, looking almost demonic. "Speaking of milk, clean up the mess you made. Don't use no broom and dust pan either. Pick up those shards with your bare hands. You owe us a deposit on that bottle too."

"We'll be late for our classes," Charlotte said. "The principal won't like that."

"He'll like what you did even less," the lunch lady said. "Get to it."

Tobias stood and let the food piled on his pants fall to the floor. He emptied his own plate into the bins and put it on the window to be cleaned. The lunch lady grabbed it and threw it away. The broom and mop stood beside the kitchen door. Tobias took them both and brought them to the table. All the food on the table top went into the floor with a swipe of his arm. Charlotte watched all this before she started picking up the pieces of glass on the floor.

The bottle had broken in large pieces. She kept from cutting herself and used the mop to clean up the leftover milk. Without him asking, she mopped around Tobias's table as well.

"I wish you would let me do this. There's no reason for you to be subjected to this kind of torture."

Charlotte leaned on the mop. "It's my choice. We're all the same below the skin, red and yellow, black or white."

"Thank you much, Miss McAdams."

"You sound like a butler or something."

"I kind of am."

"Call me Charlotte. We don't need the formality. I might be the only friend you have at this place. "

Principal Faircloth burst through the lunchroom door, startling both Charlotte and Tobias. He looked flustered and angry at the same time.

"Abernathy, I think you should head on home," Principal Faircloth said. "I'm sure you know what to tell your folks."

"Yes, sir. I'll go as soon as I clean up this mess," he said, turning his eyes to the floor.

"No, go now," the principal said. "When you come back tomorrow, I suggest a brown bag lunch and eating in your car, which you need to park down the street by the boarded-up shoe store."

Tobias nodded and hurried out of the cafeteria. Charlotte quit leaning on the mop and stood at attention like a soldier.

"Come with me, Charlotte," he said.

"Somebody is cleaning up this mess," the lunch lady protested.

"She will be back in a little while," Principal Faircloth said. "I will also remind you that I'm your boss, and if I wanted you to clean this up, you'd do it. I'm a little bit upset that you and the other staff in here let this get as far as it did. When somebody ends up dead, you'll wish you'd done a sight better."

"No, you'll be the one wishing for better," the lunch lady said, "after letting that darkie come here. You should've known what would happen."

Principal Faircloth took Charlotte by the arm and pulled her out of the lunchroom and down the hall toward his office. Although his grip was firm and authoritative, it was not aggressive or painful. As soon as they stepped into his office, he let her go. Charlotte stood looking at the principal as he closed the door and sat behind his large wooden desk littered with way too much paperwork.

"Sit down, Miss McAdams," he said.

Charlotte sat across from him, making sure to straighten out her skirt as she did so. Principal Faircloth leaned back in his chair. It creaked like it might give way. The principal was a rather large man. Supposedly he'd played football at the University of Alabama years ago. Before he'd taken over as the administrator of Pinehurst High School, he'd been their winningest football coach. A state championship plaque hung behind him over the window that looked out on Raider Avenue, the street that passed by the school, named for the mascot.

"How much trouble am I in?" Charlotte asked. Other students might get caught up in the trappings of Principal Faircloth's office, but she wasn't like other students. Direct and to the point was the only way to get things done.

"I don't know. How much are you in?"

"You're the one who determines that. Although I was trying to keep that poor boy from being picked on. You saw the condition he was in. Everyone, even some of the girls, were throwing their leftovers on him."

"He's colored. What do you expect them to do?"

"Treat him like any other human being. The color of his skin doesn't mean he's a bad person. They did that because he is different and *has* to be at our school. It's not his fault the closest colored school is two counties away."

Principal Faircloth leaned forward and started digging in his desk drawer. He brought out a pulpy looking magazine. It was already opened to an article. He handed it over the desk to her. A picture of black boy hanging from a tree took up most of the page. The caption beneath stated that Amos Agnew of Louisiana was hanged by his fellow classmates when he was forced to attend a white school due to circumstances very similar to Tobias's. Charlotte quickly handed the magazine back.

"That's what's going to end up happening to Tobias," Principal Faircloth placed the magazine back into the drawer. "If you keep commiserating with him, you might end up the same way."

Defiance built up inside of Charlotte. "They won't lynch me. I'm white."

"If they think you are—how can I say this—in a *relationship* with Tobias, folks might do worse to you. I watched French girls stoned for being in relationships with Nazis when I helped liberate Paris. Think about that."

Before Charlotte could retort, the door opened and Miss Timmons, the probate judge's secretary's spinster sister-in-law, poked her too-long turkey neck into the room. "I'm sorry to bother you, but you have a telephone call."

"Take a message."

"It's very important," she said. "It's Mr. Harrington."

Charlotte looked from the secretary to the principal. He pushed back from his desk and hurried out of his office, leaving the door opened. She could hear him talking with Tobias's father's boss, and the most respected and feared man not only in Pinehurst but also in the whole county. The linebacker-built principal said a lot of *sorry*s and *yes sir*s while talking. Principal Faircloth's demeanor changed. He hung up the phone with a last *very sorry* and walked back to his office, not bothering to sit down.

"Charlotte, I'm going to tell you to be careful. Ain't no telling what these kids or their folks might do to you."

"I'm not in trouble?"

"No," Principal Faircloth said. "Apparently, you've piqued the interest of Mr. Harrington, who specifically said that I was to make sure nothing happened to you while you are here at school."

Charlotte smiled. "What about Tobias?"

The principal swallowed hard. That much pride took a large gulp to swallow. "He'll be back tomorrow, and Mr. Harrington will make sure nothing else happens to him either."

In a small way, Charlotte believed a great victory for civil rights had been accomplished. She might write President Eisenhower to tell him about this triumph. Perhaps it might help him ensure that other black kids could go to school anywhere. Principal Faircloth swung his hand out as an invitation for her to leave his office. She skipped out the door.

Chapter Seven

Josh walked into the library. He usually tried to find something else to do during study hall, but today he had come up short. A smattering of students sat at every table. Since his aunt had lost it last night, many of them had been asking him questions. In their small town, Charlotte McAdams was famous as the crazy old woman. The popular phrase some of the creepier kids had started using was psychobiddy. A group of the black-clad, horror-loving clique started cruising past her house. Apparently, psychobiddy had something to do with old movies like *What Ever Happened to Baby Jane?*—which he had seen several times, despite what he'd told Jessica. He walked past a table with three of those kids at it.

"Hey, McAdams!" Marcus Smithson tapped him on the arm as he passed by. "Whatever happened to Auntie Charlotte?"

Josh flipped his large history textbook around and took it in both hands. He reared back, ready to knock the geek in the head. Marcus wouldn't find things so funny when his head slammed into the table and he bled real blood all over his stupid Guns N' Roses shirt. *Welcome to the jungle*, Josh thought as he swung the book.

The tune of that terrible song echoed through his head as the book made solid contact with the side of Marcus's face. The impact was hard enough that blood splattered out of his mouth. Marcus listed to the side, hit the table with the other side of his face, and then the floor.

Josh tossed the book at Jamie Morris, who charged him as soon as his head-banging buddy had gotten his head banged.

The textbook made solid contact with Jamie's chest and sent him stumbling back into a shelf full of encyclopedias.

By this time, the room buzzed with energy. The other students clambered out of their chairs and formed a loose circle around him and the three heavy metal kids. Bill Foreman came around the table at him. Josh balled his fist and readied himself. Of the three burnouts, Bill was the most formidable. He was the only one who took an interest in any kind of sport, and unfortunately it was wrestling in the heavyweight class. Josh swung as hard as he could as soon as he was in the strike range, following it up with a swift kick to the nads. A shock strike might work.

Both blows landed solid. The fist to the jaw did little but make Josh's hand hurt, but the foot to groin did the job. Bill's knees buckled, and he toppled down on top of Marcus, who was trying to get back on his feet. The chant of *fight* rose in the air and bolstered Josh as Jamie recovered and came at him. His right hand still stung, so he threw his left, which was a weaker blow. The impact stunned Jamie for a moment, but he flung a haymaker square against Josh's jaw. Josh stumbled to the side. Bill grabbed his leg and pulled on his jeans. Josh jerked away, but couldn't free himself. Jamie came at him with another wound-up punch like Popeye.

Josh didn't fight often, but he could. That came from growing up with a younger, larger brother. He slammed his palm into Jamie's nose at the tip and shoved up with as much force he could muster. Blood exploded, and the nose bone crunched, which meant he'd made that move right. Jamie covered his spewing nose and backed out of the fight.

Bill tugged harder on Josh's leg. He almost toppled to the floor, but now that the rush of adrenaline welled up in him, Josh felt like some sort of Spartan. His free foot rammed Bill under the chin with enough force to send the big headbanger's skull cracking into the underside of the table. His leg came free.

Marcus made a move as if he were trying to get to his feet. Josh readied himself to stomp down on the other boy. Someone grabbed him from the crowd. A battle fog had settled over his mind, and without looking, he shoved against the grasp, sending the person backward. The chant of *fight* stopped, and everyone gasped.

The pressure changed in the room. Josh came out of his rage and looked around. Through the gap formed in the circle of classmates, he saw Jessica sprawled on the floor. Corey Aaron knelt beside her. She didn't appear hurt, only stunned. Josh stepped through the gap and offered his hand to help her up. Corey knocked it away.

"I don't think she needs any more help from you," he said with his fake California accent.

"I didn't mean to do that. I was caught up in the fight. Someone grabbed me." He held his hand out again. "It happens."

Corey stood and put himself between Jessica and Josh. He helped her up. "You're the one who knocked her down in the first place."

"You act like you've never been in a fight before," Josh became aware that his jaw hurt pretty bad and that he tasted blood in his mouth.

Corey looked him up and down and tossed his bleached hair out of his eyes. "Clean yourself up, dude."

He took Jessica by the arm and pushed past Josh. They walked toward the door. Bill and Marcus had gotten into chairs. Jamie stood with his head bent back, and his nose pinched, trying to stop the bleeding. Josh had never unleashed anything like that before. It shocked him. His hands trembled from the thought of it.

"I'm sorry, Jessica. I didn't mean to knock you over," he yelled at her as Corey pulled her closer to the door.

"Whatever," Corey said back in his fake singsong accent.

"You're from Buck's Landing," Josh yelled at him. "Not L.A., poser."

Corey walked out. Josh would have loved to knock him down a peg or two as well, but he'd never had the opportunity. Looking at the havoc he'd wreaked on the headbangers, he swore to himself that he'd never fight again.

Thomas rushed into the library. He looked around as he stopped by his brother. "I got here as soon as I could. Looks like you handled it."

Josh rubbed his jaw. "How did you know about this?"

"I was in shop class, and news of an epic fight like this travels fast. They said it was you against three dudes, so I hauled it down here to help you out."

"Why?"

"Brothers do that for each other, and Harvey was in trig. You had no backup. It looks like you didn't need it."

Josh blushed. "I think I lost control a little bit." He looked at Jamie, who couldn't stop his pouring nose. "Sorry, man."

"Don't apologize to that dick," Thomas said. "Never apologize for kicking ass."

"Language, young man," Principal Chapman said, walking into the library. With the cool of Harry Callahan, he scanned the scene. "Where's the librarian?"

"Smoking," one of the students said.

"That's interesting," Chapman looked at the boys sprawled around. "Christ, Josh, what did you do?"

"He kicked their asses," Eric Dill said.

"Language," Chapman yelled. "You four boys come with me and leave the fight here."

Bill rubbed the back of his head. Josh could see a lump growing on his shaved head. "Don't worry about that," the big headbanger said. "I've got a splitting headache."

Josh, the headbangers, and Principal Chapman left the library. When they passed the nurse's office on the way to the main office, the principal dropped Bill, Jamie, and Marcus off with her. He told Josh that he could wait to be checked out. They headed into the principal's office. When they walked in, Alan sat in one of the visitor chairs. He grimaced when he saw them. Josh ran his hand across his mouth to wipe blood from his swelling lip.

"Trust me," Chapman said. "The other boys look worse."

"Where are they?" Josh's dad asked as Josh sat in the chair beside him and the principal closed the door.

"In the nurse's office," Josh said.

"The nurse's office?" Alan said in a surprised tone.

"Apparently, Josh here beat up three guys singlehandedly. One of which was Wild Bill."

"Bill Foreman?" Alan asked.

"Yep," Chapman answered.

"I taught my boys not to fight," Alan protested before the principal could say anything. "I taught them how to win if they had to."

Principal Chapman smiled as well. It seemed the administrator didn't mind the carnage left in the library. Josh started to feel like he might get off pretty light.

"Those guys probably deserved what they got," Chapman said, "and if you hadn't completely wiped the floor with them, and probably broke that one kid's nose, I could get away with a week's detention and a good old-fashioned paddling, but not in this case."

Josh rubbed his aching jaw and ran his tongue across his split lip. "Great, just my luck."

"Three-day suspension effective as of now."

Alan nodded his head. "Seems fair." He gave Josh a look that said something far worse was coming. "Part of your time will be spent with your grandfather."

"What?" Josh said. "The punishment is not worth the crime. He calls me a faggot to my face."

"Maybe not after this dustup, but he needs to go to a funeral tomorrow. Since you're free, you'll take him, and I can save my personal days for when your Aunt Charlotte's commitment hearing comes up."

"He can drive," Josh said.

"He'll probably be drunk," Alan said. "It was an old friend that died."

Josh looked back at the principal. "Can't you let Marcus, Bill, and Jamie paddle me as many times as they want? It's got to be better than that."

"Sorry," Chapman said. "I guess you'll think a little harder before you get in another fight like that."

Josh sighed and settled into what his punishment would be. He hoped that his Aunt Charlotte would at least appreciate what he'd done.

Alan walked through the empty school building. Coach Turnbuckle had gotten him back for blowing off yesterday's practice. It seemed silly that he should have to do some kind of makeup work for a position he was more or less forced into because it was part of his job. He didn't like coaching football. Basketball was Alan's first love, and he accepted the assistant football coaching position to secure the ability to be the head coach for basketball. Usually head coaches of different sports gave each other a little more respect than he got from Coach Turnbuckle, but at Pinehurst High School, football was not the king of sports, it was the messiah. Alan found himself scrubbing down the disgusting equipment in the weight room because the football players, including his lazy son Thomas, refused to clean up after themselves. It took him hours, but he had an ace in the hole to help him through it. He forced Thomas to pitch in.

The halls were dark, lit only by an occasional fluorescent light. Alan never liked being in the school after hours. Something about it gave him the creeps. It shouldn't, but some places did that. The school had been around a very long time. FDR had it built by the WPA back during the Great Depression. The wooden floors creaked underfoot and echoed down the hall. At night, the place smelled like years of education, ghosts of lectures past.

He'd left his car keys in the drawer of his classroom desk. As he turned down the offshoot hallway to his room, he hoped the janitor hadn't locked it. If that were the case, Alan and Thomas would be walking home in the dark. His son would be none too pleased about that. He already fumed from having to help.

Alan stopped at his classroom. The door stood half-open and a single fluorescent light glowed within. He didn't know how Thomas had gotten past him without being noticed, nor how he made only one fluorescent in the whole room work. His payback was coming, but Alan was smarter than his younger son gave him credit for. It took an early morning wake-up to pull one over on Alan McAdams.

He pushed the door open quickly and jumped into the room. "Ah ha!" he yelled, taking a quick survey of the place.

No one was in the classroom. There was no reason to look under desks, because they were almost too small for Thomas to sit in, much less hide under. Alan nodded and pursed his lips as he reached into the middle drawer of his desk to get his keys. Josh beating the snot out of those three boys and this elaborate payback trick Thomas was in the midst of proved to him that he'd done a pretty good job raising his boys. He was definitely a better father than Sim.

He flipped the light switch as he walked out the door. The single light went out. He closed the door and locked it. The floorboards at the opening of his hallway creaked. Alan jerked his head in the direction of the sound to see only a fleeting shadow passing by. Something cold ran through him. He shivered with the kind of shake people blamed on possums running over their graves. Despite knowing all this was a very good trick put together by his son, it still creeped him out.

"You're not going to pull one over on me, Tommy Boy," he yelled down the hall.

As he turned onto the main trunk hall to head to the exit, a boy chuckled, the sound of a teenager feeling very full of himself for getting away with something deemed "awesome." Alan would ruin his boy's plan, for the fun of proving he was still the master. He started to run down the hall, not at full speed but at a good trot. His slight paunch of a belly bounced more than he'd like. He needed to join the boys in running bleachers instead of watching them. Every time he passed a cross hall where the lights were on, he tried to catch a glimpse of his son, coming up short cach time.

As Alan approached the final cross hall before the exit door, a stitch started to form in his side. He slowed to a quick walk. The chuckling came from behind him. Alan turned quickly to catch his son; instead there was nothing.

"Tommy Boy," he chanted in a singsong tone trying to sound as creepy as possible. "Tommy Boy, I want my tail."

The line came from an old scary story he used to tell the boys when they were younger. Every time he did, Josh and Thomas would jump out of their skins. Occasionally when they were very young, one of them might even cry. Sim had told him the same story, making sure to make him cry every single time. Alan didn't know why he'd ever told his boys that story. Maybe to try to make them tough and realize that stories couldn't hurt them.

The exit door opened. Alan turned to see Thomas sticking half of his body through the door. The streetlamp outside the door made his hair looked green instead of auburn. His skin looked pallid, too. It took Alan a moment to realize that he was staring at his son because of the strange effect the light had, but also because he had convinced himself that Thomas was somewhere in the building.

"What do you want?" Thomas asked. "And why are you doing that old creepy voice?"

"How did you do that?" Alan turned completely around.

His son looked at him with the *you're crazy* look. "How did I do what?"

"Get outside so quickly. You were behind me laughing."

"I've been out here like forever, waiting on you. I was about to start walking home. I'm hungry."

The chuckling echoed down the hall again. Alan perked up his ears. Thomas did the same.

"Who is that?" Alan asked.

"I don't know. I haven't seen anyone around since the guys left," Thomas said. "Maybe they're playing a trick on us."

"All right, you can stop it now," Alan called. "If Principal Chapman hears about this, y'all are going to be in trouble. If you come out now, I won't have to tell him. Who's there?"

"Tommy Jones," the voice said and chuckled again. "Don't tell the principal."

"I don't know a Tommy Jones," Thomas said.

Anger rose in Alan. All of this hadn't bothered him much as long as he'd thought it was Thomas playing a trick. Even if it was another one of the football players, he wouldn't have turned them in to the principal, but this was a whole lot different. Alan knew who Tommy Jones was. One of those stupid kids who were planning the massacre anniversary party had sneaked into the school to play a very unfunny prank. Of all the teachers to pull it on, he had chosen the wrong one.

"That's not funny," Alan said. "Show yourself, this minute."

Thomas stepped inside and stood beside him. Together they took up most of the space in the hallway between the lockers. No one would get past them. It made Alan feel better to know that he'd instilled a sense of family and moral fortitude in his boys besides brute toughness.

"Make it easy on yourself," Thomas said. "You're not going to get past us."

"Please don't tell the principal, mister. It was all in good fun. I'm sorry I scared you, but if I get any more detention my folks aren't going to let me go to the Homecoming dance," the voice said.

"Too bad. You shouldn't have said you were Tommy Jones," Alan said.

"But I am Tommy Jones, and you're a McAdams, aren't you?"

"I'm Alan McAdams, one of the teachers here."

The air in the hallway started to move like wind blew down it. The posters on the wall rustled, and a few pulled free and flew against the back door. Thomas grabbed his arm, which had burst out into gooseflesh as soon as the voice identified itself. Whatever was going on, whether a good trick or not, he didn't want to find out what was next, and if his son actually touched him for support, it meant Thomas was scared, too.

"Let's get out of here," Thomas said.

"I'm not going to argue."

Both of them took two steps backward and turned. Thomas rushed for the door ahead of Alan. He disappeared outside before Alan got a good trot going. As Alan exited the building, he turned back to look down the hallway. In the dim light, a shadow walked up the hall. The wind appeared to have died down. Alan didn't watch for too long. He beat feet as quickly as he could, leaving the school unlocked and not caring if they fired him for it or not.

Josh sat on his bed with his back against the headboard, far enough within the edge of the bedside lamp's circle of illumination to let him read. He didn't have to worry about studying for the next few days. When his mother found out about the fight—which he had tried to dodge talking about, but his lip was swollen to the point that it couldn't be ignored—she had made sure the next few days wouldn't be filled with television, watching tapes, or playing video games. That left him with nothing better to do than sit in his room and read for fun.

He didn't mind reading. A good book could actually be better than anything on TV, but the idea of that being all he had to do made him angry toward the book and the author. He looked at the back cover of the book jacket. Stephen King stared back at him in black and white, sitting atop an old car. The author had a dopey grin on his face, and the caption at the bottom read *Stephen King and friend*. Because of all of that and nothing else, *Christine* blew hard.

Thomas knocked at the same time he poked his head into the room. He looked both scared and excited.

"Try knocking and waiting for me to say 'come in,'" Josh said.

"What was I going to see that's more shocking than you reading one of Mom's prized Stephen King books?" Thomas asked.

"I could have been doing other things."

"Doubtful. You've got all day for the next three days to do that. Come down to the kitchen. I've got to tell you what happened to me and dad." Thomas' voice was tinged with overexcitement that comes from either having something completely awesome happen or something completely bogus.

"Tell me up here. I don't want to go down there, because Dad might pile some more punishment on top of me."

"He's taken his supper plate into the living room to watch that stupid program he can't miss, and I'm hungry. I can tell you while I eat. Plus, Momma already told him what judgment she levied on you. He said that sounded like enough. I told him while we cleaned the weight room why you got into that fight. Dad told Momma that you had to drive the old man to a funeral tomorrow. She agreed that your current punishment was enough," Thomas almost spat the words out. His manic speech told that he had something wondrous to tell. "Come on; I'm not getting any less hungry."

Josh carefully laid *Christine* facedown on the table, opened to where he was reading. The book tented upward. Being one of his mother's prize possessions, he would not dog-ear it or break the spine for fear of her wrath. Thomas didn't wait for him to follow. Josh walked down the stairs. The blaring of the television with his dad's program made him a little homesick for the warm glow of TV. He walked into the living room on his way to the kitchen. His mother looked up from a magazine she read while the television blared.

"Are you trying to watch TV?" she asked.

"No, Thomas wanted to talk to me while he eats. Is that okay, or am I restricted from talking to my brother?" he asked.

"If you keep up that smart mouth, you will be," his dad said with a mouthful of spaghetti. "You've got a hefty amount of grounding already. Do you really want to tempt fate?"

"I'm sorry. Can I go on in before he's completely scarfed down his dinner and forgotten what he wanted to tell me?" Josh asked.

His dad twirled more spaghetti on his fork. "Don't worry; he won't forget that."

Josh gave his dad a strange look. "What was it?"

"I won't steal his thunder." Alan shoved the wad of pasta into his mouth.

Josh hurried into the kitchen. Thomas sat at the round table, already making quick work of the pile of spaghetti and a quart of sweet tea. Tomato sauce smeared across his face almost like a Glasgow smile. His brother always ate like a man starving in the desert.

He sat down across from Thomas, pulled one of the leftover rolls out of the basket, and picked at it. "What's this fantastic story?"

Thomas swallowed and took a slug of tea. "We saw a ghost."

It took everything Josh could do to keep from laughing in his brother's face. A mouthful of roll helped. "What are you talking about?"

"A ghost, a real live spook. If I hadn't been with Dad and seen his face, I'd've thought I was imagining it, but his face said everything."

"Where at?"

"The school. He thought I was playing a joke on him. He did that creepy 'I want my tail' thing he used to do. This laughing came from nowhere, and wind started blowing down the hallway. I hauled it after that, but he said on our way home that he saw a shadow walking up the hall."

Josh rolled his eyes. He couldn't resist it. "You heard a ghost."

"Don't be like that. I've never seen Dad look like that. It was the real deal. *Ghostbusters* or *Scooby-Doo* stuff."

"The ghosts on *Scooby-Doo* are fake," Josh reminded his brother.

"Why can't you get into this? You like reading those dumb horror novels."

"Ghosts aren't real."

Thomas swallowed more spaghetti. "I thought so too, but there one was."

"You say Dad looked like he was scared shitless?"

"I was," his dad said, walking in behind him, "and watch your language."

"You think it was a ghost?" Josh asked.

Alan put his plate in the sink and rinsed it off. "I know it was a ghost, but I think it was the ghost of Tommy Jones, one of the kids killed at the massacre."

"Why?" Thomas and Josh asked at the same time, both with a mouthful of food.

"Because when I thought it was Tommy Boy playing a joke on me, I yelled his name. The ghost responded to it. I saw those lights in the window of the gym. Of course he said, 'Tommy Jones' when I told him to identify himself. The thing that really scared me was, he knew we were McAdamses."

Thomas snapped his fingers, "You said that something made you run to the old gym the other night, and there was that explosion no one else knows anything about."

"Those can't be related." Josh stood to go back to his room and read some more of *Christine*. "Y'all are weird. Let me know when you call Kathryn Tucker Windham, and she can tell Jeffrey to add Tommy Jones to her next *Thirteen Alabama Ghosts* book."

He popped the last bit of roll in his mouth and walked back to his bedroom. Things seemed too quiet when he settled in to continue reading. Josh turned on the stereo with the remote. The music flowed out a little louder than he'd intended. He cranked the volume down as a song ended.

"You're listening to 105.9 the X. We'll get back to the music in a minute," the far too perky British-accented DJ said. "I was talking today with Coyote Jay about creepy things. Halloween will be coming up soon. He was telling me about this massacre that happened years ago in a small town over in West Alabama. Now apparently, some local kids want to have an anniversary dance related to it. Bad show is what I say. What do you think? Give us a call."

"You don't want to know my opinion." Josh hit the button on the remote that started the CD player.

Melancholy music started playing from the speakers. He took his book and started reading. His mind wouldn't focus on the words. He read paragraphs over and over again. The only thing that occupied his mind was what had happened to him the other night. Thomas had been right: something had compelled him to run to the old gym. Even if no one else in the whole town had experienced it, he had felt a giant explosion. The idea of ghosts seemed too far-fetched, though. He looked at the words of the book again. The idea of continuing slogging through a novel about a possessed car didn't seem all that appealing. He slipped the front jacket flap over the pages he'd read, careful not to crease it, put the book down, and flipped off the lamp. The music continued to play as he stared at the dark ceiling, waiting to fall asleep.

Josh wandered through the cemetery while his grandfather stood graveside at the service for his friend. He yawned. That's all he had done for most of the day. His mother had woken him up at his usual time for school. Despite the lack of entertainment and hauling his cantankerous grandfather to a funeral for another cantankerous old man, Josh hoped that he'd at least get to sleep in. No dice. As he drifted deeper into the cemetery, he wondered how rude it would be if he perched atop one of the gravestones. If he got deep enough into the old part that was high with weeds and snuggled among old cedar trees, no one would notice. Of course, that part was far from the service, he wouldn't know when it was over, and Grandpa Sim would have to come find him. A horrible lecture with a fair amount of swearing and derogatory name-calling would ensue.

He wandered around and looked at the names on the gravestones. It had been a while since he'd been to the cemetery. When he was younger, his folks would drag him and Thomas up there what seemed like every week, for things like funerals for his dad's great aunts and uncles. There was always the special Decoration Day visit sometime in the spring, when everything laid heavy in that greenish-yellow pollen that made him sneeze. Ever since Grandma Sally had moved to Birmingham, those visits had dwindled to none.

Back then, Josh and Thomas—who were both not very good readers yet but loved to try—would attempt to outdo each other reading the names. When they got a bit older and understood humor a little better, like the hilarity of fart jokes or farts themselves, they looked for funny names. Eventually, it turned into finding names that sounded dirty. During those searches, they'd found one particular tombstone that had a picture of the deceased on it. It wasn't etched into the stone. Instead, it was a photograph that looked like an old senior portrait trapped in a plastic bubble. The thing creeped him out back then. Josh tried to find it again.

It was somewhere near a big tree. Josh remembered stepping barefoot on a sweet gum burr near that grave. Why he'd been running around in the graveyard without his shoes, he wasn't sure. Any time you stepped on one of those stupid things, it left an impression. A glance around the expansive old cemetery found a large sweet gum tree, with a few yellow leaves, back toward the funeral service. It was probably better to get closer to the ceremony anyway. It had to be wrapping up soon. No one could be interesting enough to have a long service in the funeral home chapel and a second one at the cemetery.

As he made his way to the sweet gum tree, he avoided stepping on the actual graves. Grandma Sally had told him to never step on the graves because it was disrespectful. His dad always said that if you disrespect the dead, they'll reach up and grab you. It was completely crazy, but Josh still didn't do it, like people didn't step on cracks in the sidewalk for fear of breaking their mother's back. He would read the occasional headstone for fun. As he got closer to the sweet gum tree, he spied Purvis Smithfield. Thomas found that one years ago while they played find the dirtiest name. He won that round and used it as a trump card until Josh had stumbled upon Ariella, which they pronounced "areola" out of ignorance. After that, Josh always won. Old Purvis had been in the ground a long time, buried way back in 1912. Thoughts about how far back in time that was filled Josh's mind when he spied the tombstone he'd been looking for.

He hurried over to it. It was close enough to the funeral service for the preacher's loud praying to be heard. As soon as "Amen" was uttered, his grandfather would be itching to go. Josh had to get his look at that creepy grave marker before that.

Something had happened. The picture in the plastic bubble was gone. Instead there was a black glob in its place. Josh reached down and touched it. The plastic itself had melted. The black glob on the inside was the ashes of the picture. It had burned somehow. He couldn't figure out how that would happen without it being straight-out vandalism—maybe someone had brought a torch out there and melted it.

The "Amen" came, echoed by different men at the service. His grandfather broke away from the crowd and headed toward his car. Josh didn't hesitate to get over there. He looked at the name on the stone to refresh his memory of who laid there so that he could tell Thomas about it.

Tommy Jones, June 10, 1939 - October 23, 1956

Chapter Eight

1956
Seven days after the massacre

Sim stood with his family at Tommy Jones's graveside service. A lot of the kids from the high school attended. He recognized most of them from around town. A few had visited Charlotte over the last few days, too. He had no idea who the younger ones were unless they looked like an older sibling. Before the service had started, a lot of those kids, quite a few of their parents, and a couple of random adults had asked about Charlotte. Some expressed surprise that she hadn't attended the funerals. Sim told them all in no uncertain terms how insensitive they were.

The overly elaborate casket was lowered into the ground, and the pallbearers, all schoolmates of the deceased, started shoveling the red dirt into the hole.

Mr. and Mrs. Jones stood and walked away from the grave. She bent over crying into a lace handkerchief while her husband kept his arm around her. They were both dressed far too warmly. The late October sun beat down on them in their long winter coats. They passed by Sim and his folks.

"Sorry for your loss," his mother said, touching Mrs. Jones on the arm.

The other woman looked up with red eyes. Sim's burned in sympathy. A little smile came on the woman's face. "Thank you. How is your girl? Having to find all that must have been something terrible for her."

"Both our kids are all right," Sim's daddy said. "Our boy, Sim, found Charlotte after she fainted."

The Joneses looked at him. Both looked so downtrodden that they might go home and blow out their brains. He hoped one day, if he got that pitiful, he'd be able to do that.

"You helped catch that colored boy who did all this," Mr. Jones said. "I want to shake your hand. You can't bring back our Tommy, but you got justice for him."

The older man stuck his free hand out to Sim. It was awkward shaking with his left hand, but he put as much gusto into as he could. Every single parent of the victims had thanked him for catching that Tobias Abernathy and taking care of him. Of course, if any of them truly knew what happened, they'd probably be less willing to congratulate him.

"Thank you. It had to be done for your son and my sister," Sim said, personalizing the message for them as he had all the mourning families.

"We'd heard rumors about that," Mr. Jones said. "We'd hoped they were false."

"They were, and now we can forget about it." Sim's mother patted him on the back. "Thanks to Sim, Marshall, and that House boy."

"It *had* to be done," Sim repeated.

That phrase had become his go-to response when people started talking about how they dealt with Tobias Abernathy. It punched people in the gut so that they would recognize the need to keep the uppity niggers in their place. It had worked.

"You ought to see the stone we have for Tommy," Mrs. Jones said. "It's beautiful. It will even have a copy of his senior portrait on it, sealed in a plastic bubble to keep the elements from harming it. I'll always get to see my boy as he was."

"Come on dear, before you get yourself all worked up again. I don't need you having a spell out here." Mr. Jones started his walk back to the car.

Mrs. Jones had been fainting from the overwhelming emotion. Sim found it all a little silly. He'd lost his fiancée, and his sister came in and out of a catatonic state, but he dealt with it fine. A couple shots of rotgut moonshine took the edge off.

Someone pulled on his elbow. He turned to see Sheriff Johnson standing in his fancy uniform with his hat under his arm.

"What is it, Sheriff?" he asked.

"Step over here with me," the sheriff said.

Sim followed Sheriff Johnson several yards from the group. The sheriff looked very concerned. Usually, the guy seemed like nothing fazed him.

"What is it?" he asked again.

"Mr. Harrington's got a guy snooping around about the Abernathy thing. This ain't some yahoo from up in Jasper or over in Birmingham. He's a Pinkerton or something."

Sim snorted as he took a cigarette out of his pocket. "This isn't the Old West, Sheriff. I'm not sure there are Pinkertons anymore."

"I know he ain't a Pinkerton, but he ain't from around here either. He's from Chicago or New York."

"And what was done had to be done," Sim quoted himself.

"Unfortunately, the law sees it a little different, due process and all that Constitutional stuff." The sheriff took a stub of a cigar from his shirt pocket and started chewing on the end. "This guy's straight up law and order. I know that boy killed those folks, and I know what he supposedly did to your sister, but this guy ain't going to take hearsay as an answer."

"What was done had to be done."

Sheriff Johnson spat his cigar on the ground and grabbed Sim by the shoulders, giving him a good shake. "This guy's a colored lover. He's got some kind of civil rights connection up north, maybe even in Washington."

"Run him off." Sim took the final drag off his smoke. "It's not like you've never done that before."

"It ain't the same. He's staying with the Harringtons, and what we did isn't exactly legal. This guy has legal legs to stand on."

"Meaning what?"

"We all go to jail. Some of us may even get the chair. You and your buddies are probably the most likely to get that."

Sim smiled. Riding in Yellow Mama wouldn't be that bad. He'd hate to fry for killing a monkey, but if it happened, it happened. "What are you worried about? Sounds like you got it easy."

"Do you know what those cons who I put in prison would do to me in there? I might as well get the chair for mercy's sake."

"I'll figure out something," Sim said. "Get out of here. An old man like you asking advice of a young buck like me is embarrassing."

Sheriff Johnson left. Sim told his folks to head home in the car. He said that he needed to think and would walk home to clear his head.

As soon as everyone left the cemetery, he walked to the old part under the cedars and perched on top of a headstone to think about what had happened. In all truth, what he and the boys had done needed to be done. Any jury in Alabama would agree with them. All the worry that Sheriff Johnson expressed was for nothing, but times were changing. Pinehurst had allowed a colored family to move in, even if they were domestics for the Harrington family. Ten years ago, when he'd graduated high school, that wouldn't have been tolerated, Harringtons or not. In those days, the sun did not set on living niggers in Pinehurst.

He took out another cigarette. As it burned down with every puff, he started formulating a plan.

Chapter Nine

Alan sat at his desk. He'd reported the malfunctioning light to the janitor, even though nothing was wrong with the light when he arrived at work. His day flew by. At the time when Josh was supposed to haul his old man to that funeral, he worried about leaving his son cooped up with his father. The punishment might have been a little too harsh. After all, the boy had been defending the honor of his aunt. As Josh had complained about, his father did call him derogatory names to his face. He'd done the same to Alan and his brother Mike. Now old Sim paid for it, because his brother never came back from Denver. He and Mike rarely even spoke.

The bell rang, and Alan's students wasted no time running out of the classroom. Seventh period was about to start, and he didn't want to walk to the field house to assist in the athletic PE class. The last thing he wanted was to go anywhere near the weight room or that football field. He wanted to go home and sleep. The last few days frayed his nerves, but he tidied his desk and shoved things that didn't need to be left on his desktop into the drawers. Jessica walked in as he got up to leave.

"I'm not bothering you, am I?" she asked.

He smiled. "Oh no, I was on my way to the field house. It's a welcomed delay. I don't want to go out there today."

"I know that Josh has been suspended, and I figure he's in big time trouble, but he fought those guys because they were making fun of his Aunt Charlotte."

"I know and we were lenient on him," he said, though he doubted his own words as he thought of the cruel and unusual punishment of being trapped with his father.

"That's good." She looked down as the late bell rang. "Would it be okay if I stopped by after school today to talk to him?"

"He'd probably enjoy it."

"I want to tell him that I'm not upset that he knocked me down yesterday during the fight. I know that he didn't do it on purpose, even though Corey has been trying to convince me otherwise."

"Corey Aaron?" Alan asked.

"Yes, he's trying to put the moves on me. I'm a little too savvy for that."

Alan was glad to hear about her ability to sniff out a snake in the grass. Disliking specific students was frowned upon, but every teacher did it. Corey happened to be one of the students he disliked. Behind his "I'm trying to save the world" fake swagger, the kid was slimy. His granola attitude only started a few years ago. Before that, he was the biggest redneck kid Alan had ever seen. Occasionally, when Corey Aaron was on the field or in the weight room working out, his red neck showed through his California-cool persona.

"I think you're late for class. I know I am." Alan escorted Jessica out of the room. "Come by around six p.m. That's when we eat supper. You can grab some with us."

"Okay, sounds good."

They walked together to the main hall before he went his way and she hers. Something wasn't quite right about that girl. Josh mooned over her, and she always acted like she was impervious to it. His son told him that she would never let him into her house or introduce him to her parents. It was like she wasn't real or something.

The noise of the field house hit Alan and brought him out of his ponderings. The smell was the next thing he noticed. It stank as if he hadn't spent hours cleaning the place. It amazed him how a couple of dozen teenage boys could bring such a pervasive funk to a place. Thomas passed by in his shoulder pads with his practice jersey over his arm. Alan grabbed him by the neck of the pads and pulled him back toward him. If they had been playing football, he would have gotten a penalty for a horse collar.

"What is it?" Thomas asked with a surprised tone in his voice. "I've got to get out on the field or coach will have my hide."

"You do understand I'm one of the assistant coaches, not just your dad, right? If I pull you aside and cause you to be late, it doesn't count."

"You're right," Thomas conceded. "What is it?"

"What did y'all do to get it stinking back in here so quickly? We worked very hard on this place for it get back in this shape."

"I don't know. It smelled like that when I got in here. Maybe one of the PE classes did weightlifting or something today."

"It smelled like this when I got here this morning," Coach Turnbuckle said as he walked out of Alan's office. "I was waiting to ride your hide, but I was eavesdropping. You two cleaned this place last night?"

"Yeah, you can check with my wife about when we got home."

"We even saw a ghost in the school building," Thomas said.

Coach Turnbuckle gave Alan a look that made him uncomfortable. He didn't like bullies, and the coach was the biggest one in the school. If his job didn't depend on being an assistant coach, Alan would have gut-punched the guy a long time ago, and probably would in the future once the economics of life were in his favor.

"Get your jersey on and get out there with the rest of the boys," Alan said. "Tell them to start running around the field. We'll be out there in a few minutes."

Thomas nodded and pulled his jersey over his pads as he walked out of the field house. The door slammed on its stiff spring hinge. It helped to snap some of the tension that had built up inside of Alan.

"Ghost?" Coach Turnbuckle asked.

"That's neither here or there. We scrubbed this place. I had it smelling like Clorox when we left."

"Maybe breathing the fumes caused you to hallucinate that ghost. I will say, though, when I walked in here this morning it smelled far worse than this. I almost gagged. It smelled like a raccoon had crawled somewhere and died."

"Maybe something did overnight."

"I checked the whole place, every nook and cranny that something could crawl in. Nothing."

"What happened to that smell?"

"It went away about noon, disappeared like it never existed. This smell remained. I know you're telling the truth. I can't figure out what happened. Maybe it's the air conditioning or something like that."

"If this smell is coming from that, we need to be worrying about Legionnaire's disease."

The coach shrugged. "If it ain't that, I got no idea what it could be."

"What was here before the field house?" Alan asked.

"You went to high school here. Don't you remember?" the coach asked.

"No, it was here when I was in school, but it was new back then."

"Let me think. I think it was a parking lot and maybe a smoking section. I don't recall too well. Principal Chapman told me ages ago. Why?"

"Just wondering. We better get outside and make sure the boys are actually running."

Coach Turnbuckle and Alan left the building. To his surprise, the football team was running around the field. They actually listened to Thomas. Alan figured cleaning for so long yesterday gave him the idea he didn't want to do it again.

Turnbuckle blew his whistle and told the players to get to the center of the field. He split them into two teams and started running plays. Alan stood on the sideline playing referee. Sweat started to bead on his upper lip. He rubbed it off. The day seemed far too humid.

The team ran a play. He trotted downfield, following Corey Aaron, who'd broken a good tackle. The field ahead of Corey was empty, and the running back headed straight into the end zone. Alan threw his hands up as the signal for touchdown.

"Outstanding, Mr. Aaron!" Turnbuckle yelled, clapping his hands. "Horrible, Mr. Otis."

The defensive player who hadn't stopped Corey's run shook

his head. Alan understood why. His block was outstanding. Corey had run though it with an expert move.

Turnbuckle yelled out directions and blew the whistle. They ran another play. The ball went back to Corey. He went to the outside with a sudden burst of speed. Neal Otis broke his assignment and went after the runner. He shot down a diagonal, slamming with full force into Corey. Both flew to the sideline. The ball came loose and soared though the air, landing with two bounces. The two players hit the ground hard. Corey huffed. Otis lay atop the other player as they skidded across the patch of sideline grass, stopping only after hitting the fence.

The defensive side scooped up the ball and headed in the other direction. Alan ran to the two players on the sideline because neither seemed to rouse. Coach Turnbuckle yelled for him to keep up with the ball, but Alan ignored him. When he got to the boys, Otis rolled off Corey. He pulled off his helmet.

Neal Otis's cheeks were red. He gasped for air, barely sitting up. Corey let out another grunt. Alan knelt beside him and helped him get his helmet off. The boy's eyes were unfocused and staring off into the space.

"Is he okay?" Otis asked. His voice sounded stunned.

Alan snapped his fingers in front of Corey's face and gave him a forceful shake. The player's eyes focused with another long moan. Alan held up three fingers in front of the player's face.

"How many fingers do you see?"

Corey squinted and blinked hard. He shook his head, "Three, but one of them is dancing around."

"I told you to follow that play," Coach Turnbuckle yelled, trotting over to Alan.

"He got his bell rung pretty hard. Neither of them moved after the hit. I needed to check on them. This late in the year, having full contact practice is going to get someone hurt."

"Otis looks okay," Turnbuckle said. "Fantastic hit, boy. Next time try not to hurt your teammate."

"I'm not okay," Otis said. "I need to get out of the pads. I'm having a hard time catching my breath."

"Does it hurt when you breathe?" Alan asked.

"A little bit."

"Probably bruised or cracked a rib," Turnbuckle said. "We need to get him in the field house and give it a look. How about you, Aaron?"

"He was dazed and unfocused," Alan said.

"Still am a little bit," Corey sounded like his redneck self and not the California persona he usually portrayed.

"He sounds Southern again," Turnbuckle said. "Get 'em both in there and checked out." He turned back to the players. "Thomas, get over here and help your daddy get these guys into the field house."

Thomas ran from midfield. He helped Neal Otis up. Alan got Corey to his feet and helped him walk back to the field house. Once they were inside, Thomas headed out. Alan helped Otis get his pads off and poked around on his ribs. The player didn't punch him in the nose or scream like a girl. Alan was sure they weren't broken.

"I'm breathing easier, coach," Otis said. "I think getting those pads off helped."

"You're out for the night," Alan said. "Go hit the showers and head home. Tell your folks what happened and if you start hurting worse, head over to the hospital."

"All right," Otis hopped down from the examination table and headed toward the showers.

Alan turned his attention to Corey, who sat in a chair and leaned against the wall. He was still conscious but looked rough. Alan helped him get his shoulder pads off. He made sure to look in the boy's eyes. They were focused, and both pupils looked the same size.

"I think you're going to be okay," Alan said. "I'm still going to call your folks and have them take you down to the hospital to be sure."

"Don't do that," Corey leaned against the wall. "Call my brother."

"Jack? How is he doing?" he asked. Corey's older brother had been a fantastic kicker on the football team.

"He lost his scholarship to Samford. Got over to Birmingham and partied too much. Momma's let him come home, but he had to start working as a logger."

"What's his number?"

Corey shook his head. "Scratch that, he's out in the woods. I'll drive myself."

"I think you might have a concussion. I don't think you need to drive. I'm calling your mother."

Corey grabbed his arm as he tried to walk away. "Don't do that, please. It will worry her. She's sick."

Alan had used that excuse a few times when he was Corey's age. Although this was the kid who got on his last nerve, Alan empathized with him at that moment.

"How much does she drink?"

"She's sick," Corey insisted.

"My father was an alcoholic when I was a teenager. I've used the same excuse." Alan walked to Corey's locker and got his T-shirt. "Bush" was written on it in large white block letters. "Put this on. I'll take you to the hospital."

"Thank you."

Neal Otis walked out of the showers with a towel around his waist as Alan helped Corey to his feet. He could tell that Corey seemed embarrassed.

"We're heading to the hospital," Alan said.

"I couldn't get a hold of my mother on the phone," Corey said, his California accent returning. "Coach here is taking me."

"That's right," Alan covered for him.

"Sorry about hurting you," Otis said.

"Don't worry about it," Corey said.

Alan and Corey walked through the building to the door. A smell like cigarette smoke, gasoline, and rotten meat flourished as they stepped outside.

"Do you smell that, or am I having hallucinations?" Corey asked.

"I smell it."

It was like someone watched them. Alan looked around like a paranoid but found nothing. He patted Corey on the back, and they headed to his car. Alan glanced over his shoulder to ease his mind. He glimpsed someone at the edge of his peripheral vision. The boy seemed to be smoking and gave him the finger.

Alan turned to catch the punk. Nothing was there.
"Are you okay?" Corey asked.
"I thought I saw something."
"Maybe you should get checked for a concussion too."

Josh sat on his bed reading *Christine*. He'd made good headway through the novel. The story gripped him even though he'd doubted it early on. He hadn't had any homework to deal with since he'd been suspended, and television was still off limits even for that short amount of time he had between bringing his grandfather back from the funeral and his mother arriving home. Grandpa Sim was having supper with them. It was his mother's idea, which shocked Josh because she tried to avoid him as much as possible.

As he read, Josh's thoughts drifted back to the car ride home from the cemetery. His grandfather had seemed in a sourer mood than usual. Josh attributed it to Sim's old friend having passed away.

"How did you get that fat lip?" Sim had asked in a gruff, uncaring voice.

"I got into a fight yesterday."

"Is that why you're out of school today?"

"I certainly didn't take off to carry you to a funeral," Josh said before he could catch himself.

"Watch your mouth, boy. You ain't so big that I won't bust the other side of your lip for you." Josh could tell he had no heart in his almost cartoonish old man threat. "What kind of a fight did you have that got you suspended—or don't they paddle for fights anymore?"

"They paddle for fights, but I beat up three guys on my own."

"Did you say you beat off three guys?"

"You know good and well what I said. They were making fun of Aunt Charlotte. I took care of it."

"All by yourself?"

"I used a textbook twice, but after that, all by myself."

"Where was your brother?" Sim gave genuine attention to the story.

"In class. He got down there after it was over. He was coming to the rescue."

"Probably thought a queer like you couldn't handle yourself."

Josh slammed the brakes on the in the middle of the street. Sim never wore a seat belt, and the sudden stop flung him into the dashboard. Josh punched the accelerator unleashing all the car's horsepower. Sim was flung back as the car quickly approached sixty and then seventy miles per hour.

"What are you doing, boy?" He pawed at Josh's arm.

"Driving."

"What kind of driving is that?"

"Queer driving. Didn't you know that all gay guys drove way crazy like this?"

He slammed the brakes again. Sim hit the dashboard much harder this time. Josh shifted into park, and pressed his hand hard into the old man's back so that he couldn't lift back up. Sim made some grunts of protest, but could do little else to free himself from the situation.

"Let me explain some things to you," Josh said. "Number one, I don't like you, and as soon as I'm eighteen, we're never going to speak again. Number two, I'm not gay, and if I were, it would be okay because this isn't the good old days that you grew your bigot ass up in. Number three, I'm not a virgin. That backseat can attest to that. Number four, I beat up three guys by myself because despite the fact that I keep a low-key attitude, I'm a tough mofo like my daddy. He taught us to handle bullies like your sorry old hide. Number five, I ain't going to put up with your crap anymore. You get it?"

"Yes," Sim made no protest, which surprised Josh.

"We're going to head on over to the house. I'm going to go to my room to read, not because I'm gay, but because I like to read and I don't want to be around you. You can watch TV or smoke on the patio, or if you feel real industrious, cook supper for my mother—who works, not because she is a women's lib dyke, but because she likes having a career. Do we have an understanding?"

"Yeah."

Josh let his grandfather up, feeling a little giddy from the adrenaline that coursed through his veins. They came home, and he did what he said.

As he sat staring at the page, still in the *Arnie—Teenage Love-Songs* section of the book, he dreaded what punishment his parents would dole out when old man Sim told them about the car ride. Josh hoped that his mom had another King book on the shelf, because he'd probably be reading for entertainment for another couple of weeks. He didn't figure his mother would mind him standing up to his grandfather, since she couldn't stand him. The language would be what got him into trouble. Despite the fact that she used it herself, she liked to live under the fantasy that her sons never said such vulgar things.

He was able to focus on the reading again, but a knock on the door interrupted him. His mother poked her head in. She managed to sneak in unnoticed, but with Sim watching TV loudly downstairs, he wouldn't have been able to hear the trumpets when Christ returned, which is what Sim said would happen if that queer Bill Clinton got re-elected in November.

"Whatcha need?" he asked. "Help in the kitchen?"

"No, someone's here to see you," his mother said. "It's *Jessica*."

Josh jumped off the bed, tossing *Christine* to the floor. "You didn't leave her downstairs with him, did you?"

His mother's eyebrows dove into an indignant look. "Of course not, she's out on the patio. What do you think, I'm stupid or something?"

"Tell her to come up."

His mother's look asked the same question again. "You go down there. She's not coming up to your room." She paused and glanced at the book on the floor. "Pick up my book, please."

Josh smiled, knelt, picked up the book, and gingerly placed it on his bed. Then, he pushed past his mother. She followed him down the steps, through the living room past Sim (who slept kicked back in the recliner with the television blasting *Jeopardy*), and into the kitchen. Jessica sat at the round wrought-iron table in the middle of the patio. The umbrella, used mostly in summer, was rolled out to block the glare of the late October sun. The same sun caught the highlights of her blond hair, making it look like it had caught fire. He started out the door as his mother took a pan from under the stove. It clanked metal to metal and cleared his head.

"If it's okay, can she stay for dinner?" Josh asked.

"According to her, your father already invited her," his mother said. "I'm surprised you'd want her to stay with *him* here."

Josh looked back toward the living room. "We don't have to worry about him."

"Are you sure?"

"Positive. He won't say a thing out of place tonight." Josh smiled and walked outside.

Jessica looked up as he walked out. She grinned. As he sat down across the table from her, she reached into her backpack and took out a glossy paperback book, more the size of a thick magazine than a usual paperback.

"Have you ever seen this?" She slid the book over to him.

Josh recognized the brightly colored pink cover that surrounded a photograph of an old grandfather clock. The clock's image was in negative black and white. A small ghost icon was at the top of this graphic.

"It's one of the Jeffrey books," he said. "I read all of these back in elementary school."

"I thought I had, too, but I've never seen this one," Jessica said. "I found it yesterday in the library before the fight broke out."

A hot flush rose up Josh's neck. The tips of his ears burn with embarrassment. He grinned bashfully. "Sorry about knocking you down. It was a mistake."

She smiled a sheepish embarrassed smile. "It's okay. I'm not mad or anything. I know you didn't mean to. Corey blew that way out of proportion."

"He has a tendency to do that. You were talking about this book."

She pointed to the title. "It's called *Jeffrey Presents 13 Modern Southern Ghosts*."

"They're all Jeffrey presents thirteen ghosts." Josh pulled the book closer to him.

He didn't recognize the cover either. The table of contents listed intriguing story titles like, "I. The Spook in the Clock" and "III. The Ghost U-boat of Dauphin Island". The copyright page showed a much more recent date, the late 1980s.

"Look at number eleven," she said.

Josh looked down the numbers at "XI. Hazel's Curse and the Homecoming Dance". He looked up at Jessica. She made a hand motion for him to read it. He had no idea what he might find but didn't feel much like delving into that particular can of worms right then.

"Can I keep the book?" he asked. "I'll read it later."

"I've got it checked out all week. I'm sorry you got suspended. I went and talked with Principal Chapman and told him they provoked you."

"He said I beat them up so bad that he had do something more than paddle me. My punishment here isn't that severe. No television while I'm suspended. It's not that bad. I've been reading some old Stephen King."

"*It*?"

"*Christine.*"

"You should read *It*. You won't sleep for a week."

"That doesn't sound fun at all."

The kitchen door opened. Josh's mother walked out wiping her hands on a dish cloth. She smiled.

"You guys want some tea?" she asked. They shook their heads no. "There's a change in menu. We're having frozen lasagna. Your dad called and had to take a player to the hospital. He won't make it to dinner."

"Who was it?" Josh asked. "It wasn't Thomas, was it?"

"Do you think I'd be standing here if it was?" she replied. "He didn't tell me, but your brother will be home soon enough. He can fill you in."

"Lasagna sounds good, Mrs. McAdams," Jessica said. "Anything sounds good. I'm starving. Lunch didn't stick with me."

"It'll be ready in about an hour or so. I hope Sim's okay with it," Josh's mother said.

"Probably won't be because it's I-talian, but beggars and choosers is the way I see it," Josh said.

"You've got some vinegar in you today," his mother said. "I'll tell your brother to pop out when he gets here to tell you who got hurt."

The door to the kitchen closed, leaving Josh and Jessica alone again in the backyard. The smell of burning leaves drifted on the air. It perfumed the moment perfectly. He stared at Jessica while she gazed into space. The sun still made her hair look fiery. She wasn't angry with him and had all but said that Corey was a loser. Ever since Corey Aaron took on his California persona, he'd been like that. Before that, he'd been a pretty cool dude, if a bit of redneck.

"I'm not allowed to go to the football game on Friday night because of my suspension."

"It applies to after-school activities too?" Jessica asked.

"Yeah, anyway, the old movie house downtown is showing *Night of the Living Dead* as a lead-up to Halloween. You want to go?"

"That Stephen King book has you in the mood for scary, doesn't it? I would love to."

Excitement fluttered through Josh. They hadn't ever been out to anything together except for football games, but that was more like a group activity.

"But I promised Corey I'd come to the game and watch him."

His heart sank. Despite all her implied dislike of what Corey had done after the fight, he was still able to lure her toward him. Josh had no idea how that fakey California stuff worked.

"All right. Maybe next week. They're showing *Blacula*, I think."

Jessica smiled. "You're keeping up with that dinky place's shows, aren't you?"

"I think it's cool the old place is trying to stay open. It's like keeping history alive. There's not many of those old places left in towns like ours."

"I've been in places like that. I know why."

"They've fixed it up. A revival of *Jaws* played there over the summer."

The kitchen door slammed open. Josh's mother yelled

something from deep inside the house. It was toward Thomas, who was the only person in the house who slammed open every single door as if he were still eight years old. Thomas hurried over to the table. He carried a tall glass of iced tea, which was mostly ice. He finished the liquid off as he sat down and sucked an ice cube into his mouth.

"Momma said for me to come out here," he said around the ice.

"Who got hurt?" Jessica asked.

"Cool," Thomas picked up the Jeffrey ghost book. "I've not thought about these in years." He looked at it. "I've never seen this one."

"That's why Jessica brought it by," Josh took it from his brother. "You can read it later after me."

"Who got hurt?" Jessica repeated.

"Neal Otis got the wind knocked out of him pretty hard, and daddy had to take Corey to the hospital for a possible concussion. Neal knocked the living sh—crap out of Corey."

Thomas stopped his swear to be respectful to Jessica. He did that around girls. It was one of his more noble personality quirks.

"Is he okay?" Jessica asked.

"Yeah, you said possible concussion," Josh feigned like he cared far more than he did.

"I don't know. Daddy hadn't called the coach with an update before I had to walk home." Thomas grabbed for the book again. "Momma's making lasagna. It smells awesome."

"I hope that he's okay," Jessica sounded worried.

"He will be," Josh said.

"He'll have to sit out at tomorrow's game," Thomas said, "but he'll be back next week. Unless it isn't a concussion, he'll play tomorrow night."

"I guess you might be able to go to that movie tomorrow after all," Josh said.

Jessica gave him a cross look. "That's a bit insensitive don't you think."

Josh turned sullen. He tried to not let it show, but Corey Aaron was like a grain of sand in his shoe. It was like his classmate had some kind of supernatural ability to make Josh look like a complete buffoon.

Sim stood in the bathroom with the water running into the sink. His daughter-in-law woke him up from his nap, which he didn't mean to take, to eat. Turns out that the sliced ham and mashed potato dinner he'd been promised ended up changing to some I-talian disaster. If he'd wanted frozen lasagna, he'd bought a TV dinner and eaten it at his own damn house.

Before walking into the bathroom to wash up for his less than desirable meal, he'd seen a book one of his grandkids had left on the couch as they walked through to go to their rooms. He flipped it open to see what it was about. A story listed in the table of contents caught his eye. It was called "Hazel's Curse and the Homecoming Dance". He had no idea what the whole story was about, but he knew about the witch named Hazel and her curse.

As he ran his hands under the water, not using any soap because all his family had to offer was Dove and that made a man's hands feel girly, he hadn't heard the story of Hazel's curse in a long time. It was a common story around campfires and hayrides during that time of the year when people started thinking about ghosts and goblins. The last time anyone told it was after Tommy Jones's funeral. He'd been sitting in the barbershop at the corner of Main Street and Maple Avenue. One of the old timers was talking about how it had come true. The old man claimed Tobias Abernathy descended from that old witch.

"Bullshit," Sim looked into the mirror as he turned off the water.

Caught up in his flashback, he forgot to avoid looking over his shoulder. Tobias Abernathy stared at him with a face that looked like it had been carved in stone. Sim blinked hard and shook his head. When he looked back over his shoulder, the face was an indistinct blob again.

"Bullshit," he repeated.

Chapter Ten

1956
A week until Homecoming

The air bore a crispness that Charlotte found delicious. She loved this time of the year. With everything going on in her life, she needed something she loved. As the light, cool breeze played with wisps of hair that had come free from her ponytail, the rumors and innuendoes about her seemed to drift away on the wind. Despite all the scuttlebutt she heard in whispers about her and Tobias, she still had to focus on getting the gym ready for the Homecoming dance. Connie was the teacher sponsor and wouldn't let her quit when she'd asked. Her brother's girlfriend assured her that if Charlotte quit the committee, the bigot kids would win. She also told her that they might even start rumors as to why she quit. Those rumors might get Charlotte sent away to an all-girls school in Mobile, something she didn't want.

Charlotte walked from the back door of the school toward the parking lot near the football field. Her friend Sheila DeLeon had promised her a ride home with her boyfriend, Ben Harris. Charlotte planned to use the short drive to convince Ben to help decorate the gym. The committee needed guys to do the heavy lifting and high work. So far she'd only talked Tommy into helping out. Tobias said he would help too, but she wasn't sure how her friends would treat him, so she'd put him off.

Sheila sat on the hood of Ben's mint green '48 Pontiac. He called it Lucille Balls—a crude joke that Charlotte didn't like, for despite all the talk, she was still a lady. Ben leaned close to his girl with a cigarette dangling from his mouth. The smoke blew toward Charlotte on the wind. It was some cheap brand that the boys smoked because they couldn't afford the good ones. Sim complained about how all the teenage guys stunk up Cardinal Drive-in with their cheap smokes.

"Look who it is," Ben said when he spied her.

"About time," Sheila said. "I thought we were going to have to leave you behind. Ben's got to get to work at the lumber mill by four."

"Wood ain't going to stack itself," he said.

"Sorry, but Ms. Dearborn stopped me at my locker. She wanted me to get some more guys to help out with the decorating committee," Charlotte said. "I couldn't get away."

"She's your brother's girlfriend. Couldn't she have told you that at dinner or something?" Sheila asked.

"I guess not," Charlotte replied. "Speaking of the committee, would you be interested in helping us out, Ben?"

He took a drag off his cigarette and smiled. "Stringing up crepe paper ain't much my style."

The football team rushed on the field. Ben watched them. The smile on his face fell to a frown. He dropped his cigarette and crushed it out with his foot. Sheila slid off the hood of the car as Ben walked to the driver's side. He got in, slamming the heavy door. The engine roared to life with a burst of gasoline-smelling exhaust.

"He's ready to go," Sheila said. "Better get in, or he'll leave us."

"That was sudden," Charlotte said.

Sheila turned so that her boyfriend couldn't see her lips. "He gets that way when the team takes the field. His chance to get out of this town was football. He can't play anymore."

"He can't help that his leg was broken," Charlotte said.

"It wasn't an accident," Sheila confessed. "Johnny House broke it with a baseball bat."

"Why?"

"Johnny was drunk, and Ben fumbled a football in the game, which caused us to lose. Johnny lost money on the game, a lot of money."

"Why didn't he turn him in?" Charlotte asked.

"Johnny threatened to do worse, but he also got Ben the job at the sawmill."

"Little consolation," Charlotte said.

Ben blew the car horn. Charlotte's skeleton tried to leap out of her skin. Sheila waved at him.

"He swears he's going to get Johnny back," Sheila said. "We better get in. He will leave us." She opened the door and pulled the seat forward so Charlotte could crawl into the back. "Don't worry—I'll talk him into helping us with the decorations."

Charlotte crawled into the back seat. Ben gunned the engine before Sheila got the door closed. Gravel flew into the air, and Charlotte was slung hard against the back seat. She closed her eyes after that, because she couldn't bear to see where they were going.

Chapter Eleven

Alan drove down the street toward the school. It was well after eight p.m., and he'd waited at the emergency room with Corey the whole time. The boy refused to call anyone in his family, even his brother. He said that his brother would bring his mother along and that meant she would make a scene. Alan agreed to his wishes against his better judgment. Had the injuries been bad, he could have gotten in a lot of trouble for not including the family. Fortunately, Corey didn't have a concussion. The X-rays and CAT scan showed nothing. The emergency room doctor said Corey had gotten his bell rung good and hard and should probably take it easy for a few days.

The marquee sign for the school shone in the distance. It was still too far away for Alan to read the black removable letters, but they announced the time of the next ball game and the opponent.

"Are you sure you don't want me to go by McDonald's and get you something to eat?" he asked Corey.

"No, thank you, Coach McAdams. I try not to eat that garbage unless it's absolutely necessary," he answered with his cool California-surfer-dude accent fully back in place.

Alan wished that the blow to the head might have changed that particular characteristic he'd acquired. "I wish you'd let me call your mother when we left the hospital. She's got to be worried about you since you're late."

Corey looked at him. "Late? I'll be home early tonight. I don't blow back into the house until around 10."

"What are you doing until then?"

For a moment when Corey rolled his eyes, he looked like the adolescent he was instead of the persona he adopted to try to make everyone believe he was better than a kid from a trailer park.

"Weren't you ever young?" Corey asked.

"A long time ago. Back then there was nothing to do in this town after the sun set, except on the weekend, and it was the drive-in or the picture house downtown."

"Things haven't changed that much," Corey said. "Before the days got shorter, I'd go to the park and swing. Sometimes I'd go fishing, but the mosquitos are bad. Lately, I've been helping plan the dance."

"The Homecoming dance?" Alan pulled up beside the only vehicle left in the student parking lot, an old Jeep that looked reminiscent of the one Daisy Duke drove, eagle on the hood and all.

"Not the school-sanctioned one," He stopped and looked Alan over. "That's all you need to know."

Alan put his car into park and turned to Corey. The dashboard lights of his Pontiac Grand Am glowed an orange-red color. It always gave the passenger a slightly ghoulish appearance. Corey looked absolutely horrific. The kid was too skinny. The lights caught in all the sunken in places on his face. It was skull-like.

"You don't mean the Massacre dance, do you?" Alan asked.

"I've already said too much. I guess I forgot you were a teacher since you've been cool about everything this evening."

"You can't think that's a good idea. You usually talk about how stuff that might offend people is wrong. Granola power and all that."

"Things that save Mother Earth are great. Parties are great too."

Corey got out of the car. He slammed the door. It peeved Alan a little bit, but after seeing the hunk of metal the boy drove, he realized that Corey must be used to having to put some muscle behind closing his vehicle's door and meant nothing by it. He pushed the button, and the passenger window slid down.

"Were you up at the old gym a few nights ago fooling

around inside?" Alan yelled through the window.

"No, and that's the truth," Corey answered.

Alan nodded at him and tossed his hand up to say goodbye. He shifted the car into drive, rolled up the window, and headed out of the parking lot. Nothing came up or down the street. It seemed strange for the town to be dead that early in the evening. Pinehurst had grown a lot since he was a kid. The interstate coming through less than fifteen miles from town helped the most. Still with all the growth, the sidewalks in this part of town rolled up at sundown. Out near the bypass, things still hopped. Walmart stayed opened a full twenty-four/seven. McDonald's, Burger King, and Taco Bell kept a brisk business until nearly midnight. Still, this part of town might as well have been twenty-five or forty years in the past.

Alan stopped and looked all the ways at the four-way stop at Maple Avenue and Raiders Street. Headlights glared at him coming up fast from Maple Avenue. The driver didn't dim them, and by the pace of the high beams' approach, the car wasn't slowing down. It shot through the intersection faster than any car should be able to drive on that street. Alan looked at the driver as he passed. The red cherry of a cigarette glowed in the dark cabin of the car. The driver flipped him off. Alan thought he'd seen him before. The car flew past so quickly, he wasn't sure what he'd seen, or how he'd even been able to make out a face in the darkness.

He glanced into the rearview mirror. The taillights of the car that had approached from Maple Avenue shot up Raiders Street. The car seemed to be accelerating. The taillights looked familiar to him. They were not modern lights but off a classic automobile from a time when Detroit made everything a little too auspicious. He hoped that Corey was either well on his way or still sitting in the parking lot, because whoever that driver was meant business.

That hope drifted away when a loud crash tightened his guts. It was the loudest car crash he'd ever heard. Alan's stomach sank as he looked back into his rearview mirror. The orange glow of fire flickered from the school.

Josh got comfortable in bed ready to delve into the book Jessica had brought with her. *Christine* lay ignored on the night table. As he opened Mrs. Windham's book to the story called "Hazel's Curse and the Homecoming Dance," he hoped *Christine* didn't decide to make its fiction reality and attack him in a jealous rage. A chuckle escaped him in spite of himself. A killer book would make a good Stephen King novel.

The story started with a black and white picture of the old Pinehurst High School gym. A little cartoon ghost floated over the title of the story on the page opposite the picture.

Hazel's Curse and the Homecoming Dance
The once sleepy town of Pinehurst is nestled in the dwindling foothills of the Appalachian Mountains in northwest Alabama. The small unassuming town holds a dark secret and a haunted past. It is a tale told in two parts. One involves a curse left by an old slave woman named Hazel. The other is a gory tale of mass murder and lynch mobs in the Jim Crow 1950s.

It is said that after the Civil War, there lived an old black woman named Hazel. Most of the folks around the Harrington Plantation near the town of Mount Pisgah, now called Pinehurst, believed this woman to be a voodoo priestess and witch doctor. Many people from the surrounding county would come to her for cures from a toothache to the gout. She seemed to cure them all. Until a man named Silas McAdams came to her for help to cure an ailment his sister had.

Josh stopped reading as soon as he saw his last name. Had Jessica read the story and passed it on to him for that specific reason, or because the story took place in their town? He skimmed over the next few paragraphs. The author's lolling prose had its time and place, but this was not one of them. He needed to get to the meat of the story.

But Hazel was not able to cure McAdams's sister's condition with her powders and potions, according to the story. She told Silas that she needed to see his sister in person.

Silas was by no means a man given to messing with former slaves. He and his family were already outsiders in the community for being rather freshly off the boat from Scotland. Their deep accents made them hard to understand, and the simple folk of Mount Pisgah were suspicious of them because they came after the surrender of General Lee and might be carpetbaggers. Despite the stigma it might put upon his family, Silas agreed to take the old woman to visit with his sister.

The meeting occurred on a stormy afternoon in October. The day had been unusually warm, a precursor to the storms. Silas's sister lay in her bed at the back of the very small house that they shared with their mother. They found her in a full fit of a seizure.

Hazel took out a special mixture of roots and herbs she had made to help stop the disease and placed it underneath the sister as she lurched in the fit. Then the old voodoo priestess chanted and danced around on the floor for a few minutes. Finally, she drew symbols on the floorboards in chalk.

"Give this dram to her two hours after the fit passes," Hazel said to Silas, giving him one last concoction.

As thunder rolled in the distance, Hazel left to walk back to her shack at the Harrington Plantation. Silas followed her instructions. Two hours after the seizure ceased, he forced the dram down his sister's throat. Instead of getting better, she died.

Josh looked at the photograph under that section of text. It was of an elaborate tombstone from the local cemetery. It was a broken column with a wreath carved into it. C. W. McAdams was carved in the base. They had taken flowers there when he was kid.

The caption underneath the picture told him exactly why Jessica had given him the book. It read "The grave of Charlotte Winifred McAdams, Silas's sister, in Pinehurst Hill Cemetery." A cold chill ran though him.

Josh skimmed over the rest of the story. Delving too deeply might freeze him to death. As he suspected, Silas went to Hazel's house that night and lynched her. As she died, she cursed not only him but the town because others in the community had helped him dispatch her. All the town needed was a little motivation to rid themselves of a witch, even if she had helped them many times. A growing unease built up in Josh's stomach. Most of the stories that Kathryn Tucker Windham wrote about in her books were campfire tales. Every now and then one appeared to have more truth to it. He thought about the courthouse in

Pickens County, where a ghostly face could clearly be seen in the window. His dad pointed it out every time they drove to the Tombigbee River to fish.

The next page picked up with the contemporary story that the title of the book promised.

The old witch's curse gave everyone forty years before she would return in reincarnated form. With her dying breath, she said it was so people would forget about it and never expect it to strike. And so nothing happened for years after that fateful, stormy night the people of Mount Pisgah lynched the old woman. However, forty years to the day after old Hazel cursed the town, a devastating tornado hit, destroying everything in a mile wide swath. It had spun off of a storm that many survivors described as coming from nowhere. Obituaries recorded in the newspapers of the day listed among the dead a few of the citizens alive at the time of the lynching. Others were the young descendants of people who participated in the lynching. Silas McAdams, who was 80, was found with a hemp rope wrapped around his neck. A self-styled preacher with a traveling gypsy revival, known as Reverend Junkins, was killed as well. This is only worth mentioning because a variety of strange articles were found in his belongings, including locks of hair and what locals described as voodoo dolls. When the town was rebuilt, the citizens called it Pinehurst for the original founding family of the town. Many thought that the destruction of the town would have appeased the old curse, but that did not seem to be the case.

The feeling of dread and anticipation wound tightly in him. Even *Christine*, written by the skillful hand of a suspense master, couldn't wind such a tight wire.

Forty years to the day after that horrible tornado, a far more devastating tragedy hit the town of Pinehurst. On the eve of the big Homecoming dance in 1956, a group of students from the high school and one of their teachers were murdered in cold blood. Although the murderer was never brought to trial, local townspeople killed a suspect. Tobias Abernathy, a black youth whose parents worked for the Harrington family, and who was the only non-white student at the local high school, was lynched for the crime. He was captured by a group of three local men, one of whom was a descendant of Silas McAdams.

Locals say that the curse is hogwash, but they talk about it only in hushed voices out of the earshot of anyone. A few openly say that the vengeful spirit of Hazel drove the boy to kill the students in revenge. Most all of them wait to see what the next forty-year anniversary might bring.

Josh closed the bright pink cover of the book and tossed it across the room into the chair at his desk. He wanted the book away from him. It was sinister. The book probably came into existence only for the anniversary. Paranoid thoughts about the author being a witch in her own right bothered him even more, because Joshua didn't believe in ghosts or witches.

He grabbed the Stephen King novel and delved back into it. The comfort of a fictional story was what the doctor ordered. It seemed strange that an author recognized for instilling terror into people would help him feel at ease, but there it was. After a while and several chapters, Josh fell asleep. His bedside lamp stayed on all night.

Chapter Twelve

1956
Three weeks after the Massacre

Charlotte sat in her backyard under the shade of a magnolia tree. The musky smell of the tree filled her nostrils. It had been like this for a few days, ever since her mind started working again even if her body still wouldn't cooperate. After giving her the series of bitter pills the doctor had prescribed, Mother would help her dress as if she were going to school, and would lead her out to sit for an hour under the tree before taking her back inside. Today, Charlotte wore a heavy sweater. It wasn't a letterman sweater or even her cheerleading equivalent. It was a long woolen one her mother wore to town on brisk autumn days.

The sun shone brightly in the November morning. She wished that maybe her mother would have set her in the sun. The shade was too cool, but the sun would have warmed her perfectly. A ray of it hit her ankle and charmed it with jovial radiance. No matter how much she yelled at herself from the depths of her own mind, Charlotte couldn't make herself move or speak on her own, but in a little while her mother would come back out and help her stand and walk back into the house. Sometime after that, she'd be spoon-fed lunch, usually a hearty soup which didn't need much chewing. Once the food was in her mouth, things seemed to run on instinct. She could chew some and swallow with no problem.

The back screen door slammed. Charlotte couldn't see who it was. The footsteps coming up behind her rustled in the leaves. Over the last few days, as she became less overwhelmed by all the stimuli entering her mind, she'd learned her family by the heaviness of their steps and cadence of their stride through the unraked leaves. In the autumn, keeping the front and back yards tidy was her chore. Her folks decided not to do it for her, perhaps as motivation to make her get up and do something. They moped around so much they probably couldn't do it. Depression gripped her parents. She'd seen her daddy come in from work; even in her current near-catatonic state, Charlotte could tell that he looked like he had aged fifteen years in the last few weeks.

Now the person behind her got into his actual true stride. Sim had come for a visit. He'd started coming more frequently the last few days, and he always brought her something.

"Hey, Charlotte, it's me, Sim," he said as if he was talking to a little kid. "I brought you something."

He bent down so that his face took up most of her vision. Charlotte noticed that her brother had started looking a lot older too. Ever since he and Sally had divorced, he'd begun taking on the qualities of a craggy old man, but her brother looked in his mid-forties now instead of shy of thirty. He held out a very beautiful, long-stemmed pink rose and put it in her hand, forming her fingers around the stem, avoiding hitting any of the pricks. Her hand would hold it there until someone changed the position.

"I brought the boys with me. I've got them this weekend. They've been asking about their Aunt Charlotte. Alan seems very concerned. He's a bit older than his age would tell." Sim smiled. "Would you like to see them? It's been a while."

Of course she wanted to see them. She loved her nephews much more than she did her brother, especially now. Every day he would come and leave a gift, whether a beautiful rose or a stuffed teddy bear. Charlotte knew what he'd done. They, her family, her friends, and other townsfolk thought she couldn't hear as well as all the other stuff she couldn't do, but nothing slipped past her attention after a few doses of the medication her mother dissolved in a glass of water every morning and evening. He and his goofy friends had caught poor Tobias and hanged him. There was no way that Tobias had killed her friends. The extremeness of the murders was too much for one person to pull off. Plus, he was a gentle soul that only she truly understood.

"I'm going to bring them out," Sim said. "I'll be right back, and they won't stay too long to bother you."

He ran back to the house. The screen door creaked opened but didn't slam shut. Her brother yelled into the house for the boys. Usually, her two nephews would bound down the stairs with lots of rambunctious boy-noise. Now, their hard-soled shoes clicked on the wooden back steps as they walked softly down them. Sim, and probably her mother, had instructed them on how to act around their *crazy* Aunt Charlotte. They probably told the boys to act like they were in church.

The screen door slammed, and feet shuffled through the leaves. One of the boys, most likely little Mikey, kicked at them. Sim hushed him down in a whisper. They walked into her view. Her bother had his hands clasped down on her nephews' shoulders, holding them fast. They looked cute, overdressed as if they *were* going to church. Each had on a wonderful little coat too warm for the weather. Mikey fidgeted a bit. Alan stood rod stiff. Both had precocious little dimpled smiles on their faces. Alan's cowlick stuck straight up from the crown of his head like Dennis the Menace in the comic strips. Mikey remained pudgy like a toddler despite nearly being old enough for school.

"Boys," Sim urged them.

"Hello, Aunt Charlotte," her nephews said at the same time. Alan's voice was clear. Mikey still had a little-boy lisp.

She longed to say hello back. They both seemed to have a longing on their face that said they did as well. The doctor must have told her family to bring them by to see if it would help break her out of this state. The doctor and her family had been talking about sending her down to Bryce Hospital in Tuscaloosa until she started walking and talking on her own. He'd given her mother and father little hope for her recovery. This had to be the last ditch effort. Everyone knew how much she loved those two boys, especially Alan.

"Aunt Charlotte, they said that you were gone someplace in

your head and couldn't find your way back out," Alan rubbed her hand that didn't have the rose in it.

Sim squeezed his hand hard on the boy's shoulder. Her favorite nephew flinched. His daddy was such a big bully. She hated to think how mean he was to his sons even at that age. He never showed it around her, but she could only imagine.

"All right," Sim said with very tight lips. "We're going to go back inside now."

"No, daddy," Alan said. "We just got here. She hasn't told us a knock-knock yet."

Sim jerked on his sons and started away from Charlotte. "She ain't going to tell you a knock-knock joke. We talked about this."

"Why?" Mikey asked.

"Because she can't," Sim sounded angrier. "We're going back inside so these boys don't bother you."

"No," protested Alan.

"Yes."

Charlotte concentrated all the effort she could. He didn't need to take her nephews away so quickly. Even if they couldn't have their usual interaction with each other, their presence alone made her feel better. Now Sim was going to take them away. They wouldn't be waiting inside, playing in his old bedroom when they brought her back inside. They'd be gone, not to be seen again until probably Christmas, when they would be whisked away as quickly to keep from bothering her. She needed those little rays of sunshine to warm her on this chilly day, in her cold existence.

"Come on boys," he said.

"No." Charlotte barely forced the word out of her lips. She wasn't even sure it was loud enough to overpower the sound of the rustling of the leaves.

Sim stopped and stared at her as if into her soul. "Did you say something?"

"No." It came out louder but still a whisper. "No." Her voice gained strength. "No." It was a spoken word, soft, but not whispered.

Sim let go of the boys and ran toward the house yelling for

his Momma and Daddy. Alan and Mikey smiled. Even at their young ages, they recognized what had happened. Alan took her free hand again and squeezed it.

Knock. Knock, she said to herself and answered who's there. *Your Aunt Charlotte.* Alan looked at her and laughed as if he had heard the joke.

Chapter Thirteen

Alan sat at his kitchen table. A glass of whiskey sat in front of him. The glass sweated as the ice melted, watering down the booze. Diane had poured it for him not long after he arrived home around 11 p.m. He'd taken two sips from the glass. The smell of whiskey usually made him queasy. He only kept it in the house because according to his father, it was a man's drink. After that evening, he needed a little bit of the manly bravado that a slug of whiskey brought.

Diane sat across from him in silence. Her glass of hot tea had gone cold a long time ago. She, too, had barely touched her drink. The grandmother clock in the living room chimed midnight—the witching hour, when nothing good ever happened.

"We probably need to go to bed," his wife said. "We still have to go to work tomorrow. I'm sure it's going to be a long day for you."

"You're right. I was hoping that this drink would make me drowsy. I'm not sure I can sleep."

"Try." She stood with her teacup in her hand. She took his glass of booze and put them both into the sink.

Alan stood and followed his wife out of the kitchen, turning the light out as he went. As they crossed through the living room, his shocked imagination flashed police lights outside his window. The real lights had dazzled him a long time that evening, and his mind didn't seem to want it to drift away.

"Do you think I should wake Thomas and Josh up to tell them?" he asked.

"It can wait until tomorrow."

"I don't want them to find out at school. They need to be prepared for this kind of thing. He was on the team with Thomas and was Josh's classmate."

Diane stopped at the base of the stairs. "As I remember, Josh didn't like him very much, and Thomas called him, and I quote, 'douchebag'."

"The boy's dead. Have some compassion."

"I do, but it's late and my ability to show it is declining. Let's go to bed. I'm too tired to filter my thoughts right now."

She disappeared down the hallway that led to their bedroom. He followed. They both fell into the bed without much production. Diane wrapped herself up in the covers. Alan slid his bare feet beneath the linen and stared at the ceiling. A sliver of light from the streetlamp at the end of their driveway sneaked in past the dark, heavy curtains. It gave him enough light to look for patterns in the textured ceiling tiles. Alan often did this when he was not able to sleep. It sometimes helped to make him drowsy, much better than counting sheep; but tonight, his mind chased invisible rabbits.

After he had heard the crash, he'd turned around in the street and headed back to the school. The old car that had barreled up the street had slammed into Corey's Jeep. Somehow the old school Detroit beast had nearly split the vehicle in two. Corey had lain on the pavement several yards from the burning hulk of his Jeep. Alan couldn't believe the distance and had even paced it off. Corey's body hadn't been thrown that far by the impact; the other car had dragged him as it kept going and disappeared into the night. There was no way that car could have done that kind of damage—but he'd seen it with his own eyes, so it had happened, despite all that his rationality told him.

The people who lived around the school had called the police before he'd gotten to the scene, and they had arrived quickly. The first officer to arrive was McDonald, whom Alan recognized as the one who came with the drug-sniffing dog and swept the school twice a year. It was McDonald who caught Alan vomiting into the storm drain. He was also the officer who took his statement. Alan told him what he knew. The car had driven past quickly, so he could only tell some vague things about it like its color— blue—and that it was from the 1950s.

Staring at the ceiling, reliving the carnage and feeling nauseous again, Alan belatedly recognized the car. It was a 1954 Mercury Monterey two-door coupe. The interior was in near mint condition, oiled and cleaned frequently since the late 1950s, and very rarely driven. The car ought to be sitting in his Aunt Charlotte's garage.

Alan waited a few more minutes until his wife breathed deeply enough that moving wouldn't disturb her sleep. He got up and left the house. For some reason, he couldn't drive his own car, so he took Josh's. The radio station played the weird late-night music that his sons' generation listened to. It was dark and twisty. Alan changed the station to Soft Rock 94.5. Elton John sang about laughing like children and living like lovers. It settled Alan's nerves enough that he backed the car onto the street without scraping the tail pipe.

The drive to his aunt's house didn't take very long. No one drove at that time of night. Even the police rarely patrolled, and tonight they certainly wouldn't be doing too much of that except to look for a hit-and-run driver. He pulled into Charlotte's driveway. The garage door was down, and from his car, the front door appeared closed.

Alan got out of the car and walked to the garage. He and his sons had installed a keypad on the outside that would activate the automatic door opener with a code number. He flipped the cover off the keypad. The rubber keys illuminated with a green light. He punched in 5700 and hit enter. The motor of the opener hummed, and the door started to lift.

He squatted and walked under the still-moving door, impatient to get a look at his aunt's car. The dim light given off by the door opener proved his deepest fear. The garage was empty. Only a dried oil stain marked where the Mercury Monterey should have been. Alan sighed. For a long moment, he stood in the pale light in the middle of the old stain with his hands cupped over his mouth to keep him from screaming in frustration.

The light clicked off. Alan made his way across the

pitch-dark garage until his leg hit the edge of the steps into the house. He fumbled with his keys until he felt the rubber cap that he kept on Charlotte's house key. With this key protruded out, he walked up the steps and fumbled with the doorknob until he got it unlocked. The air that rushed out into the garage smelled like Aunt Charlotte's house always did. Despite all the other things she had wrong with her, she kept a clean house and always had it smelling of eucalyptus.

Alan flipped the light switch, and the laundry room lit up. He reached back into the garage, hit the button that closed the garage door, then made his way through the maze of laundry-room clutter to the kitchen door. The light spilled into the kitchen as he entered it. Everything looked exactly like it had the night he'd sent her to the hospital. If she'd been home at any point, she'd avoided coming in there. Unless she'd escaped from the psych ward that evening, though, she wouldn't have been able to do that.

He used the light from the laundry room to navigate through the kitchen into the small sitting room between the kitchen and the main entrance hallway. This room was windowless, and the light didn't fall far enough to illuminate it. As Alan walked through the open door, something brushed across the top of his head. He reached up to swat at it, imaging some kind of giant spider web. Instead of sticky spider silk, his hand entangled in paper. He jerked it down, and a long strand of crepe paper fell. Some of it hit him on the head, and he could tell more of it fell to the floor ahead of him. He shook it off and hurried to the nearest table to turn on a lamp. The lamp clicked on after two turns of the switch. The red shade cast crimson light though the room except for directly above and below.

Streamers scalloped across the ceiling in crimson and a strange purple color. The ends dangled in the two doorways like tentacles. Alan went into the hallway, knocking the streamers away from his head as he did. He flipped on the light. More crepe paper hung in this room along with a tissue paper ball. The paper was its true color, baby blue and gray. Alan ran through the rest of the house turning lights on in every room. Baby blue and gray crepe paper hung from the ceiling, some hanging straight down in small pieces. In other places, scallops of it sagged.

Alan stood in the middle of the living room. The swags of crepe paper dropped low and touched the top of his head. A large punch bowl that he didn't recognize sat on the coffee table. Paper cups the same colors as the streamers sat beside the bowl. Speaker wires ran from the sides of a turntable sitting on the television, but someone had twisted the crepe paper around them to make them more festive. He walked to the record player and switched it on. The needle was already in the groove, and music blasted out.

The Crew Cuts sang "Sh-Boom." Alan knocked the needle off the record. A loud scratching sounded out almost like feedback as the needle shot across the vinyl. He started grabbing at the crepe paper, ripping it down. Something primal and fearful built up in him at that moment.

He ran to the door. On a banner above it, written in baby blue and gray poster paint, were the words "Homecoming 1956."

Alan flung open the front door and slammed it behind him as he stormed across the porch and hurried back to the car. Every light in the house glowed through the windows. In those few rooms that had open curtains, the decorations hung ready for a party. The sight of them infuriated him more and more. He gunned the car too much backing up. The rear end crashed on the street. If Josh had been there, he would have given the teenage boy the lecture of his life, but his son wasn't there, and Alan wasn't in the mood anyway. The tires squealed as he shot off down the streets. Neighbors would call the cops, but he didn't care. The Pinehurst PD was too busy—and would be even busier after he reported this sick break-in, or whatever it was.

It took only a matter of minutes to get to the hospital. Alan had driven far too fast, but he was a man on a mission. The elevator took him to the third floor. Two large steel doors blocked the ward immediately to the left of the elevator. A call button hung on the wall. He punched it and waited.

"Can I help you?" a gruff male voice asked, sounding a bit confused.

"This is Charlotte McAdams's nephew, Alan McAdams. Her

patient number is 2250. I need to speak to someone," he said back into the box.

"Sir, it's 2 a.m. Can't this wait until morning?"

"It is morning, and no it can't wait."

The voice now sounded a bit miffed. "You can't come on the unit. It's after visitation time, but I'll be out there in a minute."

When one of the metal doors opened, Alan stood with his arms crossed, patting a foot. It took the far too fat nurse far too long to get to the door, at least five minutes. Alan's face showed his frustration. His skin pulled tight around a grimace.

"Can I help you?" the nurse asked. A big smile came on his ruddy, moon face when he noticed Alan's look.

"You could have helped me five minutes ago. It's late," Alan said. "I need to see my aunt."

"It's after visiting hours."

"You've already told me that, but someone has broken into her house and stolen her car."

"We can tell her that tomorrow. Right now she's sleeping."

"She is here?"

"I looked in on her before I came to the door. That is why it took me five minutes."

"She's been here the whole night?"

"Of course—those doors are locked. We have to let people in or out."

His aunt hadn't put the slip on the zookeepers and gone on a psychotic rampage. This relieved Alan. The fact that *someone* had stolen her car and done that to her house disturbed him more than the idea that she had caused the wreck.

"Sorry to bother you," Alan said. "I'll try to come around to see her tomorrow."

"Have a good night and a safe drive home. Take extra care; you look a bit stressed."

Alan nodded and hit the button for the elevator. The doors slid open, and he stepped back onto it. He would have to wait until daylight to notify the police about the break-in. After everything that had happened, he wasn't sure that he would be coherent enough to give them a sensible-sounding report tonight.

Sim was at his kitchen table, drinking a strong cup of coffee and reading the paper, when his phone rang. He reached up and grabbed it off the wall.

"Hello."

"Is this Simeon McAdams?" a very serious voice asked on the other end.

"It is." The person either meant business or was trying to sell him something, because no one ever called him Simeon.

"Sir, this is the Pinehurst Police. We've found your car."

"My car? I don't have a car. I've got a beat-up old pickup truck that I can see through the window," he said back, a little confused.

"We found a 1954 Mercury Monterey out on Harrington Road. There was a registration in the glove box with your name on it," the officer said.

Sim stood up. "That's my sister's car, but she's in the hospital."

"It's in pretty bad shape, and we think it was involved in a hit-and-run that killed a young man last night. Are you sure your sister is in the hospital?"

"I'm positive. Officer, let me get in my truck, and I'll be out there in about fifteen minutes."

"Sir, they've got an active investigation going out there, I don't know if that's advisable."

"I don't care. If my sister might be involved in this, I need to be there."

Sim hung up the phone. He took the keys from the hanger at the door and headed to his truck. The morning was cool, bordering on cold, and he'd walked out wearing only an old pair of jeans and a white undershirt. His jacket lay in the passenger side as did an old ball cap. He pulled the cap over his mussed hair and slipped into the jacket before getting into the truck.

It took him exactly fifteen minutes to get to the car. The police had both sides of Harrington Road blocked off, which didn't mean too much, because the only people who lived down that road were the Harringtons. A black police officer stopped him. Sim pulled onto the shoulder and got out of the pickup.

"Sir," the officer said. "I need you to get back into your truck, and head back toward town. This is an official police investigation. We don't need any bystanders."

Sim pushed past the cop, not giving his position any respect. "Don't worry, boy, I'm not a looky-loo. I'm Simeon McAdams. The car is registered to me."

"Dispatch got a hold of you, good." The officer walked with him toward a group of three more officers. When they got there, the black officer took the lead. "Chief, this is the owner of the car."

The chief nodded his head with complete recognition and put his hand out. "Sim, I had no idea this was your car."

"What happened?" Sim asked.

"We've got no idea. All we know is that a car matching this description cut through a Jeep Wrangler last night like butter and killed the driver, a student at the high school. From the look of the front end of the thing, I believe it is the culprit, but I can't figure out how it kept driving with that much damage."

"They made them tough back then," Sim said.

He looked past the chief to the car. It sat in the middle of the road. The right rear tire was flat. The trunk was popped. Two tow truck guys were changing the tire. Now the black officer who greeted him was bending over into the trunk compartment like he was going to climb inside. Sim flashed back forty years to the night that he, Johnny, and Marshall caught Tobias Abernathy. The car was even in the same spot.

"It belongs to my sister," he said, "but she's in the nut ward at the hospital. Somebody must have stolen it."

An old memory came to Sim's mind as he looked at the car and processed the idea that it had killed a boy from the school. A tingle streaked up his arm, and tightness clamped in his chest before everything went black as his head hit the road.

Chapter Fourteen

1956
Six weeks after the Massacre

Charlotte sat in the living room. Her mother had moved a tin TV tray in there with her. A thick ham sandwich with lots of mayonnaise, some potato salad, and a sweating glass of tea sat on the tray. In the middle of the day, nothing much was on television. Charlotte sat staring at an awful soap opera. A knock on the door echoed from the front as she picked up her sandwich and bit into it. Lifting the food was like lifting heavy rocks, but she had done it.

Ever since the day Sim had brought the boys over, Charlotte had kept improving from her near catatonic state, thanks to the barbiturates she now took three times per day. When the doctor visited, he no longer secretly talked to her parents about Bryce Hospital. Instead, they all discussed her progress. Every day, she did something else on her own. Those things progressively got easier. Feeding herself was a priority this week. Last week it was moving her shoulders up and down. All this after the torturous effort of speaking again.

Charlotte shoved the spoon into the pile of potato salad. Mastering the use of utensils still gave her some trouble, but like a little kid, she took the spoon with both hands to retrieve it from the pile. After that, one hand guided it to her mouth.

Someone knocked on the door again.

"Momma," she yelled, physically forcing the air up to do so. "Someone's at the door."

"I'm coming," her momma yelled toward the door, while

hurrying through the living room wiping her hands on her apron. She disappeared into the entryway.

The door opened, but no one stepped inside. The floorboards in front of the door always creaked when someone stepped on them, which made sneaking in extra-hard. There was some soft talking at the door. She strained to hear, but the television interfered.

"I don't know if you should," her mother said. "The doctor said we should not cause her anymore stress than necessary."

The person at the door whispered back. Charlotte couldn't hear the words. She wished they'd speak up.

"I can't let you in," Momma said. "It isn't proper, and she can't walk yet. I suppose that's that. I'm sorry. Thank you for coming by."

The door closed, and her mother walked back into the room, this time wringing the end of her apron. She looked worried.

"What's the matter, Momma?"

"Nothing. Go on and eat your lunch." Her mother looked at her with more sympathetic eyes. "Are you handling that spoon okay, or do I need to help you with it?"

"Watch."

Charlotte took the spoon and fed herself from the potato salad. For an added spectacle, she used both hands to take her tea glass and drink from it. Everything went back in place without making a huge mess. Her mother smiled and clapped her hands together like she'd watched some kind of magic trick.

"Thank you, thank you," Charlotte said as if she had pulled a rabbit out of a hat.

"That's wonderful. Soon you'll be up running around," her mother said.

"I hope so. That way I can change the television to something better."

"I can do that," her momma said. "What do you want it on?"

"Turn it off. There's nothing good on during this time of the day, but a bunch of stupid soap operas."

Her mother switched off the set and headed back to the kitchen. Charlotte took another bite of her sandwich. The doorbell rang. Her mother looked back to the entryway. Worry lines formed around her eyes and forehead.

"Are you sure everything's okay?" Charlotte asked with a mouthful of sandwich.

"It's fine, and don't talk with your mouth open, or you'll choke. That's the last thing I need."

The bell rang again. Her mother twisted the bottom of her apron. With the third ring from the bell and a heavy rap on the door, she let go of the apron, stood straight and walked into the entryway. The door opened.

"I told you that this wasn't a good time," her mother said well before the door was opened all the way. "I'm sorry."

"I would like to see your daughter, Mrs. McAdams." Charlotte recognized the slow, drawly female voice. It was pitched higher than most while it lulled out with molasses thickness.

"The doctor said," her mother protested.

"I'm sure the *doctor* would not think a visit from me too stressful," Mrs. Harrington said with an entitled tone. "I know him well."

"But it's not proper, and my husband isn't at home," her mother protested.

"Don't worry. I'll come in alone. Everything will stay peachy keen," Mrs. Harrington said.

The boards at the door creaked. The door closed as Mrs. Harrington, fashionably dressed in a green dress with matching hat and handbag, walked into the living room. Charlotte's mother swept in behind her. She grabbed the TV tray and whisked it into the kitchen. Charlotte didn't have time to protest about her food being taken away.

"You didn't have to do that, Mrs. McAdams," Mrs. Harrington perched on the edge of one of the wingback chairs that sat to the side of the windows. "I've seen people eat sandwiches before, and Charlotte is convalescing. She needs her strength."

"She can have it back when you leave," her mother said, coming back into the room without her apron on. She sat in the chair on the other side of the window.

"Charlotte, I've come to see how you are doing."

"Thank you, Mrs. Harrington. That is very nice of you," Charlotte said. "As you can tell, I am talking very well."

"I had heard that. What about walking?"

"Not yet. But I'm feeding myself and hope to be up and about soon."

"We're more than pleased with her progress, as is her doctor," her mother said.

"It is very wonderful, especially after such horrible circumstances. No lady should have to hear those kind of things, much less see them." Mrs. Harrington said this with a sound of horror in her thick accent. It sounded somehow genteel and didn't bother Charlotte any.

When other people had mentioned the massacre, Charlotte would sometimes swoon. Her mother looked tensed ready to spring into action, but she relaxed when Charlotte kept focused. Mrs. Harrington must have noticed the change in her mother's body language because she smiled and laughed softly.

"I may be here for a short spell, but I am awfully parched. Mightn't I have a glass of water?" she asked.

Charlotte's mother jumped to her feet and almost slapped her cheeks as she threw her hands up to her face horrified that she'd forgotten to offer the Harrington woman a drink. She controlled herself.

"Would you like sweet tea instead?"

"Tea sounds lovely," Mrs. Harrington answered.

"Could you please bring my glass back out when you come?" Charlotte asked.

She had been around long enough to know that it was rude to let a visitor drink alone. While they waited for her mother to return, Charlotte and Mrs. Harrington stared at each other in awkward silence. The notion dawned on Charlotte that her visitor hadn't intended on being one. They had never met each other. The only common bond they had was Tobias. Her mother came back into the room, carrying both glasses of tea on the TV tray. She sat the tray in front of Charlotte and took the other glass to Mrs. Harrington, who graciously took it and sipped from it before sitting it on a low table between the chairs.

"Can I be frank, Mrs. Harrington?" Charlotte asked.

"That will be fine," she replied.

"Why did you come to see me? We've never met. Is this some kind of charity like the Daughters of the Confederacy?" Charlotte asked. "Because I might be a little on the crazy side right now, but I'm not a charity case."

"Charlotte," her mother barked at her.

Mrs. Harrington laughed. It wasn't a polite high society chuckle, but a real *I'm glad the elephant in the room has been addressed* laugh. The tension broke with an almost audible crack like thunder.

"It is okay, Mrs. McAdams. We both know she is absolutely right. I didn't come to see her. I never intended to set foot in your home, no offense. I came with the Abernathys so they could see her and not be looked at strangely for being in this neighborhood alone."

"Tobias's parents are here?" Charlotte asked.

"They are waiting in the car outside. Your mother, quite rightly, would not let them in. It is not proper. I should have known better."

"Let them in," Charlotte said.

She wanted to jump out of her skin. What did they want to say to her that would bring them into town? She needed to see them.

"We can't do that," her mother said. "The neighbors would talk. Your daddy would find out."

"Daddy wouldn't mind. You know that. At least let them on the porch and help me to the door."

"No," Mrs. Harrington said. "I think your mother is right."

"She's not. Daddy's not one of those cross-burning bigots."

"But your brother is," Mrs. Harrington said with a cold tone that chilled Charlotte more than the ice in the tea. "I'm sorry, Mrs. McAdams."

Charlotte looked at her mother, who cast her eyes to the floor in shame. "I know what he is."

Her mother's admission shocked Charlotte more than the tone of Mrs. Harrington's voice. Sim was the golden child who never did a thing wrong. He'd been the yardstick her parents held Charlotte strictly to.

"I'm surprised they would even want to touch their feet on my lawn, having raised him," her mother said. "He did such a horrible thing to their boy."

"It speaks to the admiration they have for your daughter," Mrs. Harrington said.

Charlotte looked out the window. Through the lace curtains, she spied a large Lincoln parked on the street. Two dark figures sat in the front. The man, Mr. Abernathy, wore a fedora. Mrs. Abernathy appeared to be wearing a hat she probably wore to church. They stared straight ahead.

Something inside her changed. It clicked like the tumblers of a lock. She pressed her hands in the sofa and pushed herself to her feet. Her mother gasped as she gained a wobbly balance on her own for the first time. She took a step forward. It was stiff-legged, and she walked like Frankenstein's Monster.

"Momma, come help me."

Her mother rushed over to her and took her by the arm to help steady her. They walked stiffly and slowly toward the front door. Mrs. Harrington stood and took her other arm as they passed her.

"Please, sit back down," her mother said to Mrs. Harrington.

"Nonsense," she replied.

All three walked to the door. Her mother opened it. The chilly December air hit Charlotte in the face like a motivating slap. Tobias's parents sat in the car. They noticed her and turned their attention toward her.

"Charlotte, let's go back inside," her mother said. "You're not dressed for this air."

"Hush, Mother."

Charlotte took hold of the handrail by the steps and went down them. By this time, she'd shaken off the training wheels that had been her mother and Mrs. Harrington. Her steps became more human. By the time she got to the Lincoln, no one would have ever guessed that she had ever had difficulty walking.

Mr. Abernathy got out of the car. He took hold of her arm before she stepped off the curb. His wife was quickly around the car to take her other arm.

"Child, what are you doing?" Mrs. Abernathy asked.

"Coming to thank you for your visit," Charlotte said.

"You should not have done that," Mr. Abernathy said. "You could have told Mrs. Harrington and that would have been enough."

"No, it wouldn't have," she replied. "I'm sorry about Tobias."

"Thank you," Mrs. Abernathy answered.

"He liked you very much," Mr. Abernathy said. "He always said you were the only person at the school and maybe the whole town besides the Harringtons who seemed to care about his well-being."

"I did."

"Here in a little while, I'm driving Mr. Harrington to the sheriff's office," Mr. Abernathy said. "We're going to get Tobias's car out of impound. The missus and I want you to have it."

"I couldn't take your car."

Mrs. Harrington joined them at the curb. "It was his—Tobias's. My husband bought it for him to drive to school and such because they wouldn't let him ride the bus. He agrees that you should have it."

She looked in her friend's parents' eyes. Hope and sadness dwelled there. It was a piteous look.

"Okay." The words barely came out, and her strength left her.

Charlotte slumped in the Abernathys' grip. They helped her back to the porch, and her mother, without saying a word, got her into the house. The car soon pulled away. Her mother closed the door after helping Charlotte back to the couch.

"That was too much," her mother said once she came back into the room. "Are you still hungry?"

Charlotte shook her head. The ability to speak had left her again, as had her appetite. She didn't want her mother to know this, so she closed her eyes and faked sleep. After a while, she dozed. By suppertime, Mr. Harrington had delivered Tobias's '54 Mercury Monterey, with the title already changed over to her name, and would hear no protests from her family.

That night, Charlotte walked to her bedroom, still stiff like Frankenstein's monster, and wrote both the Harringtons and the Abernathys five-page long letters in a shaky child-like handwriting, expressing her gratitude and utter regret. Her body healed, but when she slept that night, her mind still showed its injury in the way of nightmares that had plagued her since she'd found all of her friends dead.

Chapter Fifteen

Josh jumped out of bed, punching at the air. Once standing, he wiped his hand across his face, pushing icy cold water away as he did. Thomas stood over his bed with an empty tea pitcher. His brother laughed with a big burst of pent-up hilarity.

"What are you doing, jerk?" Josh asked. "Mom said I could sleep in today."

"You did," his brother pointed to the alarm clock on the bedside table.

The large red numbers showed the time as 9 a.m. Josh looked at the clock and at his brother, who was clearly dressed for school but all the same standing in his bedroom, not realizing how dangerously close he was to getting pounded.

"Why are you still here?"

"They canceled school," Thomas answered. "I was about to walk out the door when Harvey called. I'm surprised the phone didn't wake you."

Josh pushed back his wet hair. "I unplugged mine, in case someone took the notion to call too early."

"Principal Chapman called to tell dad school was out, but the teachers needed to come in about lunchtime."

"No one said why classes were canceled?" Josh asked.

"No, and I didn't ask. I know that Dad wasn't going in today anyway. Momma wouldn't say why."

His father only missed school unexpectedly when he was sick unto death or when something major came up. School didn't get canceled this early in the year except for a threat of a tornado. Thomas still grinned a little bit like an idiot. It was fun to get a free day from school, but he'd been having free days for the last two days. After a little while, it lost its luster.

"Go on," Josh said. "Quit bouncing up and down like a little kid who's got to go potty."

Thomas flung the few drops of water remaining in the pitcher at him and walked out of the room still smiling. Josh took off his wet T-shirt and pulled out a dry one from the drawer. He'd wait a little while to dress. There was no reason to be uncomfortable. It was his last weekday to be off before having to return to school. His dad slept, so the place would be left to him and Thomas. With his brother there, video games would be played despite his grounding, and probably some TV watched. Perhaps they'd luck up and some R-rated movie with a lot of boobs would be on the premium channels.

He walked downstairs and into the kitchen to eat breakfast. Thomas sat at the table, gnawing on a biscuit. Their mother had left a few in a pan. They must have been for his breakfast, because there was fried bologna alongside them, and his brother hated the stuff. Josh broke a biscuit in half and shoved some bologna in it, got the mustard and chocolate milk out of the fridge, and closed the door. The mustard squirted out with separated liquid draining first, then the thicker sauce. Josh made a face. He hated the liquid stuff. The mustard squished out of the edges when he topped the biscuit.

He stuck the biscuit in his mouth, poured himself some milk, and sat down. Thomas grimaced at him as he bit off a chunk of his breakfast. Josh chewed it with great exaggeration, making pleasurable sounds as he did. He slugged down some chocolate milk with his mouth full of bologna biscuit. Thomas acted like he was gagging.

"How do you eat that stuff with chocolate milk?" Thomas asked.

"How do eat those disgusting fish on pizza?" Josh answered still chewing. "It's an acquired taste."

"That's as gross as Dad putting mayonnaise on his pinto beans."

"Don't knock it until you've tried it," said their dad as he walked into the room.

He passed them and made himself a bologna biscuit to match Josh's, including a glass of chocolate milk. The three of them sat at the table for a moment, gnawing on their too hard, cold canned biscuits.

"I knew they'd cancel school," Alan said.

"You're not off the hook. Principal Chapman called and said that all teachers had to come in at noon," Thomas said.

"What made you think they'd cancel school?" Josh asked.

"I wish I could have slept longer. I'm wiped out," Alan answered.

"Why didn't you stay in bed?" Thomas asked.

"How could I with all this noise? The phone ringing. You two carrying on out here."

"We haven't been doing anything but eating," Josh said.

"I heard y'all yelling in your room." He looked at Thomas. "Did you do the cold water thing or the burning paper between the toes?"

"Cold water," Thomas answered.

"Excellent choice, and you don't set off the fire alarm that way," Alan said.

"How did you know they'd cancel classes?" Josh asked. "You dodged the question."

Their dad looked very tired, beyond not sleeping well. He looked like a man who had been up for two days. The hollows of his eyes were dark, his cheeks sunken. All of his facial features seemed to be framed in gray tones, a worried face if Josh had ever seen one.

"Corey Aaron was killed last night," Alan said.

Thomas twitched his head in disbelief. "From the hit in football?"

Their dad shook his head. "Everything was okay from that. After I dropped him off, a car came by, driving way too fast. It passed me going at least 80 miles an hour. It slammed into his Jeep and tore it almost in two. The wreck killed him. I'll spare you the gorier details."

"What did it do to the other driver?" Josh started to feel a little queasy. "Did you know him? Was it someone from school?"

"It was a hit-and-run."

"How?" Thomas asked. "I don't know that much about cars, but it had to be a tank to split another car and keep going."

"I don't know. It literally cut the Jeep in two," Alan said

"That's impossible," Josh swallowed back the need to vomit. It was like getting kicked in the nads, a deep queasiness from way down in the gut.

"I'm pretty sure it was your Aunt Charlotte's car," Alan said. "I got enough of a look to recognize it."

"I've driven it. Can that car even go fast enough to do something like that?" Josh asked.

"I don't know," Alan said.

"What does all this mean?" Thomas's voice pitched with fright and concern.

"I don't know," Alan answered.

"What's going to happen?" Josh asked.

His father shook his head and looked older than when he walked into the kitchen. "I don't know. I went to Charlotte's house last night, and her car was gone. Then I went to the hospital where she is. They said she was still there and had been since I admitted her."

"No wonder you're exhausted," Josh said.

"Does this mean that the game is canceled?" Thomas asked.

"Of course," Josh answered, feeling miffed that his brother would ask such a question.

He didn't care much for Corey Aaron, but the death of someone you know always hits hard. Josh's own mortality worried him at the moment, but the cause of Corey's death bothered him even more. Flashes of the plot of *Christine* came to him. If the old car had taken a mind of its own and went out on a murderous rampage, he wanted nothing to do with that reality. Charlotte's Mercury had belonged to the black boy that was killed after the massacre. Corey was one of the students advocating hard for the anniversary dance. He was pretty sure that Corey was related to one of his grandfather's friends, not the one who killed himself but the other one. The three of them had captured the boy in that very car and hauled him in its trunk to the sheriff.

"Do you think it might have been a ghost?" Josh asked.

Thomas blew a raspberry at him. "The other day you were

making fun of us for saying we had seen a ghost."

"Explain how a car cut a Jeep in two and kept going," Josh said.

"I don't know," his dad interrupted the argument. "All I know is that I'm sure it was Charlotte's car."

The phone rang. Thomas got up and answered the one on the kitchen wall. He said "Yes" a few times before putting his hand over the mouthpiece and holding it out to his father. Alan took the phone and listened for a moment and said "Yes" himself. A few questions received answers, and then he got to his feet and hung up the phone. The worry lines were etched deeper into his face.

"I've got to get to the hospital," he said. "It's your grandfather."

"What's the matter with him?" Thomas asked.

"They think he's had a heart attack. They don't know for sure. You two stay here. I'll call if I need anything."

Their dad hurried back to his bedroom. In a few minutes, he left the house, speeding out of the driveway, scraping the back end of his car as he did. Josh watched through the window. There might be some truth to the curse that he'd read about in the Jeffrey ghost book. Although he was very familiar with the massacre, the tale of Hazel's curse eluded him. Over time the legend must have faded from retelling, especially after the massacre. Most of the town folklore and ghost stories revolved around it.

His friend Harvey claimed that he ran into one of the girls killed that night at the old drive-in restaurant. Aunt Charlotte talked about that girl before. Her name was Sue something or other. She would say that Sue—Sue Browning, that was it—carhopped at the Cardinal. Charlotte told stories about how jealous she was of Sue, especially in the summertime because Sue got to make money, hone her roller-skating skills, and eat malts and French fries at a discount. *Harvey needs to come over*, Josh decided.

For the second time in less than twenty-four hours, Alan walked into the emergency room. Only a couple of people sat in the lobby, a big difference from his last visit when the place was standing room only. He walked to the counter where a nursing assistant sat.

"Sign in," she said not looking up.

"I'm not here for services," he answered. "I got a call that my father is here. He's had a possible heart attack."

She looked up at him. "What's his name?"

"Simeon McAdams."

She looked down at her computer screen. "Walk to that door over there, and I'll buzz you in. He's in room eleven."

Alan hurried to the double wooden doors. The lock buzzed, and a small green light flickered on. He pushed his way into the emergency room. The staff were spread here and there, but no one looked in a giant rush. He walked down the hallway past the nurse's station until he came to room eleven. It was little more than an alcove with a sliding glass door to cut it off from the hallway. His father sat in the bed, propped up with pillows. His eyes were closed. An IV drip was attached to one of arms. A heart monitor beeped occasionally.

"Dad?" Alan walked into the room.

"What?" Sim kept his eyes closed.

"How are you feeling?"

The old man's eyes popped open. They looked a little bloodshot, but not weak or tired. Alan was surprised at how strong the gaze was.

"I'm fine. These idiot doctors think I had a heart attack, but I ain't had a durn heart attack."

"What happened?"

"I don't want to talk about it in here," Sim said. "I'm afraid if they catch wind of my story, they'll throw me in the looney bin with Charlotte."

A black nurse, wearing bright blue scrubs came in. She smiled at Alan. Her nametag read *Rita*.

"Are you Mr. McAdams's son?" she asked.

"One of them," Alan said.

"The only one who even tries to help me," Sim said.

"The police called the paramedics to bring your dad in after he fainted out on Harrington Road," the nurse said.

"Blacked out," Sim corrected. "Only ladies and queers faint."

"Daddy, there's no need for that."

Rita gave Sim a sour look. She had no idea how bad it could be. Alan smiled for her to continue.

"They believed he had a heart attack. The doctors have run all the tests, and he's clear. They think it was a giant anxiety attack. He's good to go, *if* you want to take him."

"What does that mean?" Sim said. "He's my son. Of course, he'll take me."

"Get him ready. I'll get him out of here for you."

"I'll be back in a minute to pull out the IV and bring the discharge paperwork and a few prescriptions the doctor wrote," she said.

She left the room. Sim sat up and started to get off the bed. Alan walked over to him.

"What are you doing?" he asked.

"Putting on my clothes. Hand me my pants and pull that curtain."

There was no point in arguing. He walked to a chair where a pair of pants lay and pulled the curtain across the door before handing the pants to his dad. The old man pulled the pants on under the gown and started to tug the heart monitor pads. The machine started to beep and made a long, high-pitched buzz. The bleeping line on the screen went flat. Rita rushed back into the room.

"Are you okay?" she asked.

"He pulled off his monitor pads," Alan said. "He's not the most patient, patient."

She rolled her eyes very noticeably and grabbed some latex gloves from a counter. Pulling them on, she walked to Sim's side. A cotton ball came out of her pocket. She removed the tape holding the hep lock against Sim's hand. The cotton ball went over where the needle entered his vein. She pushed on it and slipped the needle out, tossing it into a red trash can. A Band-Aid covered the cotton.

"You can sign the paperwork at the nurse's station," she said, "since you're in such an all-fired hurry to get out of here."

Rita walked out. Sim walked past Alan and grabbed his shirt off the chair his pants had been on. He pulled it on.

"Let's get the hell out of here. This place is nothing but jigaboo nurses with too much attitude. They need to remember their place."

"*Their* place is the same as yours."

Sim said nothing else. He left the room. Alan followed him to the nurse's station where a very young orderly handed him his paperwork, which he signed with a quick flourish. Sim shoved the prescriptions into a pocket and walked out of the emergency room, not even giving Alan a side glance.

"I'm sorry, everyone," he said loud enough to be heard by the staff at the station. "I've only been here a few minutes, but I'm sure you didn't deserve whatever kind of abuse he gave you."

Alan followed his father out of the emergency room. It wouldn't have surprised him if the workers had applauded after their exit.

Sim was not in the lobby. Alan found him standing by his car, smoking a cigarette. His father looked at the prescriptions in his hand. He took the lit cigarette and set the edge of the squares of paper on fire. They flamed up and curled into black ash. When the heat touched the old man's fingers, he let them drop to ground. The remaining paper succumbed to the fire. The ash blew off on the wind.

"What did you do that for?" Alan asked.

"I ain't taking that."

"Did you even look at what it was?"

"Xanax and Prozac. I don't need no crazy pills. Let's get out of here. Take me back to Harrington Road. I need to get my truck."

"Why is it there?"

"I'll tell you in the car."

"Put out the smoke," Alan said. "You can't smoke in my car."

Sim gave him a sour look and took a draw off the cigarette. Alan could actually see the paper receding back into a long tail of ash. The old man flicked the butt onto the ground and got into the car.

Alan started out of the parking lot and headed to the far side of town where Harrington Road headed out to the old Harrington place. His father told him what had occurred as they went. Sweat beaded in Alan's hairline. He flipped on the air conditioner. It *had* been Charlotte's car involved in the accident. He told Sim about finding it stolen.

After that they rode in silence all the way to Harrington

Road. Sim's old truck sat on the shoulder. The police had moved it and removed the Mercury. Sim sat in the car for a moment before opening the door.

"Did Charlotte do it?" he asked.

"I checked on her. She's still safe and sound in the psychiatric unit."

"Nobody could have driven that car in its condition when I last saw it. As smashed up as it was, nobody could have survived the crash."

"I know."

Sim looked at his son. Alan had never seen such an expression on his father's face. It was a mixture of borderline terror and complete perplexity. He didn't like it.

"What did?" Sim asked.

"I don't know."

Sim nodded his head and got out of the car. Alan watched him until he got into his old pickup, start it up, and pull away. He had lied to his father. He had an idea what might have done it, but he was afraid to say it out loud. Sim told him that the car was parked exactly as it had been the night he and his friends had caught Tobias Abernathy. It was even at all the same angles.

Alan looked at the clock on the radio. He had to get to the school meeting.

Harvey arrived an hour after Josh called him. His friend looked like he'd been enjoying his day off. All of his clothes were wrinkled like he'd been wallowing in bed, which he probably had been. His blond hair stuck up at all angles. Josh got in his friend's car before Harvey could get out.

"Couldn't you have spruced up?" Josh asked.

"What, is this a date?" Harvey asked. "Because I need to let you know, I put out on the first date."

"No one wants what you're giving."

"What did I need to get over here for? I was having a good nap."

"I can tell." Josh made a hand gesture for Harvey to drive. "Tell me about that ghost at the old Cardinal Drive-In."

"Why?"

"Because."

"Have you seen a ghost?" Harvey asked. "Because you made fun of me something fierce when I said I had."

"Tell me about it, and take us out there."

"I said I wasn't ever going back there again," Harvey crossed himself despite not being the least bit religious and especially not Catholic.

"It's daylight, and I'm with you. Plus, you go there all the time."

"It was daytime that time."

Josh smiled to himself. He hoped they'd get lucky today and see this supposed ghost again—exactly why, he didn't know. They drove away from his neighborhood toward downtown.

The Cardinal was literally on the wrong side of the tracks, in the part of town that had become run down sometime in the 1970s and attracted the least acceptable citizens. The street changed when they crossed the railroad track. The pavement was rougher, with potholes here and there. Ridges, like that of a washboard, left the surface uneven. Harvey's car started to jitter along this stretch of street as if he was driving on four flats. He hummed with his mouth open. It sounded like he was speaking into a fan.

"Pretty soon you'll need a tank to drive over here," he said, his voice sounding almost mechanical due to the vibrations.

"Why would you want to come over here?" Josh asked.

"You know good and well why I come over here. It's why I was here the day I saw that ghost."

The old Cardinal Drive-in came up on the right. The once bright-red head of a bird on the large sign had faded pink. Someone had painted the part below the bird white. Black letters spray painted on with a stencil said, Red Bird's Wings and Things. Someone had attempted to make a go of a soul food restaurant at the location. Josh had eaten there twice—one time with Harvey on one of his pot runs, the other because his dad wanted to try something different for takeout. Both times had been disappointing, probably the reason it had closed.

The car entered the parking lot. The cement was a bit smoother than the road, but the entryway gave both of the boys a jolt. Harvey parked in one of the old berths. A black guy with a green bandana tied around his head like Tupac came from behind the building. His right pant leg was rolled up.

The butterflies in Josh's stomach acted up. He looked over at Harvey, who seemed very nonchalant. "Are we safe?"

"Yeah, that's Peanut. He's cool. You usually have to honk the horn three times, but he knows my car."

"Are you going to score some dope while we're here?" Josh asked.

"I'm here. We've not got class, and one of our dear classmates died. I'm depressed. I need something to help me out."

"You're going to Hell for using that as an excuse," Josh said.

"Okay, I like to get high," Harvey answered, getting out of his car.

"You're going to Hell for that too."

Josh sat for a minute, watching his friend walk around the car and move toward Peanut. The two slapped hands and did some histrionic and elaborate handshake that ended in a loose man-hug. Harvey waved for him to get out. He always hated going with Harvey on a pot run. He'd sworn the last one way up in Jasper, with a redneck guy who seemed to be on crack, would be his last. He got out of the car and walked to his friend and his friend's drug dealer.

"Peanut, this is Josh Mc—

"Josh," he interrupted. "You understand."

Peanut nodded his head and looked from shoulder to shoulder. "Cops. It's cool man. That's why I go by Peanut. Only this fool is stupid enough to use both his names and write me a rubber check that time."

"You got me back for that," Harvey gave him the thumbs up. "We're cool now. No reason to rehash the past."

"Is that how your thumb got broken last year?" Josh asked.

"No need to rehash the past," Peanut said. "Speaking of rehashing, I guess you're in need of some."

Harvey had his cash already in his hand visible for Peanut to see. "Sure enough, and my friend wants to snoop around a little bit."

Peanut took the money, counted it, and dug into his pocket.

He handed Harvey a baggie of pot. "What kind of snooping? We don't like nosy people around these parts. Long noses end in long snoozes."

"We're cool," Harvey bent over and shoved the baggie into his sock. "He wants to see if we can knock that ghost back up."

"Why would you want to do that?" Peanut asked.

"Curiosity," Josh said, feeling strangely more comfortable with the pusher.

"She's usually around back," Peanut said. "I've already seen that creepy bitch today."

"Really?" Josh asked.

"She's getting to be as regular as Harvey. I'm thinking hard about shifting store locations. I can't take too much more of her creeping around."

"Can I walk back there, or do you need to go with me?" Josh asked.

"You can go by yourself, but I'll go with you," Peanut said.

"I'll be waiting in the car," Harvey said.

Josh started walking toward the back of the building, "Crack a window. I'm already grounded. The last thing I need is to get covered up in your sticky bud stink and get a contact high."

"You need to mellow," Harvey said, "but I can dig it. Be careful, Peanut, he's suspended right now for beating up three dudes by himself."

Peanut slapped Josh on the shoulder with the back of his hand. "You that guy? You interested in joining a gang? We need some tough guys."

"I'm good," Josh said.

"Don't matter none if you're white," Peanut said.

"I'm fine. Can we go back there?"

Peanut shrugged his agreement. They walked to the shady area behind the building. A lawn chair sat at the edge of the pavement. A small Sony portable radio sat on a tin television tray. An ashtray with a smoldering blunt sat beside the radio. A Biggie Smalls rap whispered from the speakers. A sweating Pabst Blue Ribbon rested on top of a redIgloo cooler.

Peanut sat down in his place and picked up his blunt. He inhaled the smoke and let it go in a long *S* curl before turning up the music. "She hates Biggie," he said. "Come over here and stand by me. Look back toward the street. She'll come rolling by."

Josh walked closer to Peanut. He stood upwind, and the cigar and marijuana smoke drifted away from him. The easy flow of Biggie's "Big Poppa" drifted from the speakers. He stared back toward the street. The whole rear cinderblock wall of the drive-in's building was tagged with different symbols. He recognized them as the signs of the Folk. This particular branch preferred the pitchfork and the Star of David.

"You said that she's been showing up more frequently?" Josh asked.

"Two or three times a day. It's driving some of the customers away. It's been getting on my nerves too. I don't care too much for ghosts. It's a bad sign. It's like a harbinger of death."

Josh looked over at the dealer as another curl of pot smoke drifted from his mouth. Peanut's use of the phrase "harbinger of death" surprised him. He composed himself and reminded himself not to judge a book by its cover. That was what Sim did.

"There she is," Peanut said.

He looked back toward the street. Between him and the building, a perfectly formed female figure floated. She wore clothes straight from *Grease* and stood on roller skates. She was in profile. Her curly hair stood up on her head and moved as if in a wind. Iciness crept up through Josh. His mouth went dry like he'd taken a toke off of Peanut's blunt.

"Sue Browning," he croaked at the apparition.

The ghost turned her head. The other side of her face was gone. The whole half was a skull grinning with missing teeth. Holes pockmarked the facial bones, left by shotgun pellets.

"Can you understand me?" Josh asked.

"What are you doing?" Peanut asked.

The ghost nodded. She moved closer. The movements looked like she skated. Josh took a step back. His heel hit the edge of the pavement, and he stopped.

"Can you talk back to me?"

She stared him head on, one eye completely normal, the other a hollow socket in bone.

"Why have you been coming back more frequently?" he forced the words out of his mouth. "Is it related to Hazel's curse and the Homecoming dance?"

Biggie suddenly quit singing. The song became an old 50's tune Charlotte played on her bad days. The chorus said *sha boom* or *ka boom*. It had been a long time since he'd listened to it.

"I ain't got time for this," Peanut said.

He tried to walk off, but the ghost of Sue Browning turned and stared at him. He sat back down and took a long puff off his blunt.

"Charlotte," a voice crackled over the speakers in heavy interference as the singers definitely sang *sha boom, sha boom*. "Tobias. Baby blue crepe paper. Mercury Monterey. Corey Aaron."

Josh trembled at the unearthly sound. The ghost started to glow orange. He reached to turn off the radio. Sue Browning's ghost looked him dead in the eyes. An eyeball with an emerald green iris floated in the empty socket.

"Sim McAdams," the ghostly voice screamed on the radio.

The speakers exploded like the sound of a shotgun blast as the ghost flared a bright red and disappeared. Peanut nearly flipped out of his chair as he fumbled for the pistol he had tucked in his waistband. Josh's ears rang from the reverberation.

"What was that?" Peanut said.

"I don't know." He yelled. The explosion had deafened him for the moment. "Has she ever done that before?"

"Hell, no," Peanut shoved the pistol back behind him. "She ain't never going to do that around me again either. I'm getting the hell up out of here. Tell your boy Harvey I'll be moving to a new location."

"Don't blame you," Josh tugged on his ears trying to get them to clear.

"You need a hit." Peanut took a long drag off his blunt and handed it out toward Josh.

He shook his head and ran as hard as he could back to Harvey's car.

Chapter Sixteen

1956
Six weeks after the Massacre

Sim sat on his parents' couch, smoking a Camel and drinking lemonade that his momma had squeezed fresh that morning. His daddy sat in a rocking chair on the other end, puffing away on a Lucky Strike and drinking a cup of coffee. Sim couldn't understand why old men drank coffee in the evenings and complained about not being able to sleep like they had when they were younger. The connection between the two should be obvious. Perhaps he gave those men too much credit.

"Explain to me one more time why you let Charlotte have that car," Sim said.

"Because it seemed to snap her out of whatever it was that had her," his daddy said. "Plus, you don't say no to Mr. Archibald Harrington, especially when you work for him."

"I would have flat-out told him no. The main thing that had Charlotte all balled up on the inside was nigger-loving in the first place."

"Don't you talk like that in my house," his mother said as she came through the door of the kitchen. "You might be a grown man with children, but in my house, you'll listen to your momma or else."

"It's the truth. I've got a right to tell the truth. All this nonsense happened because she was fooling around with a nigger."

A sharp sting on the side of his face made Sim aware that he'd been slapped. Other women had slapped him, and he'd been punched more than few times by men. None of those blows were like this one. It had a sharp sting to it like an insect bite and a thin welt like a bullwhip produced. He put his hand over his injured cheek and looked up at his momma. She patted a rubber-mesh flyswatter in her hand. The look she gave him made Ma Barker look like Martha Washington.

"Say something like that again, smart mouth, and see what it gets you," she said. "You ain't so big that your momma still can't whoop you."

"There's no need for that, Trudy," his daddy said. "He ain't going to talk like that anymore. Are you, son?"

"Both of you are turning on me because y'all can't raise your own daughter. My sons will have no regard for those *coloreds*. You'll see that."

"If you want to raise your boys to be like that, fine," Trudy said. "But I didn't raise you to be like that, and I ain't got no idea why you came out such a ways."

"Life, Momma. It's no rose garden. Uppity nig—Negroes don't help anything either." He looked at his watch. "How long has she been gone?"

"I sent her to the store about half an hour ago, but I told her not to hurry. I don't need the stuff until tomorrow. None of it will ruin. I told her to take the change and head over to the Cardinal and get her a malted or something."

"Get a malted. Drive to the store. You realize that she couldn't walk last week, and before that, she couldn't do anything without one of us propping her up. Now you let her drive around like there's nothing wrong," Sim said. "Don't you care about her at all?"

"A sight more than you." His daddy stood up to his full height. Sim had forgotten how large a man he was. His father meant to use the full intimidation of his presence right then and there.

"Her doctor said it would be good for her," Trudy said. "The doctor approved it. Do you understand that?

His father stepped closer to him, rolling his shoulders. "The last time I checked, you wasn't a doctor."

"What if something happens? " Sim asked. "What if she sees something that jars her memory and puts her back like she was?"

"We'll deal with it. She's our daughter, not yours."

"What if she hits someone in that thing and kills them?" Sim asked.

"That won't happen," Trudy said.

"What if someone recognizes the car for who it belonged to and does something to her?"

His father put his hand on Sim's shoulder and squeezed with enough pressure to crack a walnut. "I'll handle it. And with that said, it's time that you best be leaving, son. Do call us next time before coming over."

Sim readied a retort but took the hint. He got up, dropped his cigarette butt in the half-drunk glass of lemonade, and left. It would be a little while before he ventured back to see them. He hoped they enjoyed not seeing their only grandchildren for Christmas. The idea of withholding his children from them made him smile. His father thought he was mean and tough, but Sim could teach him a few lessons from that book.

It took less time for Sim to drive home than usual. His foot grew heavy when he was angry, and his boot was made of solid iron that afternoon. When he pulled up into his driveway, Charlotte's new car sat parked in front of his house. She sat on the trunk, twisting the hem of her sweater. He parked and got out.

"What's the matter with you?" he asked.

"Something bad's happened," she said, then pointed to the front of the car.

The front fender was dented in, and the headlight dangled down. Sim helped her off the trunk and listened to her story. His daddy might think he knew how to raise his daughter, but when trouble came, she came to him first.

"Don't worry. Walk home, and tell the folks you hit something, a deer ran out in front of you. Tell them it was Blitzen for added holiday fun. I'll get the car fixed, and I'll talk with the sheriff. Okay?"

"Are you sure?" she asked, starting to sound panicked.

"Yes, and don't get yourself bothered and back like you were. Your big brother will handle everything."

She smiled and headed off down the street toward her house,

carrying a sack of groceries. Sim smiled. He would indeed take care of everything. Her big brother handled all kinds of problems.

Sim drove out toward the graveyard on the outskirts of town. He could think of only one reason why Charlotte had gone there. The Abernathy boy was buried in that cemetery, over many a protest of the townspeople with loved ones interred there. She couldn't have known that, however. His burial happened while she was still in a stupor.

Deep inside him he knew that she had driven out there to see the boy's grave. Someone had told her he was there. Their parents encouraged such a relationship to bend to the growing norm that coloreds and whites were equal. The real question that burned inside him was why Johnny House was there. He had absolutely no reason to be at that cemetery. None of his family rested there, nor did any friends. Not a single person killed in the massacre was there. The only reason Johnny would have been there was to visit that Abernathy boy's grave as well.

He pulled his pickup onto the gravel driveway that circled the cemetery. All the tombstones faced away from Sim as he drove around. He saw the mound of red dirt with no marker but some dead flowers atop it. Johnny's Hudson sat on the side of gravel road, but Johnny wasn't near it. Sim parked behind his car and got out.

The gravel crunched underfoot as he approached the vehicle. A few feet from it, he could see tracks where a car had skidded, piling up gravel into two small lumps. Sim followed the skids to the end. Johnny lay secluded in the high brown weeds. He held pressure on his leg. Sim could see the fracture was compound. Johnny bled from the wound.

"What have you gotten yourself into," Sim asked.

"Your crazy sister ran me over," Johnny yelled. "Broke my leg. The bone's torn through the skin. I'm going to bleed out."

"I'll help you, but you're going to help me too."

"Anything."

"Good."

Sim helped his friend up and got him to his truck. He put Johnny in the bed and made him as comfortable as he could. Without much fanfare and without much care for the agony his driving put his friend through, Sim drove as quick as he could to the hospital where he dumped Johnny off with a story he could tell the doctors. He headed over to the sheriff's department.

A new deputy, who looked a little older than Charlotte, was on duty. The deputy sat behind the desk at the entry of the station. He looked very official in full kit, sitting board straight. His badge shone like a real star.

"Do you need some help, sir?" he asked Sim.

"Is Sheriff Johnson in?"

"Gone for the day. I am Deputy Gilreath, and I can be of assistance."

Any port in a storm would do, Sim told himself. He walked to the counter and propped his arms on it to lean toward the deputy.

"My name is Sim McAdams," he said. "I need to report an accident."

"I can handle that. Go in there." The deputy pointed to an open area to the right with several desks. "I'll get the form and join you."

Sim sauntered into the other room and sat at the desk nearest the door. The deputy disappeared into a small room that looked like a closet. He came out carrying a form and sat across from Sim.

"Is this an automobile accident?" he asked.

"Kind of," Sim answered.

"How do you mean?"

"My sister, Charlotte McAdams, hit Johnny House at the Round Hill Cemetery," Sim said.

"Did she do it purposefully or by accident?"

Sim smiled. Despite Sheriff Johnson not being there, putting a slight kink in his plan, an even better solution came with the gift of this naïve deputy.

"You aren't from Pinehurst, are you?"

"No, I'm from Birmingham. I came here to get some experience so I can get on with the Jefferson County Sheriff's Office."

"Come out to the sticks, huh? Good experience here. Apparently you aren't paying very good attention, son. You've heard of the massacre?"

Deputy Gilreath looked a little astonished. "Yes, who hasn't?"

"My sister is the one who found them. It made her go crazy for a little while. Maybe you've heard of that, too?"

"I didn't know her name," Gilreath said. "So, was it purposeful or accidental?"

"Accidental," Sim said. "The Harringtons thought it appropriate to give her the car that belonged to the boy who killed those people. She was driving it around to see his grave. It was a little too much for her, and she had another bout of her problem."

"He was a colored boy," Gilreath said. "Why would she be going to his grave?"

"Exactly. She's still not in her right mind. My dear sister's only been walking on her own for about a week, and she goes driving. I need you to keep this in mind on your report. She wasn't in her right mind. Now, Sheriff Johnson would understand and make exceptions."

"I understand, but that would make a good alibi for attempted murder. I do recognize the name Johnny House, Mr. McAdams, just like I recognize yours. You both helped apprehend that Abernathy boy. She might have had reason for revenge and faked having a relapse."

"Are you a psychiatrist, Deputy Gilreath?" Sim leaned in on him.

"No."

"Well, a psychiatrist diagnosed her with catatonia. Did you learn about that in school?"

"No."

"It means she sometimes gets trapped in her own mind, unable to do things. He said it might make her do things that she normally wouldn't because she loses control over herself."

"I see. What happened with Mr. House?"

"I took him the hospital. They're going to call you with a hit and run, but we know different, right?"

The deputy nodded. "I've got it. There's no need for your poor sister to have more troubles than she already has."

"Glad to hear it." Sim got up, shook the deputy's hand, and left.

On the way back to his house, he pondered over a brain full of information. That stupid smashed-up Monterey sat in his driveway. Charlotte meant to run Johnny over. She *was* trying to get revenge because Johnny helped to kill that nigger. Sim didn't like it, but lucky for her, he didn't need any more attention. Now, he had something to lord over his holier-than-thou folks. Alan and Mikey would get to visit their grandparents for Christmas after all. Ho, ho, ho.

Chapter Seventeen

The front door closed while Alan sat at the kitchen table. Josh wouldn't know that he had come home early. Despite his son breaking his grounding, Alan wasn't mad. His classmate had died. Thomas would take it hard because Corey was on the team with him. Josh might eventually take it harder than he seemed to because he'd been in class with Corey since the third grade.

Footsteps came through the living room toward the kitchen. Somehow Josh had missed seeing his father's car in the driveway or didn't care. "Dad, there you are," he said from behind him.

Alan turned to look at his son. Josh looked very pale, as if he had been vomiting. He shook, and his eyes stared wide and glassy.

"What is it?" Alan asked, getting up.

"Don't be mad at me, but Harvey drove me to the old Cardinal Drive-in."

"Are you stoned?" Alan asked. The old drive-in was a hot spot to score some dope, but Josh had never shown interest in marijuana.

"No, I'm scared."

He believed his son. Now that he paid closer attention to Josh's appearance, it was definitely white-knuckle fear.

"What happened? Harvey didn't get into anything bad, did he?"

Josh shook his head. "I think I did."

"Is it drugs?" Alan asked. "Please don't tell me you did

something to a drug dealer. They're all in this gang called the Folk. The Birmingham PD put on a workshop about them."

"It has nothing to do with that. I might be dumb enough to blow off my grounding, but I'm not stupid enough to tick off a drug dealer."

"What's got you so scared, son?"

"A ghost."

"Are you serious?"

"You and Thomas claim to have seen one. Can't I?"

"You can, but you look like when you were a kid watching reruns of *Scooby-Doo*. Sit down and explain it to me."

Josh sat across from him and explained everything. Alan listened as his son talked about running all the way to the old gym the night, he had seen the lights there. Josh talked about the tremendous explosion that no one else noticed. He talked about the burned picture on the tombstone. Staring at that thing in the cemetery was one of Alan's strongest memories from childhood. His father would often take him and his brother to the cemetery and look at the graves of the kids killed in the massacre.

Then, Josh told him about the ghost of Sue Browning. "It blew up a boom box?" Alan repeated.

"I've never seen anything like it, Dad. I think something evil is after us. Is that even possible?"

"Go get your brother from upstairs," Alan said, "and call your friend Jessica. Tell her we'll be by her house in a little while to pick her up."

"What's going on?" Josh asked.

"You'll find out when we get there."

Alan sat at the table staring at the wall. He listened to Josh's footsteps above and could even hear the conversation with Thomas. His boys were anything but quiet. It made it easy to know when they were conspiring, which wasn't that often. The great thunderous noise Thomas made running down the stairs made Alan think of a herd of elephants. He couldn't imagine how one kid could produce so much noise.

Thomas loped into the kitchen. "What's up, Dad? When did you get home?"

"A little bit ago."

Thomas looked guilty. "Like before Josh got home?"

"I was waiting for him," Alan said. "Don't worry, he's not in trouble. He won't come after you for not covering for him."

Thomas let out a relieved sigh. "That's good. What did the teachers have to say about Corey? I got the call about the canceled game."

"They're concerned that this might be related to something bad Corey was involved with. We had a workshop back in the summer about gangs. Apparently, the Folk are active in our town."

Thomas crossed his ring and middle fingers on both hands and spread the remaining fingers out to form two Ws. "Westside!"

"It's not funny. For some reason, they think he might have been involved with them, double-crossed them perhaps."

"It wasn't a drive-by."

"That's what I told them, but apparently Coach Turnbuckle and Principle Chapman are convinced that Corey was a drug dealer."

"His brother was the dealer. Corey just smoked a lot of it."

"It doesn't matter because that's not what happened."

Josh walked back into the room. "I couldn't get a hold of Jessica, but if you need an unbiased opinion, I can give Harvey a call."

"No, I want Jessica," Alan said.

"So does Josh," Thomas said.

Josh punched his brother in the shoulder. Alan stood up and pulled them apart.

"This is serious. We'll go by her house and pick her up anyway," Alan said.

"What's so important?" Josh asked.

"She moved to town and is familiar enough with your Aunt Charlotte but not completely biased against her."

Without saying anything else, Alan walked out of the kitchen toward the front door. His sons followed. All of them got into his car. Josh and Thomas got into the back seat without the usual argument for shotgun. His boys weren't mysteries to him. More than likely, Josh sat in the back, thinking Thomas would naturally take shotgun and thus shoving Jessica into the back with him. Thomas knew that's what his brother would do and foiled his plan. He drove away from their house. Josh gave him turn-by-turn directions to Jessica's house. Within a few minutes, they pulled into the driveway of an older house in an aging part of town that hadn't quite gone to the other side of the tracks yet. As they drove into the neighborhood, Alan spied a spray-painted symbol on a telephone pole, one of those that the Birmingham PD had said were associated with the Folk.

Alan stated the obvious. "There are no cars here. Do you think anyone is at home?"

"There's never a car," Josh said. "I'm not sure that they own a car."

"How do they not own a car?" Thomas asked.

"Some people don't own cars," Alan said. "They may be poor. This house has seen better days."

"And what's up with those shutters?" Thomas asked. "Who has red shutters?"

"What do her parents do for a living?" Alan asked Josh, ignoring his other son.

"I've never met them," Josh said.

"How have you never met them?" Thomas asked.

"I've never been invited inside," Josh said. "Is that strange?"

"Maybe a little, but we've got more important things to worry about," Alan said. "Hop out and see if she's at home."

Josh got out of the car. He walked up the broken sidewalk to the door and knocked. After no one came to the door, he used the heavy knocker. Still no one came. He walked back to the car and sat shotgun.

"She's not at home."

"All right," Alan said. "We'll have to go without her."

He backed onto the street and headed toward Charlotte's house. They passed Hickory Avenue and turned onto Fourth Street. At the next intersection was a four-way stop. As they slowly rolled through it, Josh pointed down Euclid Avenue and patted the dashboard.

"There she is. Jessica's walking this way."

Alan turned down the street. He almost hit the opposite curb due to being so far into the intersection, but he made it. Josh rolled down his window as they pulled to the sidewalk. Jessica stuck her head in like a carhop.

"Hey, guys. I didn't expect to see you down this street," she said.

"Get in," Josh said. "Dad wants you to go with us."

"Where to?" she said.

"My Aunt Charlotte's house," Alan said. "I want some folks to go with me to look at something."

"Why me?"

"Because you're unbiased," Josh said.

She gave him a strange look.

"He's quoting me," Alan said. "Please take a ride with us over there. I'll take everyone out for a pizza afterward."

"How about Mom?" Thomas asked.

"I left her a note," Alan answered. "She can either meet us there or eat alone."

"Sounds good," Jessica said.

"Will your folks mind?" Alan asked.

"They don't care," she answered. "One less thing to worry about."

Thomas moved across the back seat, and she got in on the passenger side. Alan could almost feel Josh's anger. He'd tried hard to get in the back with her, and it was foiled again, this time by sheer dumb luck. Still, they'd be at Charlotte's in few minutes. After that, he could sit with her in the back and at the pizza joint.

Taking Euclid Avenue was a bit of detour over to Charlotte's house, but Alan hadn't been down that street in a while. They passed a faux Tudor house. He recognized one of the boys Josh had gotten into the fight with, shooting basketball by himself. He elbowed his son.

"You want to get out and take care of him again?"

"I'd rather not," Josh said. "I didn't even know he lived this close to Aunt Charlotte. He should know better than to make fun of her. She's almost his neighbor."

"He said that he's sorry he did that," Jessica said. "I was

walking home from his house when you caught me."

"Why were you there?" Thomas asked. "He's a loser."

"Marcus gave me a ride to the library and back to his house. He gives me lifts occasionally when I can't catch one with Josh."

"Why were you walking?" Alan said. "Is he such a brute that he wouldn't drop you off at your house?"

Jessica shook her head. "I don't want him to know where I live. He's creepy."

Josh and Thomas giggled like girls. He agreed that the kid was a creepy loser, but laughing with his sons would have been wrong.

"He was trying to convince me to help set up the Massacre Dance. I told him that he was nuts," she said.

"They're still planning that?" Alan asked. "When and where?"

"At the old gym on the actual anniversary of the massacre. There's a pretty hardcore group of them bound and determined to have it."

"Even after Corey was killed?" Thomas said. He leaned over to Alan. "He was one of the ringleaders of the committee."

They pulled into Charlotte's driveway. Alan kept anything else about the Massacre Dance to himself. He wanted to give the kids a clean mental slate before walking into the house. Years ago when he had taken abnormal psychology in college, he'd written a paper about a strange mental illness called *folie a deux*. It was a disorder where people shared psychoses. If he had hallucinated all those decorations, there was a chance, with all the strange things that had happened to him and the boys, that if he mentioned the crepe paper, it might cause them to see what he had experienced the other night. He didn't need that.

Sim sat in a deer stand high enough in a pine tree for him to see over the hedge bushes, but not high enough that he couldn't climb into it. The pine sat far enough back in the thicket that no one paid much attention to him unless they were looking for someone to be there. To help matters, he wore real tree camo. Mike had given it to him for Christmas despite the fact that he hadn't hunted in nearly ten years, which might have been the last time he'd seen that ingrate of a son. The gift had come with a large-brimmed hat of the same material, which he also wore. The kids that broke into the old gym never even knew he watched them.

If Alan ever found about this clandestine operation, he would blame it on the paranoia related to his condition. Ever since scuttlebutt started going around that some stupid smart-alecky kids from the high school were planning to throw an anniversary dance, Sim had been staking out the place. At night he could park at the very edge of the parking lot secluded behind some old privet hedges. When Johnny's grandson died and school was canceled, he started staking out the place in broad daylight. Now his plan was working. For the first time since his surveillance began, some kids were breaking into the building.

These kids were stupid, too. They went in the side door that led into the old boys' locker room. All four of them walked by as plain as day, not even trying to be stealthy. They even parked by the door. He jotted down their license plate numbers. The teachers at the school were doing a bang-up job teaching those kids common sense.

Sim perched in the tree, waiting. He expected more to show, especially since the football game was canceled. The hoodlums would have nothing better to occupy their time but to vandalize the old gym for their stupid idea.

Another car pulled up. It was an older model Chevy, something from the 1980s. For a time, Sim had owned one himself, a dark blue Caprice Classic. The black kid who was good on the football team got out. His Pinehurst High School baseball cap in the blue and white school colors was on backward. Sim hated that trend. The white kids had picked it up. Even his grandsons were prone to doing it, Thomas more than Josh.

The running back strutted to the door that Sim watched. A deep loathing welled up inside the old man. There was no reason something like that should be good at sports, but he could run like a bunny—a jungle bunny.

Sim laughed out loud. The boy stopped and looked toward him. For a brief moment, he thought he'd been caught, except the sun hung at an angle that seemed to blind the boy. He put his dark hand over his eyes to shield them and strutted into the building.

"Stupid coon," Sim whispered to himself. "Doesn't know what that ball cap was for."

He snorted again, this time purposefully. While he waited and the sun drew closer to the horizon casting more shadows, he jotted down the names of the boys who had broken into the gym. Every one of them was connected to someone he knew, even that jungle bunny. It made identifying them easier. It would make getting back at them even sweeter, because he couldn't stand most of their people.

In his quivery handwriting, Sim jotted down: *Arnold Smithson's grandson—Marcus?* Next, he struggled to write out, *Jeremiah Black, Deacon Black's grandson, Neal Otis, jungle bunny football player, Thad Tucker's grandson by his daughter and that Foreman boy,* and *Jamie Morris, who used to deliver my paper.* He needed the notes to help solidify the names and faces. His Parkinson's disease made it harder to remember details.

Sim schemed in the tree until sundown. Only when they had to turn on the lights in the building did the boys leave. Sim didn't come to himself until the deep bass from the Otis boy's car thumped through him. The two vehicles left.

He climbed down from his seat in the tree as best he could in the dark. Everything worked like he'd wanted it to. Right now, he needed a drink, and not the watery stuff he kept at home to satisfy Alan. He needed to visit with Johnny and then head over the county line for some stuff off the tap.

It was deep sunset before Sim got to Johnny House's place. After knocking on the door for a long time, he found Johnny sitting alone on his back porch.

"What are you doing out here?" Sim asked, walking up the whitewashed steps.

"Watching the sunset," Johnny sounded someplace between reality and a dream.

Sim sat down in the wooden rocking chair beside his friend. "Why aren't you over at your daughter's house with your family?"

"No reason to be." The other's voice remained dreamy. "They aren't doing jack squat about that boy's death. My no-good drunk whore of a daughter isn't even planning a memorial service." He finally looked at Sim. "Can you imagine that? The boy's a crackerjack football player. The whole town knows his name, and she's going to throw him in a hole."

"A shame. What's happened to those kids we raised? My smart-alecky grandson told me off yesterday after Marshall's funeral. Told me stuff no boy should tell his grandfather. Why? Because his daddy didn't raise him no better. Today that boy of mine told me as good to shut up in front of a nigger nurse at the ER."

Johnny looked at him again. The pink light of the sunset made his wispy silver hair look like cotton candy. "Why was you at the ER?"

"That's part of why I came over to talk to you. I heard about how your grandson got killed."

"Hit and run driver. The sheriff says he hasn't got any idea how the other car kept driving after splitting Corey's jeep in two. He said he's never seen anything like it."

"Did he tell you anything else?"

"The condition my grandson was in. He said it was one of the worst wrecks he'd ever worked. Sheriff told me he hasn't seen anything like that since Vietnam."

Johnny turned back to the sunset. His expression went soft and blubbery. Sim hated seeing a hard man cry. Although he could barely stand to see his friend cry, he'd shed a tear if something like that happened to his grandsons, especially Thomas. His hand shook as he put it on his friend's shoulder. Ever since climbing down from the tree, his palsy shaking had worsened, and the face in the rearview mirror had grown clearer. Now the face had a fuzzy body below it.

Sim took his hand back and clasped it over his knee to prevent Johnny from noticing how badly it quaked. "The sheriff called me out to Harrington Road bright and early this morning," he said.

"What for?"

"They found Charlotte's car out there all torn up to the point they couldn't figure out how it was still driving."

Johnny looked back him. "You don't mean it was the car that killed Corey, do you?"

"They think so."

"Did they find the driver?" Johnny asked. By his tone, he was asking if Charlotte had gone off her rocker again and run his grandson down.

"No, Charlotte's in the hospital. She has been for days." Sim shook his head, mostly to hide the strong trembling. "No one could have survived that wreck, much less driven that car from the high school to Harrington Road."

"What are you saying?"

"Why do you think Marshall killed himself?" Sim asked.

"Guilt."

"Is that it?"

"I suppose. I'm not a mind reader, Sim."

The growing clarity of the face in his reflection scared him, worse than seeing that Mercury Monterey sitting like it had forty years ago. It frightened him more than what happened the night of the massacre. The face staring over his shoulder in his reflection scared him worse than anything he'd ever experienced.

"That car was in the exact spot it was the night you shot out the tire. The same tire was even flat. The trunk was up when I arrived, and a black deputy leaned into it," Sim said. "Gave me the heebie-jeebies so bad I passed out."

"That's why you were at the ER? They must have thought you'd had a heart attack."

"Exactly. Let me tell you something. That car didn't end up there by sheer luck."

"Are you trying to tell me a ghost drove the car there, and a spirit killed my grandson?"

"You tell me," Sim answered as coolly as he could.

A steely calm descended on him for the first time that day. Perhaps it was the first time he'd felt that way for a while, if he was completely honest with himself. Johnny looked very uncomfortable.

"Have you seen him?" Johnny asked.

"Who?"

"Ben Harris."

"No, I ain't seen him since his funeral. He looked pretty rough back then."

"His ghost looks a lot worse now. I take Lasix every night, and I have to go about two times most nights, maybe three, depends on what I drink. Anyway, for the last few months, he's been staring in my bathroom window while I take a piss."

"You can tell it's him? He didn't start out fuzzy and get clearer?"

"The first night scared more than the piss out of me. It was like his corpse stood there plain as day." Johnny squinted his eyes at him. "What have you seen?"

"Nothing. Except that car this morning sitting like it had *that* night."

"Marshall said he heard Sheila Deleon's screams every night for two years. He told me not long before killing himself that he'd not slept a whole night in three weeks. Apparently she started appearing at the foot of his bed, glowing blood red and screaming too loud for him to sleep."

"My son claims to have seen Tommy Jones the other night at the school."

"Does he know?"

"Do I look like an idiot? Of course he doesn't know. Did your grandson know?"

Johnny shook his head. "I've never told anyone."

"Why him?" Sim asked.

That particular question had been burning in his mind most of the day. Why had Johnny's grandson been killed in such a horrific way? That led him to think about what might be in store for others, especially himself.

"Some high school kids are planning on having a Massacre Anniversary dance. What you reckon about that?" Johnny asked.

"My son works over at the school. He mentioned it, but he told me that the principal shot down the idea, for good reason."

"Principal Chapman shot down the idea of them having it at the school, but some of them still planned on putting it on. Corey was one of them."

Sim entwined his fingers and stared out into nothing. Johnny did the same thing. The two gray-haired men sat on the porch saying nothing until well after the sun slipped behind the pine trees. Even the purple halo of the setting sun was gone before Sim even recognized that he was thinking. He looked over at Johnny. His old friend appeared trapped in a catatonic state like Charlotte had been long ago.

"I reckon I'll be heading out," Sim stood. "Don't drive well at night these days."

"Thanks for coming by." Johnny's voice had taken on that dreamy quality again.

His friend ruminated over his lost grandson. He left, not bothering to say another word. The only good thing about driving at night was that the darkness kept him from seeing the reflection in the truck's mirrors.

Chapter Eighteen

1956
Two days before Homecoming

Charlotte sat on top of Connie Dearborn's desk while her math teacher tried to grade freshman test papers. She popped her gum, which she wasn't supposed to chew but it was overlooked because of her special relationship with Miss Dearborn.

"Sim told me that he proposed," Charlotte swung her crossed leg in and out to the rhythm of her chewing.

"Yes, he did," Connie answered with curtness in her voice.

"He said you didn't give him an answer."

"That's right."

"Why not?"

Connie put her red grease pencil down and looked at Charlotte. "Because I don't know if I want to marry him."

"You've been going with him for a year," Charlotte said. "Don't you think you ought to?"

"I don't know if I want to spend the rest of my life with him."

"Why not? He's got Alan and Mikey. They're sweethearts."

Connie nodded. "I like the boys a lot, but they're part of the reason for my worry. Your brother has been married before. He's got children. That's a lot of baggage to drag into a marriage. I don't know if I'm ready for that."

"But y'all have *sex*, don't you?" Charlotte asked.

"Do you and Tobias have sex?" Connie asked, not lowering her voice.

Charlotte hopped off the desk and looked around the room

as if someone had come in without being seen. The nerve of her teacher asking such a question, even if she was about to marry her brother. Indignation welled up in Charlotte. No one had the right to ask her that question. Yet it seemed to be coming up frequently. Sim himself had asked her that the other day.

"That's none of your business."

"Same to you. Remember there are questions too personal, even in our modern times."

"You're a war widow. What does it matter?"

The end-of-school bell rang. Connie shuffled the papers she was not going to get finished grading and put them into her desk drawer. She stared at Charlotte until the sound of scuffling feet at lockers in the hall outside the door died away. It had to be five minutes of complete silence. It nearly drove Charlotte nuts.

"My fiancé died in Korea. We weren't married, so I'm not a widow. Sim is divorced. The marriage ended because either Sim or his ex-wife did something wrong."

Charlotte could see the true dilemma in Connie's face. "It was his fault."

"I know. I don't think I can keep on with him. I haven't found the right time to tell him."

The bobbysoxer's heart sank. Somehow she had fallen prey to those cheesy love stories at the pictures. Love prevailed over all, even though her brother was an aggravating man. It saddened her that Connie wouldn't be her sister-in-law. She liked her a lot.

"Are you going to help us decorate the gym tomorrow night?" Charlotte asked.

Connie smiled. "If you'll shut up long enough so I can grade those tests."

Charlotte pulled an imaginary zipper across her lips, snapped a make-believe padlock over it, and tossed away the invisible key. Connie nodded.

The front door slammed shut while Charlotte and her folks were eating dinner. Her father jumped to his feet, fists balled and ready to fight. Sim charged into the kitchen. Her father let his hands relax but didn't sit back down.

"What do you mean storming into this house like that?" her father demanded.

"That stupid bitch turned me down," Sim said.

"Watch your mouth," her father said. "There are ladies present."

Sim looked down at Charlotte. His eyes told her that he didn't believe she was very much of a lady. Despite how much she loved her mother's fried pork chops and creamed potatoes with brown gravy, her appetite vanished.

"Connie told me she couldn't marry me. And what's worse, she wants nothing to do with me." Sim sat at the empty chair. He put his hands over his face and started to cry.

Charlotte pitied him. The idea of true love still made her think that Connie would change her mind. She put her hand on his shoulder, but he jerked away as if she had burned him.

"Don't touch me, whore," he snapped.

A loud pop echoed across the table. Sim favored the cheek closest to their mother. She held her right hand in her left, rubbing it, her lips drawn into such a tight angry slit that they nearly disappeared. For a stunned moment, the family sat around the table like a Norman Rockwell painting gone wrong. Charlotte's daddy walked around the table, snatched Sim up by arm and shoved him through the house and out the door.

"Don't you dare come back here until you learn some manners," her daddy yelled from the entryway.

The front door slammed again. This time it was her daddy who'd done it. He walked back into the kitchen, red faced and puffing like a bull. Her mother continued to rub her hand. Charlotte cradled her ego, which stung from the verbal slap her brother had given her. Yet she still loved him despite how horrible he could be.

"Something bad is going to happen to that boy one day," her father said, sitting back down to his plate. "If it ain't already."

"Don't talk like that, Herman," her mother said.

"You can't ignore what he called his sister," her daddy said. "No one who does good things in good places talks like that to his family." He looked at his half-eaten meal. "I ain't even hungry anymore."

"Neither am I." Charlotte could barely keep from crying. "May I be excused?"

"Of course," her mother said.

She left the table, went to her room, and cried.

Chapter Nineteen

For reasons he wasn't entirely sure of, butterflies fluttered in Josh's stomach. His dad had been acting strange all afternoon. He caught a glimpse of Thomas as their dad fumbled with the key in Aunt Charlotte's front door. His brother looked as confused and anxious. His dad seemed a little deranged as the key failed to turn the tumblers.

"What's the matter with this thing?" Alan asked. "I don't even remember locking it when I ran out last night."

"Dad, relax," Thomas said. "Let me try."

Alan stepped back and let his son try the door. He had a near-panicked look on his face. This puzzled Josh more than anything. Alan's reaction was extreme. The butterflies fluttered harder.

"I don't get it." Thomas let go of the door handle. "It's like someone superglued the lock."

"Kick it in," Alan said.

"Whoa, Daddy." Josh put his hand on his father's shoulder with a firmness he hoped would imply calm, even though he continued to get increasingly jazzed up by his father's behavior. "Why don't we try the back door?"

"That's a good idea," Alan said with a calmer voice. His shoulder slumped to a more relaxed position.

"If that doesn't work," Josh said, "we can try the door from the garage."

"And there's always the window she leaves unlocked," Thomas said.

"I'll go around back," Alan said. He held his hand out to Thomas for the keys.

"We'll all go," Josh said.

His father might still try to stomp the door in if the key didn't work. Thomas kept the keys, and the three McAdamses walked off the screened porch. Jessica stayed.

"Aren't you coming?" Josh asked.

"If you don't mind, I think I'll sit in the glider swing," she said. "You can come and get me when you get in," she added as she sat down.

"All right."

They walked around the house. The grass was high for the time of the year. Usually it had already stopped growing by now, and sometimes even died. He needed to come over and mow it to keep it from looking ratty.

Thomas got to the back door before the others. He tried to unlock it. The key fit, but his brother couldn't turn the lock. He jiggled the knob.

"It's like the front door," he said.

Alan walked up the narrow stairs and nudged Thomas down a step. He fumbled with the door and had as much success.

"Let me try," Josh said. Sometimes he had a way with pesky locks. It came in handy with lockers and sneaking in at night.

Alan moved aside, which reassured Josh that his father was giving way to more rational thinking. He took the key out of the lock and blew on it. Sometimes wayward fluff from pockets would stick to the teeth. The same could happen with the tumblers, so he bent down and blew into the lock as well. The key went in easily, but when Josh twisted it, nothing budged. He moved the key out a little and tried again, with the same result. Another try, shoving the key in very hard, came up the same.

"I think someone might have put something in there, but that can't be," Josh said.

"Because the key will fit," Alan said. "I thought about that, too. Epoxy or even superglue would plug up the keyhole."

"Hold on," Thomas said. He walked to the kitchen window that was over the sink. He was tall enough to reach the bottom of it without a boost. He pushed on the pane hard enough that it should have sent the window sailing open, but nothing happened. Thomas stood on his tiptoes to put forth extra effort.

The veins stood out on his brother's neck as he strained at the window.

Thomas relented. "It won't budge."

"Maybe it's locked," Josh said.

"Nope, I can see the lock."

"Let's go to the garage," Alan suggested. "I know I left that door unlocked."

"Hold on, Dad," Josh said, a little tired of the whole charade. "Why is it so important to get in there?"

"If I tell you, I'm afraid you won't be able to give a clear answer," Alan said with an irrational tone returning to his voice.

"No, tell us," Thomas said. "You're sounding crazy."

"It was your aunt's car that killed Corey. I knew that last night. I came over to check. The car was gone. When I went into the house, I saw something. I need you two to tell me I'm not crazy."

"You're acting a little bit that way," Thomas said.

Josh punched his brother in shoulder. He got a froggy in return.

"Let's check the garage door," Josh said.

The three of them walked around the other side of the house and came up beside the garage. Alan punched in the number of the garage door lift. It rumbled to life. As they stepped into the gloom of the garage, the bulb on the lift had burned out. Jessica poked her head from the porch.

"I got the door opened."

All three of them stopped. No one said anything for a moment. They looked at her dumbfounded. Thomas spoke first, as he tended to do.

"How?"

"I'm good with locks," she said.

"You don't have a key," Josh protested.

Jessica showed them something, but she was too far away for them to see. "Hairpin."

"Does that actually work?" Thomas whispered.

"I suppose so," Josh answered back. He had no clue.

"It always did on *Scooby-Doo*," Alan said.

The McAdams men walked back to the porch. Despite the

mania that seemed to have gripped them, they hung their heads a little defeated. Despite how much he liked Jessica, Josh never liked being one-upped by a girl, and Thomas hated it. He supposed it was the only negative character trait they had inherited from Sim.

When they stepped on the porch, the front door stood open. Josh looked inside and saw nothing out of the ordinary. Alan rushed into the house like a man on a suicide mission. Josh and Thomas followed. They stuck in the door for a moment as both tried to enter at the same time. Josh felt like slapping his brother on the back of the head, impersonating Moe from the Three Stooges, but his father's manic behavior made him quickly squeeze his shoulders inward to break the logjam. Jessica entered last.

Alan walked quickly from the kitchen into the living room and back into the entryway before going into the sitting room. Josh watched him, thinking he looked like a mouse in a maze that couldn't quite remember how to find the cheese.

"What's the matter with him?" Jessica asked.

"He's gone crazy," Thomas answered.

Alan stopped in the entryway, bent over panting. His eyes glared around the room. It scared Josh a little. By the expression on Thomas's face, it scared him as well.

"It's gone," Alan said between gasps. "It's all gone."

"What's gone?" Josh asked. "Everything looks okay to me."

"There was crepe paper everywhere. It was hanging in here, and over there." Alan flung his hands frantically. "The record player was playing some old song from the 50s."

Thomas walked into the living room. "Was it some guy named Pat Boone?" he yelled. "Because that's what's on the record player."

"No." Alan put his face into his hands. "No, it was a song called 'Sh-Boom'."

"'Love Letters in the Sand'," Thomas yelled back.

"I'm not crazy," Alan said to Josh. His face looked tired and old. "There were baby blue and gray streamers everywhere. This place was decorated for a party."

"Or a dance," Josh corrected.

His Aunt Charlotte would talk about getting the wrong colored crepe paper for the dance. She would have been killed that day if she hadn't gone for the decorations.

"Jessica, was everything like this when you opened the door?" Alan asked.

"Yeah. The only thing was it smelled a little bit like Cool Water cologne," she said.

Thomas walked back in from the living room. "A lot of the guys on the team wear that stuff, Dad. You've smelled it before. You've had to. Some folks douse themselves in it."

"Do you think someone broke in when they stole the car and decorated the place?" Josh asked. He was trying to confirm his own suspicions.

"Maybe," Alan said.

"They must've come back in and cleaned up everything," Thomas said. "To cover their tracks."

"Why?" Alan asked. "That doesn't make sense."

"I bet it was Marcus Smithson and his buddies," Josh said. "They knew that Aunt Charlotte had to go to the hospital. I bet they did it to scare her back into the place when she got out."

"Do you think they stole the car and killed Corey?" Thomas asked.

"They wouldn't be alive," Alan said. "Your grandfather saw her car. He said no one could have survived the accident. I saw Corey's Jeep and completely agree."

"Marcus drove me to the library a little while ago," Jessica said. "He would brag if he'd set up a prank like that."

"Maybe it was Corey," Thomas suggested. "He loved that stupid cologne. He almost bathed in it."

"I was with him the whole afternoon and a good part of the evening," Alan said.

"And he ended up dead." Josh knew it sounded cold, but it needed to be said. "It still wouldn't answer who took it down."

"Let's go," Thomas said. "I'm getting the creeps."

Jessica shivered. "Me too."

Alan looked around. Josh could tell he was desperately searching for some scrap of paper that would prove he hadn't imagined it. He didn't think his dad would find any. After everything that happened lately, it was enough to make anyone believe anything. He had seen the ghost of a girl who died forty years earlier. Even now he was unsure that hadn't been his imagination.

His father led the way out of the house, the others following. Josh locked the door behind him as he pulled it closed. They walked off of the porch single file. Every one of them seemed down and worried—even Jessica, who had no connection to any of it.

When they got into the car, Alan turned on the radio. For some reason it was set to the local golden oldies channel, 91.7 WALA. Four guys sang the chorus. It was "Sh-Boom." Thomas punched the button for 105.9 The X out of Birmingham. "Peaches" by the Presidents of the United States started playing. Josh absolutely hated the song, but he welcomed it over the golden oldie.

"Thank you," Alan said. As he backed down the driveway, he added, "Let's go get something to eat."

The sun set over the river. Its warm pink and orange glow reflected on the water like fireworks. The colors of the leaves added to the impressionistic look of the scene. Josh and Jessica sat in his car at the River Park picnic area. He'd parked all the way at the edge of the bluff over the Buxataloosa River. Few people came out there anymore. It had a small swimming beach at the base of the bluff. A set of steps led down to it, but a little boy had drowned at the beginning of the summer.

"It's pretty this evening," Jessica said after they had sat there for a long time.

"It's hard to believe that something that horrible happened yesterday," Josh said.

Over dinner, they had all talked about Corey's death. Despite how much he didn't want the death to affect him, Josh felt something deep inside of him. He couldn't deny that he didn't like Corey, but equally, he didn't want him to die.

"You never realize how fragile life is until someone you know is gone," Jessica said. "Who do you think did it?"

"I've got no idea. My Dad said the other car was so smashed

up that no one could have survived driving it."

"Do you think it was an accident?"

"I hope so. Who would want to kill him?"

"You."

That single word, uttered from her lips in a flat matter-of-fact tone, set Josh's teeth on edge like fingernails scraping across a long chalkboard. The last thing in the world he wished for Corey was death. Josh had been taught a long time ago never to wish for someone's death, because it might happen. The warning was always lodged in the back of his mind.

"I did not. I would never wish that on anyone."

"Not even Marcus Smithson and his buddies?"

"No. I gave them what they deserved."

"But they trashed your aunt's house." Jessica never looked at him.

"You were there. The house was fine."

"How about your grandfather?"

Josh looked at her and touched her arm so that she would look at him. Her eyes were very serious, like she had been focusing hard on something outside that wasn't the sunset.

"I don't want anyone to die. Why are you asking me about it? Do I come off like some kind of serial killer?"

"Psycho killer, *qu'est-ce que c'est*," she sang.

He stared at her like she had lost her mind. At that moment, in his mind she had. She must have noticed. Her eyes softened to a look of playfulness, and she let out a good-natured cackle like she impersonated a witch.

"It's the Talking Heads. Lighten up. I know you wouldn't ever want to kill anyone. It's getting close to Halloween. You needed a good scare."

"Is that what it was?" he asked, not quite believing her.

"Of course! We should go costume shopping."

"We've got no reason to wear them. You don't trick-or-treat still, do you?"

"We can throw a party—or even better, wear them to the Homecoming dance. We'll get matching ones." .

"I don't think they'll be having a dance after what happened with Corey. People won't much be in the mood. Plus, why would we wear matching costumes? People would think we were a couple."

"That would be horrible, wouldn't it?"

Before he could say another word, she grabbed him by the face and pulled him close to her. They kissed without him completely grasping what was going on. Only when he tasted the flavor of her mouth, salty and exactly what he'd imagined, did the gravity of the situation pull him back to earth. Josh put forth the effort to make their initial kiss a memorable one. Mediocrity had no place in that moment.

A million things rushed through his head. Jessica was very much into making out. He couldn't remember ever making out with a girl who was that enthusiastic. During the time they pawed at each other, one of them turned the radio on. Snippets of music floated in the air during that time. Cake followed Bush. At some point a Nirvana song came on. He heard it clearly enough to think about how ironic it was that "Rape Me" should play during that particular moment. Finally things broke off.

"Jane Says" played after they finished. Jessica smiled as she stretched her lips out. Josh giggled. He couldn't help it. It was like she'd bewitched him. He had wanted nothing more than to kiss her since they'd met.

"I need to get home," Josh said. "I'm pretty sure that Dad didn't intend for me to be gone for long."

She looked around. "Yeah, the sun has gone down. I hope that you don't get a worse punishment."

"I'll have to hurry home. I'll tell my folks you needed to run some errands. Dad knows that you have to rely on the kindness of strangers." He backed up and started toward the park exit.

"What do you mean?"

"You told us that Marcus gave you a ride to library. When we went to your house earlier today, there was no car. I've never seen one there any time."

"You went to my house earlier? Did you go inside?"

"No, that would be rude. No one answered the door."

Jessica nodded. The glowing green of the radio display caught in the highlights in her hair. "Of course the car wasn't there, my folks were at work."

She turned up the radio and settled into her seat before he could say anything else. Josh could tell he had made her angry. He concentrated on driving. Something about all of her questions about who he wished would die still bothered him. He rolled down the windows and let the cool evening air blow in. Her hair flurried up before she caught it and pulled into a ponytail, producing a hair band from her pocket to hold it in place. She smiled at him. The dusty aroma of autumn wafted in.

They rode in silence, listening to the collection of alternative tracks the radio played. Josh basked a little in the glow of achieving a goal he had longed for. He wished he could read her mind.

Alan congregated with all the teachers from Pinehurst High at Corey's wake. They stood on the right side of the funeral home's chapel midway down the room. A couple of Gary Springs Middle School teachers stood with them as well. Students and their parents packed the place. A lot of townspeople sat in the pews as well. It seemed that the death of a young person always brought out a crowd.

He'd spoken very briefly with Corey's mother. She thanked him for taking her son to the emergency room the evening he died. The reek of booze came off her skin. It would have carried on her breath if she hadn't covered it with very strong peppermint. Probably one of the chalky aspirin-looking mints that came in the tin. He hated being there.

Thomas laughed with Steven, one of his football buddies. They relived some *awesome* plays from the game against Fayette County. One of them had jumped off a blocker's back. Josh admitted it was pretty awesome, but they should have more respect at a wake.

He stood with Thomas and a group of the football players. Harvey was with them. The reek of Cool Water came off of him like stink off a dead skunk. There were undertones of skunk weed as well. His eyes looked glassier than normal. A permanent smirk rested on his lips. It had started when he saw Jessica holding Josh's hands for all to see, but he had said nothing. The pot had mellowed him out, which was good. There was no telling what he would have said to Corey's mother. Instead, she and Harvey shared a looked that said they partook of a shared communion, THC.

"This is horrible," Steven finally said. "I can't believe he's gone."

"I know," Jessica replied. "I'd seen him at the end of the day on Thursday. I woke up on Friday, and he was gone."

"It makes you think," Thomas said.

"Yeah, about why he has a closed casket," Harvey said, starting to get louder. "Let us see the carnage."

Josh was able to quiet his friend before the whole phrase was blurted out. Several of the adults glowered at them. He took Harvey by the arm and started leading him toward the exit.

"Maybe you need some air," he said.

"No, I'm fine," Harvey said.

Josh put pressure on his friend's arm. "I am positive you need some air."

They walked past the stream of sympathizers waiting their turn to speak to the grieving mother. At the door, Josh looked up to see Marcus Smithson, Bill Foreman, and Jamie Morris standing in the receiving line. They were all dressed in their black jeans with holes at the knees and various heavy metal T-shirts. All the shirts feature grinning skulls. Marcus wore the same one he had been wearing when he and Josh had gotten into their fight—Guns N' Roses' "Appetite for Destruction." They all stared at each other like cagy gunfighters in some old Clint Eastwood movie, but said nothing. Once in the lobby, Josh shook his head at their ridiculousness.

He hated being there.

The coffee Sim swallowed tasted scorched. It had come from the orange-topped pot, which meant decaf. He reckoned he needed to lay off the leaded stuff. Sleep hadn't been coming too well for him lately. Last night he had dreamt about the massacre, but instead of it being the original bunch, it had been those kids breaking into the old gym and Johnny's grandson. The nigger running back on the football team who had been with the others hanged from one of the rafters in the old gym like one of the streamers. They were even baby blue and gray.

Johnny sat across from him drinking a bad cup of coffee as well. They both smoked cigarettes. The snack room was the only place in the funeral home where smoking was allowed. They hadn't said much to each other since Sim had arrived, after the family-only visitation ended. They didn't have to.

The death of a young person made everyone feel bad, and Sim understood that the old hated it even worse because they had lived life and seeing one cut short seemed unfair. He and Johnny knew their fair share of death. A few days ago, they had sat in the same room at the same table drinking the same too-bitter coffee. That time, it was for a friend.

"I'm sorry about your grandson," Jack Tomlinson said to Johnny, shaking his hand. "Do they know what happened?"

Johnny shook his head. "The police are stumped. They found the car that did it, but it was stolen and in such bad shape that they don't think the driver could have survived."

"That's horrible. If you need anything, give me a call," Jack said and walked off.

"That's probably the fifteenth person who has told me to call if I needed anything," Johnny said. "What am I going to ask for—another tuna casserole?"

"Have y'all gotten a lot of those?" Sim asked.

"One is too many. Why folks think everyone who has lost a loved one wants some sort of casserole is beyond me."

"I remember when Momma died. It was the time of the year when the gardens had started to come in. We got at least five squash casseroles from people who planted too many of them." He took a drag off of his cigarette. "I still won't eat the things. I'm sorry again about your grandson. I hope they catch the guy who did it."

Johnny leaned into him. "You know they won't. Wasn't no man that did it."

"Don't be crazy," Sim's hands begin to tremble. His symptoms worsened under stress. "It had to be, couldn't have been anything else."

"It was that thing that looks through my window. Maybe

the one that your boy seen at the school, or whatever it is that you stare at over your shoulder."

His head started to move as well. His tongue wanted to move from side to side. "What are you talking about?"

"I've seen you glance over your shoulder when you catch your reflection in mirrors and shiny objects. You've even done it a couple times tonight in here without the mirror. You see something there, don't you?"

Sim cut his eyes over his shoulder. "No." He snuffed his smoke. "Listen, I've got to go. If you need something, let me know. I don't mean a casserole either."

"Why you leaving so early?" Johnny asked.

He showed him his tremulous hands. "My Parkinson's is acting up a bit tonight. It does that sometimes. I'll be at the funeral tomorrow though."

Johnny shook his head. "We're not having one. His momma wanted him buried without any more fanfare. Corey's brother and I had to talk to her a long time to get this."

"Let me know if you need anything."

Sim hurried out without waiting for Johnny to say another word. The face actually felt as if it floated over his shoulder like a child's balloon. The nearness of it made the hairs on his neck stand up. He hated being there.

Chapter Twenty

1956
Three days after the Massacre

The funeral director's office smelled faintly of formaldehyde. The acrid smell nauseated Sim. If he had to sit there much longer, looking at the dark-paneled walls, he'd have to open the window. It faced the alleyway between the funeral home and the dry cleaner. The whole neighborhood probably loved the smell the two establishments generated. This was the second time in a week he'd sat in that very office.

After the murders, the coroner had sent Connie's body over to this place. He'd come to give the director the information for her family so that they could make appropriate arrangements. After several days and all of the other funerals had been announced, the mortician got back with him. Now he sat waiting, staring at the posters advertising coffins.

Mr. Weinstein, the funeral director, walked in. "Sorry to keep you waiting, Mr. McAdams," he said.

Sim didn't stand or accept the man's hand. The last time, the lanky man's hand had been cold and damp. The mortician might have returned from tending to the dead. Mr. Weinstein even looked like a vampire, if Jews could be that kind of bloodsucker.

"What did Connie's parents want for her burial? Are they having her shipped back to Georgia?"

"No, there is a slight problem," Weinstein said. "The information you gave us for her family didn't work out. I'm sorry it took us so long to get back with you, but we've been rather busy, as you might understand."

"What was wrong with it?"

"The address that we sent a telegraph to wasn't her parents'. A couple named Johnston lived there. They said that Connie's parents haven't lived there for three years."

"She talked about them all the time. I addressed a Father's Day card for her back in the summer. That was the address, because I remembered the funny street name."

"Connie never told you?"

"Told me what? Frankly, Mr. Weinstein, I don't have time for riddles. I've missed a lot of work lately. My boss will fire me if I spend much more time off."

"I'll cut to the chase. They're dead."

"Her parents?"

"Murdered three years ago. According to the Johnstons, who called me on the phone, the killer remains at large."

Sim shook his head. It didn't make any sense. There were recent pictures of her family from her visit in August, and she'd been talking on the phone with her mother several times when he showed up at her house.

"You've got to be wrong," Sim said

"I called the town's police department and local funeral home. I know the director of funeral services there. Both confirmed they were murdered coming home from a picture show one night. The killer was never caught."

"Give me a minute," Sim took a very deep breath of air. His nostrils and lungs filled with the low odor of the embalming chemicals. Another wave of nausea came over him. This time, he didn't know if it was the news or the chemicals. "What do we do?"

"Did she have siblings?" Weinstein asked.

"A brother, but he's stationed in Germany."

"It will take a while to get a hold of him. Why don't you plan the arrangements? You were her fiancé."

"Ex-boyfriend," Sim corrected. "She broke up with me the night before she was killed. That doesn't matter. I'll pay for her burial. Given me that coffin." He pointed to one of the posters that displayed a beautiful golden oak coffin with a light pink silk lining. "Do you sell plots?"

"Only to Round Hill Cemetery," Weinstein said. "You'll have to call First Baptist to purchase a place in Pinehurst Hill Cemetery."

"You got their number? I won't have her put up there where they buried that Abernathy boy. Isn't that old witch Hazel supposedly buried there too?"

"It used to be a potter's field of sorts," Weinstein answered. He pulled a business card from his desk and handed it to Sim. "That's the church's number. We have the coffin in stock, and once you secure a plot, we can do the service."

"No service. Lay her in the box, and put her in the hole. I'll get the preacher from the Baptist church to pray over her."

"What about her family and friends?"

"Obviously, she's not got any family, and her friends are probably tired of going to wakes and whatnot." He pointed to the coffin poster again. "That coffin." He pointed to a date on the calendar lying on the director's desk. "That date. I'll call you with plot location. You call me when you've got a price, and I'll pay you."

Sim didn't give the old Jew time to tell him to pay up front. He walked out of the office and the building. The sun shone on him, warmer than he'd expected. He got into his car and drove to Connie's house. Her car sat in the driveway like it had since he'd had it towed from the gym. He parked on the curb, got out, and walked to the house.

The front door opened into the living room. Everything sat around like it had the day after she passed away when he'd come over to get her folks' address. Sim had been waiting for them to get back with Mr. Weinstein before he took care of her belongings and house. He hadn't felt right liquidating her things without her family's permission, especially after she had broken things off with him. The point was now moot.

He went to her bedroom, pulled the long middle drawer out of an antique rolltop desk she kept back there, and let the contents tumble onto the patchwork quilt neatly made over her bed. Overstuffed envelopes piled into a small mound. A few stray coins rested around the perimeter of the stuff. Sim sat the drawer on the floor and sat on the corner of the bed. He started rifling through the papers in the envelopes.

Most of them were receipts. He even found the one for her parents' funerals. He couldn't figure out why she'd kept up such a long, drawn-out charade about them being alive. Another envelope contained the Dearborns' death certificates. Death by homicide was clearly listed as the cause of death. In that same envelope, he found a few newspaper clippings, yellowed from age.

The first article looked like a front-page story about the murder of her parents. The police at that time suspected they might have picked up a homicidal hitchhiker. All motorists were put on alert to not pick up anyone they didn't know. Another article was about the hitchhiker theory being ruled out. The final article talked about how the police were giving up on the investigation. This article was dated a few weeks before Connie moved to Pinehurst.

Sim gathered up the loose coins and put them in his pocket. Any little amount would help get her in the ground. She supposedly had a bank account, but there was no way for him to get access to that. He gathered up the papers and picked up the drawer. Something in a larger manila-style envelope was taped to the bottom. He tore it off.

The envelope had heft. When it opened, a book fell out. It looked old with a red fabric binding. Sim picked it up and read the flaking gold title, *Legends of the Deep South 1864-Present*. A thin piece of yellow ribbon marked a place in the book. He flipped to the page. The title of a legend jumped out in large block letters—THE WITCH NAMED HAZEL.

He dropped the book. It landed open and face-up. The name of the town was underlined with a red grease pencil. In the margins, Connie had written *this is the place* with the same pencil. A few strange symbols were on the margins on the other side. One looked like the pyramid and eye symbol on a dollar bill. Another was definitely the Star of David.

After the first surprise, Sim's curiosity got the best of him. He picked the book back up and flipped to the next page. The red pencil underlined something else, his family name and the name of the Harringtons' ancestor. He closed the book and shoved it back into the envelope. All of Connie's other papers went into the drawer, and it went back into the desk. Sim took the book and started out of the room. He looked under the edge of the mattress before he left. By sheer luck, he found another envelope secreted there. It had about $500 in it. Enough money to bury her with a few bucks to spare.

Clutching the book in one hand and the money in the other, Sim would let the probate judge handle the rest of Connie's affairs. He suddenly didn't care what happened with them.

Chapter Twenty-One

The psychiatrist walked into the small visitation room where Alan waited. He looked middle-aged, with graying hair in a high horseshoe shape around a central bald spot. He didn't wear a lab coat, just a pair of roughed-up blue jeans, a western shirt, and cowboy boots scuffed at the toe.

"Mr. McAdams, I'm Dr. Vanhouten." He shook Alan's hand before settling into a vinyl recliner across the room. "I'm sorry to have kept you waiting, but we had to give a patient an injection. I find that my presence sometimes helps ease the process for the staff. It didn't."

"I could tell." Alan said. By the sound of the yelling, the staff had been dealing with a large, angry man delusional about something he called the stump of Babylon. "Is my aunt okay?"

"She's perfectly safe. We have rarely had patients harmed by other patients."

"That's not exactly what I meant."

"You are right; I didn't call you here on a Sunday to chat about a Haldol PRN." Dr. Vanhouten rubbed his chin. "Your aunt has been with us for nearly a week. We were making good progress until Friday."

"What happened then?" Alan asked.

"We were getting ready to call you and let you know that she could have visitors when one of our night nurses documented her talking to herself in her room. She was saying things that bothered us."

"Like what?"

"Violent things. Killing people, specifically someone named

Corey. Our nurse noted that name in the chart. As you may know, a student at the high school named Corey was killed Thursday night."

"I was the first on the scene," Alan said. "He was one of my football players."

"I'm sorry. Your aunt talked about other people being dead when I spoke with her late Friday. She talked about a Sue and Sheila. I think I remember her mentioning a Tommy."

"Those are all the kids she found dead back in 1956. You do know about that, don't you?" Alan asked.

"Of course. She carries a diagnosis of posttraumatic stress disorder. It can cause dissociation and can manifest alongside catatonia or even psychotic symptoms in some recorded cases. All these things have presented in your aunt to some degree."

"Why are you concerned? You can medicate her, can't you?"

"Of course, the problem is this. Today, I learned that your aunt's car is believed to have killed that boy."

"It was stolen. I came the night he died to check and make sure you hadn't discharged her without letting me know. I was afraid she might have done it. The nurse told me she was in her room sleeping and had been for a while."

"That may not be the case."

Alan looked at the doctor like he was the crazy one. "What do you mean?"

"We record video of all the patients. On Sundays, I review the tapes to watch for any behaviors or symptoms they may be masking. On Thursday evening, the tape for your aunt's room malfunctioned. Before it went out, she wasn't in her room. During the span, no other cameras on the unit recorded her. When the tape came back on, well after lights out, she wasn't in bed. Fifteen minutes later, she was. The tape has a delay of few minutes, but none of the tape shows her coming back to bed."

"What are you saying?"

The doctor looked very concerned. "Your aunt may have busted out and killed that boy."

"Then returned? Not Charlotte. She hates these places. If she busted out, even to commit homicide, she wouldn't come back."

"Let's hope so, but I am going to have to report this to the police. I wanted you to know so that it wouldn't come as a shock."

"That's fine. I'm sure they'll find she was in the bathroom or something," Alan said. "Can I see her before I leave?"

"That will be fine, but do me a favor. She has not been overly cooperative as of late. Ask her if Connie has come to talk to her today, and what they talked about."

"Connie? Is that who she says she's been talking to?"

"Yes, she told me that was the person who told her about Corey dying. Is she a relative?"

"No, another victim of the massacre. She told me that Connie visited her the day we brought her in. It's what prompted us to bring her here."

"Please try to find out if she's still talking with her and let me know."

Alan nodded to the doctor. They sat for a few moments, looking at each other. This made Alan feel a little uncomfortable. He believed that when doctors stared at you for no reason, they were trying to figure you out. The last thing he wanted was for a psychiatrist to analyze him. With everything that had been going on, Dr. Vanhouten would certainly find something.

"So?" Alan asked.

"I was waiting for you to say you were ready."

"I'm ready."

They walked out of the small room into the main area of the ward. The nurse's station sat in the middle. Three halls radiated off of this central spoke. Dr. Vanhouten led Alan to the right. A sign above this hallway indicated it as the women's wing.

They stopped in front of room 307. "This is Miss McAdams's room," Dr. Vanhouten said, tapping on the door.

His aunt gave permission for entrance. The doctor pushed open the door. Charlotte sat on the edge of her bed, staring out the window.

"Charlotte, you have a visitor," Dr. Vanhouten said.

"It must be someone special," she said. "I haven't gotten visiting privileges yet, and the doctor is bringing him in. It must be Alan."

The doctor nodded for Alan to step inside, and he closed the door behind him. Alan looked around the room. The only window was double-paned with a set of blinds between the glass panes. They looked shatterproof. A small, rolling tray table was near the bed, which looked like a standard hospital bed without the electronic doodads. A door led, undoubtedly, to a bathroom. Beside it was a sink with a highly polished metal mirror. A fluorescent light hummed above that.

Charlotte patted the bed beside her. "Have a seat," she said. "It's the only place available. We aren't allowed chairs in our rooms."

Alan sat down beside her. The mattress dipped in too far. He could feel the springs poking him. "Not a comfortable bed."

"It'll do in a pinch."

"So, how have things been since you got here?" he asked.

Charlotte looked at him funny. "How do you think? It's a psych ward—crazy."

She laughed in her real manner, not the way she did sometimes when she was sick. He joined her.

"Everything is okay at the house?"

"Yes," he said, almost telling her about the car but deciding it was better to let it pass. "Me and the boys went by to check on it Friday."

"That's good. How's Sim?"

"The same."

"How bad is my car damaged?"

It took Alan a second to realize what she had asked. He gave her a perplexed look. "What do you mean? It's sitting in your garage. I told you that Josh, Thomas, and I checked on things Friday." He tried very hard to make his voice sound normal instead of surprised.

"No, it's not, and it hasn't been since Thursday night."

"How do you know that? Did someone tell you? Was it that night nurse?"

"Connie told me."

"Is that a nurse or a patient?"

"Neither."

"Who is it?" Alan asked.

"You know good and well who Connie Dearborn is. She nearly married your daddy," Charlotte said matter-of-factly.

"She's dead, Aunt Charlotte. She's been dead a long time. I think you might've been hallucinating or having delusions. The doctor told me that you haven't been doing very well."

"Don't be stupid. Connie was here Thursday night. She said she needed the car for a while. I asked her why, and she told me that some troublemakers had to be taken care of. Her intention was to run them over."

"And you let her?"

"No, I told her that she couldn't use my car for that. I told her that I never wanted anyone to get hurt, but she insisted. I had no choice."

"What did she do to you that made you not have a choice?"

"She took me to this place. It was dark and cold. Sue and Sheila greeted me. Debbie Eva and the boys were there. They were chained together."

"Where was this?"

"I don't know, and I shouldn't have told you anyway."

"Has Connie been back?"

"Every night, if only to say hello."

"She's dead."

"Tell *her* that."

Alan looked at his aunt. For a moment, he saw deceit in her eyes. She was very bad at lying. Over the years of caring for her, he'd learned the look when she was telling a bald-faced lie. She had that look.

"Why are you lying?"

"I'm not." Her face looked even guiltier.

"Did you break out and kill that boy in your car?" Alan whispered, afraid that if she said she had, the doctor would hear.

"Of course not. I've never tried to kill anyone," she said. "Much less a teenage boy I don't know."

"What about Johnny House?" Alan asked, remembering his father talking about her attempt at running him over.

"Whatever your daddy said happened didn't. It was self-defense."

"Did you think it was self-defense when you ran Corey over?"

"It wasn't me. I've been in this god-awful place since you and your daddy put me here. I told you that Connie needed the car."

"What did Connie look like?" Alan asked. He had seen pictures of the woman in Charlotte's yearbook.

Charlotte described a person completely different than those yellowing yearbook photos. She described a much younger woman with the wrong-colored hair and none of the features Connie Dearborn had in her yearbook picture.

"That doesn't sound at all like pictures of her," Alan said.

"I told her the same thing, but she knew things that only Connie could." Charlotte's face no longer looked like she was lying. "Things that I told her and only her. Things about Tobias and me. Things I would never tell anyone, even today. The others in the place told me they were chained to her. They called her Connie"

"She comes every night?" Alan asked, feeling a deep unsettled feeling in his gut.

"Always about an hour after supper."

"When's supper?"

"5:30."

"Did she kill the boy?" Alan asked.

"No, Ben Harris and Sheila Deleon used my car to go necking. They accidentally ran over him."

"Ben and Sheila are dead," Alan said. "They have been for forty years."

"Don't be silly. They borrowed my car on Thursday and accidentally hit that poor boy."

Alan could see that she had drifted back to 1956. There was little point in continuing their conversation. She would only recognize him as Sim, and her general distrust of him kept her from saying too much.

"I'll see you later," Alan said.

"Come back around suppertime, and you can eat with us. Momma's been cooking swell lately. It's the new stove, I think."

"I will."

Alan left her room. The doctor met him as he came to the nurse's station. He shook his head at Dr. Vanhouten.

"She's still talking to Connie. She claims that she comes

every day at around 6:30 p.m. Keep an eye on her with that camera you have," Alan said. "I'm not sure she's making it up."

Dr. Vanhouten smiled broadly, "Of course she's not *making it up*. It's a delusion. Her brain is doing it, and she believes that it's happening."

"Please watch the monitor."

Josh sat in trig class as long as he could. He and Thomas had stopped at a gas station to fill up the car before school. They'd both gotten giant bladder busters of Mountain Dew. Now he felt close to bursting. When Mrs. Watkins paused to pick up a piece of pink chalk, he raised his hand and asked to go to the bathroom. She let him. As he hurried out of the room, much faster than he intended, his classmates giggled. Mrs. Watkins called for quiet as he broke into a run down the hall.

The nearest restroom was at the end of the hallway. Josh usually avoided that place because the smokers and burnouts usually hung out in there. It was a risk when going in there that the principal would bust everyone, but he didn't have enough time to get to his preferred restroom. The smell of the room hit him like a rank gust of wind when he pulled open the door. The janitors didn't spend much time cleaning the place. The faint sweet odor of a clove cigarette barely registered as he hurried to the bank of urinals against the far wall. He rushed by the wooden toilet stalls painted royal blue, paying no attention to whoever was there for a smoke.

"Look who it is," Marcus Smithson said from the stall nearest the door.

Josh stopped halfway to the urinals. He turned quickly enough to see Bill Foreman and Jamie Morris rush from the other two stalls. Bill pinned his arms behind his back. Josh tried to kick out, but Jamie grabbed his legs and smiled up at him. Marcus stepped out of his stall. The dark-wrapped clove cigarette dangled from his mouth. The sweet smoke curled around him. In his all black clothes, he looked like some kind of low-budget thug from a motorcycle movie in the 1950s.

"Let me go," Josh said. "I'll fight y'all again, but not like this. It's not fair."

"I don't care," Marcus said.

He cracked his knuckles as he formed a fist. Josh tightened his stomach muscles in anticipation of the gut punch. The fist landed solidly in his solar plexus. Air escaped from his mouth despite his preparation. With no time to recover, Marcus knocked him across the face with another solid punch. His bladder had given way with the gut punch. His legs grew warm as the urine ran down them.

Jamie let go of his legs when he realized what had happened. Bill let him go as well. Marcus pulled the cigarette from his mouth and laughed.

"He's pissed himself," Marcus said.

"I think I got some on me," Jamie said.

"Wait until everyone hears about this," Bill said.

The restroom door opened. Josh tried to stop his urinating but couldn't. He let it finish as the three headbangers turned to see who had intruded on their fight. Harvey sauntered in, pulling a Kool from his shirt pocket. He had it to his lips when his eyes registered what he was seeing. He smiled.

"I see you guys have your hands full," he said. "I can wait."

Bill jerked at him like he intended to attack. Harvey rushed back out of the restroom. Josh felt let down as his friend abandoned him. He stood alone against the three boys, pants wet and morale drained.

"He's probably running to Chapman's office right now," Jamie said.

"We better get out of here," Bill said.

Marcus nodded his head. "All right."

He took the half-smoked clove from his mouth and pressed it against Josh's bare arm. His skin sizzled and blistered as the cherry snuffed on his skin. He gritted his teeth against the pain. Marcus dropped the cigarette on the floor and walked out with the other two. As soon as the door shut, Josh walked to the sink and stuck his arm under the cold tap, letting it cool the burn. It was already swelling around the circular sore. While keeping his arm under the water, he finagled his shoes off to pour out the urine that had puddled in them.

Once this was done, he looked at his watch. There were

fifteen minutes until classes changed. He had enough time to run out of the building, get into his car, and drive home. Marcus and his buddies would announce to everyone about his pissing himself, but he'd have to deal with that later—in dry pants.

He walked out of the restroom and started around the corner to the main hall that led to the exit nearest his car. As he rounded the corner, a leg jutted out, tripping him. Josh splayed out on the floor, pointing down the classroom-lined hallway. Bill Foreman made a goofy chuckling sound as someone jumped on Josh's back and pinned him to the floor.

Jamie Morris leaned into his ear. "We've got you again," he whispered like he was expressing sweet nothings.

The sensation of the boy's hot breath blowing on his ear gave him goosebumps of disgust. Josh tried to lift himself up. Jamie threw a hard punch to his kidneys, and his arms collapsed below him. He turned his face to keep his nose from slamming into the tile floor. Two heavy black boots paced toward him. Josh strained to look up while Marcus strolled by like a shark waiting to strike. He stopped directly in front of Josh, inches from his face.

"Don't kick me with those steel-toed boots. You'll break my jaw."

"You broke Jamie's nose," Marcus said.

"I hope Jessica likes a man who can drink supper through a straw," Jamie whispered in his ear again. This time he flicked his tongue inside his ear canal.

In something like slow motion, Marcus drew his foot back. The sheer disgusting feeling of Jamie's tongue licking his ear gave Josh a renewed focus. As hard as he could, he flung his head backward. The bulbous part of his skull slammed into Jamie's face. Something soft gave way with the blow. Jamie's weight fell off his back. Josh rolled out of the way as Marcus's Doc Marten slipped past his face.

Josh got to his feet as quickly as he could, but not quick enough to block Marcus's punch. It landed under his left eye and stung. He stumbled back, catching himself on the wall. Something warm ran from below his eye. He wiped blood away and felt the swelling. In a normal fight, he would not resort to dirty tactics, but he wasn't faring as well in this fight as he had the last. Marcus advanced on him. He kicked out, flattening his foot as if punting a football. His foot made hard contact with Marcus's crotch. The boy grabbed his junk and buckled to his knees.

But Bill was still coming at him. "Let's call it quits," Josh urged him. "Y'all won."

Bill shook his head. "I'm going to get revenge."

He threw a hard punch. Josh dodged it, and the meaty fist broke through the plaster on the wall beside a classroom door. Bill let out a yelp and pulled out his hand. His knuckles bled and a piece of plaster stuck out of one. He threw a hard unexpected left that caught Josh on the chin. It stunned him, and he toppled to the floor. His teeth bit into his cheek. The coppery taste of blood filled his mouth. He hoped the blow hadn't loosened any teeth.

Bill came at him again. Marcus had recovered and advanced as well. Josh scooted across the floor until his back was against the end of a bank of lockers. He started to crawl upward to stand against the beating that would probably knock him out.

Bill's fist came directly at his face. Josh braced himself for the pain of his nose breaking, but the blow didn't make contact. He opened his eyes. Thomas had hit Bill from behind, knocking him clear off the ground before they hit the floor in a full tackle. He must have run down the hall at full speed to accomplish that. His brother was big, but not enough to manhandle Bill Foreman.

Thomas straddled Bill's back and starting whaling on his head with his fists. Josh stood ready for what Marcus had to offer, but Harvey had him in a headlock. Jamie curled on the ground, cradling his smashed nose. Blood seeped from between his fingers.

Teachers and students stared out of the classroom doors all the way down the hall. Principal Chapman stormed toward them from the far end of the hall. He carried his paddle by his side like a riot police officer might carry a billy club.

The fight ended while adrenalin still rushed through Josh. Chapman had Thomas, Harvey, and him lined up against one wall, and Marcus and his boys against the other. The classroom doors closed, as students still tried to catch a glimpse of the fight.

"All right, you birds," Chapman said. "My office now."

Without argument, all six of them walked in a line ahead of the principal. Once they made it to the office, they sat across a small space from each other, staring like gunfighters. Not a word was uttered. The principal called them into his office one by one. No one returned. The last two to go in were Thomas and Josh. Principal Chapman called them over at the same time. When they walked in, their father sat in a chair between two empty ones. The principal closed the door and sat down behind his desk. Their father eyed Josh as he sat on his right, farthest from the door.

"What's the matter with your pants?" he asked.

Josh cut his eyes over at him with what he hoped was an expression of pure disgust. "I pissed myself."

Thomas snorted a laugh. Josh gave him the same deadly look. He put his hand up as an apology.

"It's the way you said it," Thomas said. "I know it's not funny."

"None of this is very funny," Principal Chapman leaned back in his chair. It creaked on its springs. "Two fights with three guys in a week's time, Josh. Didn't you learn anything from your vacation?"

"I didn't start it," Josh felt not the least bit comical. His face hurt. The cut under his eye had stopped bleeding but had swollen to the point that he couldn't see very well. His chin was bruised too. The interior of his mouth stung and swelled.

"Harvey saw it," Thomas chimed in.

"He told me," the principal said. "And that's why I'm not expelling you, Josh."

"I would hope not," their dad chimed in. "They jumped him. Look at that arm."

Alan took Josh's arm with the cigarette burn and showed it to Principal Chapman, who nodded his head and waved his hand for it to be put away.

"Don't worry. Marcus and his chums are on a vacation for

the rest of this week and the better part of the next," Chapman said. "Nonetheless, I have to punish Josh."

"Why? They jumped me, three on one."

"It was three on one last time," Chapman said.

"They had the advantage of surprise this time," Josh said. "If it hadn't been for Harvey running off to find Thomas, I'd look a lot worse."

"Still, you broke Mr. Morris's nose, again. His parents will have something to say about that, and if I let it go, they'll come after me."

"I see your point of view," Alan said. "He is right, Josh."

"It doesn't mean I have to like it," Josh answered. "So, what do I get? Another week off?"

"Alternative school," Principal Chapman said.

"That means I have to ride the school bus," Josh protested.

"It is part of the punishment, but it's only for three weeks. If I expelled you, which is the other option, you'd be driving forty-five minutes one way each day to go to school up in Walker County or over in Fayette."

"It's out in the old library annex," Alan said. "It will be like *The Breakfast Club*."

"I hated that movie," Josh said.

"So did I. Give me *Pretty in Pink*," Thomas said.

"You can watch that at your leisure, Thomas," Principal Chapman said. "You're suspended for two days."

"I was getting them off of him," Thomas protested.

"Still, rules are rules," Chapman said.

"It's okay," Alan patted him on the arm. "You did the right thing."

"I'm not going to get to practice with the team," Thomas said. "That means I don't play on Friday night. It's Homecoming."

"It doesn't matter," Alan said. "We're not playing on Friday night anyway."

"We've canceled the next two games because of Corey's death," Principal Chapman said. "Before you say anything, I know it's Homecoming, but this was sent down from the Board of Education."

"Are we done?" Alan asked.

"Yes."

Josh, Thomas, and their dad stood. They walked toward the door. Principal Chapman stood behind his desk.

"Before you go," he said, "I know those guys started it. I'm glad you two and that pothead Harvey gave them the business. I find Smithson, Morris, and Foreman a little bit creepy," the principal admitted. "Also, why don't you boys go on home for the day and relax. I'll tell your teachers."

"Thank you," Thomas said. "I get to start this thing early."

"I was going anyway," Josh said. "I'm not staying at school in peed pants."

"Guys, politeness. Principal Chapman didn't have to do that," Alan said.

"Thank you," Josh said.

The three McAdamses walked out of the office. Alan patted his sons on the back and assured them that he'd handle their mother and that no further punishment was coming.

Chapter Twenty-Two

1956
Two days before Homecoming

Sim sat at the kitchen table in his shotgun house. It was all she could afford after the divorce. Most of his money went to keeping up his ex-wife and sons. A bottle of bootlegged beer sweated on the table. He'd already drunk three of them. They were too expensive to chug, but he needed to get drunk. The hangover from them was easier than from the rotgut.

He thought about Connie as he finished off the bottle. She had no right to deny his marriage proposal. Her excuse was flimsy. She said that he carried too much baggage with a previous marriage and two kids—but every time Alan and Mikey had been around, she ate them up like they were candy. It was something else, and he knew exactly what it was. The next beer came out of the fridge, and as he emptied the bottle, it bolstered his ideas about Connie's retraction. The plain and simple fact was that she was a nigger lover.

She never had liked for him to talk bad about the coloreds, especially that Tobias Abernathy. That monkey had ravaged his sister, stealing from her the most precious thing she had to offer a man. No real man would ever have her with the taint of the jungle on her. Connie probably joined them in wild orgies, like they were on the African continent with the rest of the free-roaming, spoon-bill jungle bunnies.

"Screwing like jungle bunnies," he said aloud as he finished the fifth and last beer in the icebox.

The bottles sat on the table in a row like Pilsner tin soldiers.

He stood and stumbled across the floor to the sink, where he found a few pint jars of moonshine. He'd bought those for labor only, helping Marshall with his still. The peppermint sticks hadn't quite melted in the liquor yet, but Sim was drunk enough not to care. He opened the first jar and took a long swig out of it. The booze lit his gullet on fire. Only the faintest hint of mint was in it. As he sat on the floor, crying and drinking more and more of the first pint of hooch, he formulated his plan to get back at Connie. No one would hurt him like that. His no-good ex-wife had, but his revenge was to be carried out on her much later in life, once his sons grew up and moved off. Connie didn't have that advantage. As he got drunker, he remembered the exquisite and erotic pain when she pulled out a plug of his hair as he came while they made love a few days ago.

Finally, the last of the moonshine slipped into his gut, and he passed out on the black-and-white-checkered floor.

Chapter Twenty-Three

Josh pulled his car into the empty driveway, in the prime spot closest to the door. Thomas jumped out and headed inside. Josh took a little bit longer. He liked the song playing on the radio and wanted to listen until the end. As soon as it faded out, he opened the door and stepped out. A stiff breeze blew, and his pants were still damp enough to make his legs a little bit cool. The smell of his urine seemed stronger on the breeze.

"About time you two got home," said a familiar voice. Jessica came out the wooden gate in the privacy fence that circled their back yard.

"What are you doing here?" Josh tried to hide behind the car door.

"Word of a fight travels fast. I skipped to come and check on you." She walked toward him.

He held his hand out to try to stop her from coming closer. "Why don't you go on inside and get comfortable on the couch? I'll be in right behind you."

"I know about your accident," she said. "You don't have to hide it. I don't mind."

Embarrassment rose from deep inside him. It was the feeling you got when you dreamed about giving a report in front of the class completely naked, but in reality, it was far worse. Everyone knew about him pissing his pants. There was no way to keep that kind of thing a secret.

He stepped out from behind his car door. Jessica smiled at him. "Why don't we go inside and get you cleaned up?" she said.

He looked at her. The comment jarred him. "Huh?"

"I said, let me help you get cleaned up," she repeated with a coy smile. "If that's too dense for you, I want to get naked in the shower with you."

"Are you serious?"

"I don't make that kind of offer unless I am." Jessica held her hand out to him.

"But Thomas is here. He got suspended."

"I know. He can go get a pizza and video or something like that."

Josh took her offered hand, and they walked toward the door. "He's fifteen."

"What does that matter?"

"He might get pulled over and get in trouble."

"Maybe I'm not being clear enough for you." She put her lips to his ear. "We're going to take a shower, and I'm going to make you feel much better."

Josh swallowed hard. Although he'd fantasized many times about her alabaster skin and nude body while alone in his room or in the shower, he'd never expected this to happen. They were inside without him realizing.

Thomas came down the stairs. "What are you doing here?" he asked Jessica.

"I came to see the gladiators of Pinehurst High for myself," she said. "It looks like you showed up the nick in time."

"I blindsided Bill Foreman. He didn't know what hit him." Thomas grabbed Josh around the waist and lifted him to demonstrate.

Josh's hand was pulled from Jessica's while he hung a few inches from the floor. His brother put him down and laughed. Josh tried to arrange himself quickly. He had some arousal and didn't want it to show.

"I was holding my own," Josh said.

"Looks like it," Thomas said.

Josh touched his swollen eye. "I'm a little worse for wear. Everything's still in functional order."

"I noticed," Thomas said dryly.

"I think he needs a little bit of TLC," Jessica said. "Something to help with the pain."

Josh handed his brother the keys to his car and dug his wallet from his back pocket. He gave Thomas a couple of twenties he kept in there.

"Go to Philly Paul's and get us a couple of pizzas," Josh said.

"That's halfway to Jasper," Thomas answered. "I need to call ahead."

"No, order when you get there. Make sure one of them is a Philly cheesesteak pizza. I don't care about the other," Josh said.

"Maybe pick up a video on the way back, something funny," Jessica added.

"See if they have *Happy Gilmore* or *Black Sheep*," Josh said.

"All right, I can drive your car?" Thomas asked.

"*Our* car." Josh pushed his brother out the door and followed him. "Drive like you've got some sense, and make sure you don't get pulled over." When he was sure that Jessica couldn't hear him, he added, "Don't hurry back."

Thomas looked at him. His eyebrow cocked up. "Really?"

"Yeah."

His brother got into their car. He revved the engine but backed out into the street like an old lady heading to church. Once on the street, he squealed the tires and jetted off down the road. Josh shook his head, then hurried back into the house. Jessica wasn't standing by the stairs, but the water in his and Thomas's bathroom was running. She sang a siren song. The melody made the tips of his toes tingle. His mind felt heavy as if drugged by the greatest opiate ever. He started stripping off his clothes as he ran up the stairs.

Josh's arm ached with pins and needles, having fallen asleep from the weight of Jessica's head. He stared up at the ceiling, studying the pattern in the tiles. Faces and objects formed from the little dots. There were the standards: the Indian head, Darth Vader, and a car. Jessica looked up there too. They hadn't said anything for what seemed like a very long time. A wonderful combination of exhaustion and exhilaration wrapped his body. His toes still tingled, and his mind spun giddily. The pain from the beating melted away. He'd never even made it with a girl, and now he'd done it back to back on his first time. He didn't even know he had it in him. Everyone lied about how bad the first time was. It had blown his mind. Although his memory was a little fuzzy.

"I'm hungry," Jessica said. "When do you think Thomas will be back with the pizza?"

Josh rolled over and finally freed his arm from under her. The blood rushed back into it, and the prickling feeling grew stronger. He shook it to try to make it quit. The alarm clock on his bedside table read that it had been nearly two hours since Thomas left.

"He ought to be here any minute. I suppose we should get dressed."

He uncovered himself and tossed his legs over the side of this bed. The few steps to his dresser to get underwear seemed like a marathon. There were many firsts today, including his first naked walk in front of a girl. Of course, they had walked together across from the bathroom to the bedroom and had stopped to use the railing on the stair's landing as a sex aid. It had been like porno stuff. He'd never imagined losing it like that. When he sat down to dress, Jessica pressed her hot body against his back.

"Not bad for your first time," she whispered in his ear. "Do you feel any better?"

He had never told Jessica he was a virgin. Did his performance seem inexperienced? During all their fun, none of his battle wounds had bothered him. With that question, his swollen eye throbbed and the cigarette burn sang out. A small thin pain ran through his temples.

"I'm aching a little bit," he said. "It just started."

"Let me see if I can help that." She ran her tongue playfully in his ear.

The action reminded him of Jamie doing the same thing during his fight. He jumped, and she tipped forward. He looked around to see her put a hand down to keep from falling off the bed. The naked line of her body still looked like nothing he'd ever seen. Jessica reminded him of some classic piece of art.

The door downstairs slammed shut. Heavy footsteps hurried across the floor below. Josh let Jessica straighten herself out.

He grabbed some jeans from his closet. His T-shirts were in the chest of drawers on the other side. Jessica sat on the far side of the bed holding the sheet around herself, more modest now that his brother had returned. She held her arms out to him. Josh walked over to her. She hopped up, letting the sheet drop, and embraced him. Their skin touching, she kissed him deeply. Something hot tore from the back of his head. He jerked away.

"Did you jerk out some of my hair?" He rubbed the back of his head.

She smiled, sheepishly. "Sorry, I got carried away."

He kept rubbing his head as he found a blue long-sleeved shirt that looked like an old baseball T-shirt. Jessica dressed quickly, and they headed downstairs.

Thomas stood in the kitchen with one of the pizza boxes opened. He had already pulled three slices of the Philly cheesesteak pizza from the box. The cheese stretched out long. He looked up at them as they walked in, a smile plastered on his face.

"Better be glad I wasn't Mom," he said, "or y'all would be in trouble."

"Did you get stopped by the police?" Josh asked.

"Nope."

"Did you get a funny movie?" Jessica asked.

"Yep."

"*Black Sheep?*"

"Nope, *Happy Gilmore.*" Thomas said.

"Good," Jessica said.

"You want your change?" Thomas asked.

"Yeah." Josh pulled a slice of the cheesesteak pizza free.

"Do you like that?" she asked.

"Oh yeah," Josh said.

"Did y'all do it?" Thomas asked.

"Uh huh," Josh said, without thinking about what he said.

Thomas started laughing hard. A blush rose up Josh's cheeks, but not much. He was proud of what they had done, like an athlete that finally made the Olympics. Jessica got a slice of pizza and disappeared into the living room.

"Good going," Josh said to his brother. "You embarrassed her."

The noise of television static echoed into the kitchen. The sound of the VCR accepting a video cassette clicked and whirred. Thomas smiled at him while he took another bite of pizza.

"Sounds that way to me," he said with his mouth full. "You can give me the blow-by-blow later."

"I don't think so."

Josh couldn't remember enough of the experience to do so anyway, although he considered himself too much of a gentleman to kiss and tell.

Sim sat in his pickup truck across the street from the old gym. He'd been there for a long time, waiting and smoking. When he noticed his cigarette had burned down almost to the filter, he flicked the ash out the window and took another good drag off of it before flipping it onto the street. The high windows of the gym glowed from the interior lights. Tonight, the kids who broke in to do their decorating didn't care if people saw them. They had grown reckless. He'd given the kids too much credit to think they would give up on holding the dance after Johnny's grandson died. Teenagers were stupid no matter the decade.

He recognized one of the three cars that had pulled up in the driveway. It was the same one that the Smithson boy and his friends had been in the other night. Sim had a particularly foul taste in his mouth relating to that kid. Alan had called him earlier in the day to check in on him. He'd told Sim about that Smithson boy and two others jumping Josh. Although Josh had apparently handled himself in a fight with them earlier, they had bushwhacked him and made him piss his pants.

No one deserved that. A boy would have trouble getting over that. The whole school would know and laugh about it. Sim hated the feeling of complete humiliation. The whole town had laughed at him and his family after his sister got tangled up with that house slave of Harrington's. Years later, it niggled at him. The Smithson boy started to seem more and more like that Tobias Abernathy. He even tried to steal his grandson's girl. Her name was Jessica. For some reason, he could remember it. She was a real beauty for a girl her age. Her peaches-and-cream skin glowed. Her pouty lips looked polished even when they weren't. As he sat staring up at the building, his thoughts drifted to that very girl, naked. He could see every line of her body, the plumpness of her breasts, and every shade of her nudity.

The air perfumed his imagination as it became more vivid. His groin tightened. It had been a while since that had happened. Jessica morphed into Connie. Not much had to change. Connie and Jessica looked a lot alike. If Connie were still alive, Jessica could have been her granddaughter. The hair color was different, as was something about the nose. Josh's girlfriend's teeth were a little more prominent than Connie's.

In his imagination, Sim felt like a man of twenty-eight again. He made love to Connie or Jessica or whoever it was. Before he had time to truly get into the rhythm of things, he felt a warm dampness. Reality came back to the old man as a small area of moisture spread across the straddle of his pants.

Headlights blinded him as the cars left the gym. He'd intended to follow and threaten them. Boys could still be intimidated, and he could be scary if he had to, as long as it didn't look like he'd peed himself. No one feared an incontinent old man.

Sim cranked his truck and shifted it into gear. He looked into the rearview mirror to check the traffic behind. The face of Tobias Abernathy stared at him from over his shoulder, as clear and real as forty years ago. The face made the sound of a woman in mid-orgasm. Sim screamed and punched the accelerator. The truck's tires squealed and left burning rubber smoke in the air. He tried to race away from the image, but he could see it even without looking into the mirror.

The clock on the wall read 7:30 p.m. Alan sat in an uncomfortable wooden chair in a cramped room. Claustrophobia began to bother him, as did the fact that he hadn't been able to enjoy his evening of freedom without football practice, but Dr. Vanhouten had called him. Apparently, the doctor needed to talk to him about Charlotte. Instead of leading him to the very nice room from his last visit, the nurse had put him in this closet of a space. A bank of television monitors against the wall made the room even smaller, and far warmer. Beads of sweat formed at his hairline under his bangs.

The door opened, and Dr. Vanhouten walked inside. He carried a video cassette. Alan started to stand, but the doctor waved for him to sit.

"Thank you for coming," the doctor said. "I did what you said and had Charlotte's room watched during the time after supper. We found nothing until tonight."

"What happened?" Alan asked.

"I'll let you have a look."

Dr. Vanhouten put the video cassette into a VCR by the television bank. One of the TVs flickered. The view was of Charlotte's hospital room, taken from a high corner. She sat on her bed with her face away from the camera.

"So?" Alan said.

"Keeping watching. When the time stamp gets to 18:35, the screen will static."

Alan watched. The screen became fuzzy. When it cleared, a woman stood in the room with Charlotte. Alan recognized her.

"Do you know her?" Dr. Vanhouten asked.

"It's my son's friend. Her name is Jessica. How did she get in there?"

"We don't know. Charlotte is still on visitation restriction, and we have no record of someone matching that girl's description visiting."

"She just appeared?"

"Keep watching."

The time stamp ran the time up to 18:40. Static obscured the screen. When it cleared again, Charlotte sat alone. Alan looked back at the doctor.

"What did she say when you asked her about it?" he asked.

"She denied anyone was there," Dr. Vanhouten said. "I was hoping you could talk to her."

"Certainly. Let's go right now."

Alan led the doctor out of the small room. They walked down a small corridor and through a large metal door that the doctor had to unlock. Alan recognized the layout of the unit after that. He made his way toward the women's wing. Dr. Vanhouten had to trot to keep up with him. As they passed the nurses' station, the doctor waved to the nurses to stay seated as two of them started out to stop Alan.

Charlotte lay on her bed reading a Harlequin novel. She propped up on her elbows when Alan hurried into her room. She looked surprised, but precocious, in her 1956 mindset.

"Alan, why are you here? I've not got visitation yet," she said.

"Dr. Vanhouten called me. Who was in this room with you?"

"Connie Dearborn. She comes lots of nights after supper."

Dr. Vanhouten walked into the room. "How did she get in here?"

"The same way she always comes. I'll be doing something, and she'll be here."

"You don't find that unusual?" the doctor asked.

Charlotte shrugged her shoulders. "I assume she walked in the door like you two, and because I'm not paying attention, I don't notice when she walks in."

"How does she leave?" the doctor asked.

"She's gone."

"Aunt Charlotte, why do you think that girl was Connie Dearborn?" Alan said. "Does she look like Connie?"

"A little bit," Charlotte said.

When Alan heard that, the resemblance between Jessica and Connie Dearborn hit him in the face. There was something about the eyes. Pictures, especially old faded ones, could be deceiving. All the real memories he had of Connie were from photographs, except for vague ones of her piercing eyes.

"But I know it's her because she tells me so, and she knows things that only Connie knows."

"Like what?" Alan asked.

"Don't push too hard," Dr. Vanhouten said. "I want to know about this mysterious woman."

"Let me handle this," Alan told the doctor. "You might have the degree in psychiatry, but I know my aunt. What does she know that only Connie would?"

Charlotte looked embarrassed and shook her head like a child not wanting to tell. Alan looked directly in her eyes—a stern look. Usually that was enough to pry stuff out of her while she was in her 1956 mind frame. His aunt sighed and appeared to deflate a little.

"I'm a virgin. Connie knows that all those rumors about me making love to Tobias were lies. I never admitted they were true, but I didn't deny them either. People assumed. I hoped if people thought I was okay with him enough to do that, they would be okay with him."

"Is that true?" Dr. Vanhouten whispered to Alan.

He shrugged. All he'd ever been told was that his aunt had had a relationship with that boy. His father had always implied that it was sexual, but in truth, everything had been circumstantial. Charlotte would never address it directly. When Sim would go on one of his rants, she'd storm out or go nuts.

"I told her right before I went to old man Shannon's store for more streamers." Charlotte stopped and stared at herself in the mirror. Her face took on its contemporary visage. She looked at her nephew. "She was killed after that. The only people she possibly could have told died with her."

"You're sure that girl was Connie Dearborn?" Alan asked.

She paused for a moment. In her present-day frame of mind, her eyes seemed to search her memory. "No, it was Jessica, Josh's little friend. Why would she say she was Connie?" Charlotte leaned toward them looking very confused. "How would she know that?"

"I don't know," Alan said.

"Can you remember how she gets into your room?" Dr. Vanhouten asked.

"She appears and disappears," Charlotte said.

"That's impossible," the doctor said. "You must be hallucinating."

Alan looked at him. "We saw it on the video."

The doctor looked confused and shook his head before walking out of the room. Alan and Charlotte looked at each other for a few minutes. During that time, she transitioned back to her 1956 persona. He had never seen her cycle so quickly.

"Alan," she said. "Something bad is going to happen to us."

"No, it's not," he said. "Don't think like that. Everything is going to be okay."

"It isn't. Connie told me so. She said bad things had to happen. An eye for an eye."

Alan looked at his aunt. Her eyes were sincere and terrified at the same time. Ice-cold terror filled him up at that moment. Something bad *was* going to happen.

"Did she tell you what would happen?" he asked.

"No, but all my friends are with her, including Tobias. She took me there the other day. I told you that. They're all mad, especially toward Sim, Johnny House, and Marshall." Charlotte changed back to 1996. "I'll have to stop her from hurting Josh. I'm the only one who can."

"What do you mean?"

"Connie wants to hurt Sim. She plans on doing more than just kill him. She wants his line gone, our family line."

His aunt's comments were like a punch in his stomach. Josh was in the most danger. Jessica, or Connie or whoever, had him in the crosshairs.

A melancholy Toad the Wet Sprocket song ended when Josh pulled into his driveway. After taking Jessica back to her house, he'd driven around for at least an hour listening to music and letting the wind blow through his hair. Pinehurst looked ready for Halloween as he meandered through the old downtown and out onto the bypass where a bunch of the fast food joints were. The stores had pumpkins and corn stalks in front of them. A few even had cutesy scarecrows propped up. A costume and decoration store had opened in the old Fred's building. It had been the first year that ever happened. He'd wanted to stop in but had no reason to get dressed up for Halloween. After driving out to River Park, Josh headed home. It was a school night and tomorrow he would have to wake up early to ride the cheese wagon into alternative school.

When he got out of his car, Bush's "Machinehead" was playing. He'd grown a little tired of that song. It had gotten too much air time over the summer. As with most of his drive around town, his thoughts were lost in Jessica and what had happened between them. He hoped that Thomas wouldn't waylay him with a lot of questions when he went to his bedroom. Although his recent after-school activity took up a lot of space in his mind, he didn't want to relive it with his little brother.

No one moved around the house when he walked inside. The television was off. It usually squawked from the time his mother got home from work until after the Nightly News. Only dim light came from upstairs, like it did when Thomas was in his room with the door closed. A hint of light brightened the hall from the kitchen. Now that his ears had time to adjust to the quietness of the house, he could tell his parents were whispering in there.

"Is that you, Josh?" his dad called down the hall.

"Yeah," Josh replied. "Sorry I'm late. I lost track of the time."

"Come in here."

His dad's voice sounded stern but not angry. Josh didn't know what to expect. His dad seemed pleased with him after the fight, although he doubted he was pleased with the punishment, and his mother may have *convinced* him to change his mind about additional grounding. She had a tendency to see things a little more black and white than he did.

His mother got up from the table when he walked in. She sucked in air through her teeth as she passed. It was the first time she'd gotten a look at him.

"It's not that bad," Josh said. "It looks worse than it feels, although it doesn't feel good."

"Put a warm cloth on your eye before you go to sleep tonight." She rubbed his face with the soft touch of a caring, loving mother. "That way if it oozes or something it won't glue your eyelids shut. I don't want to have to pry your eye free from goo tomorrow."

"I will, and thanks for being loving," Josh said in a joking tone.

His mind eased as he took a seat by his dad at the table. If his mother was joking, additional punishment was not coming. However, the look on his father's face made him quickly change his mind. Deep worry lines furrowed his father's brow. He rubbed his chin like he did when he was about to tell Josh something disturbing, or when he punished Josh.

"Do I have to take Grandpa Sim to another funeral?" Josh asked.

"No, I want to talk to you about Jessica."

A hot rush of embarrassment rose through Josh's face. He hoped that the blush didn't show, but it certainly would. His mind raced, trying to come up with how to answer a question before his dad asked anything.

"What did Thomas tell you?" he asked.

Alan shook his head. "Nothing. Should he have?"

Now instead of embarrassment over the impending dad talk about the importance of responsible sexual behavior, he almost revealed something that he didn't have to.

He tried to cover up the mistake. "No, but you know how he can be."

"How well do you know her?" Alan asked.

Josh immediately started to panic a little again. What did his dad mean by that? He might in fact get a sex talk after all. "What do you mean?"

"How much do you know about her? Where is she from? What's her family like? All I know is they have only one car, and she's a pretty good student."

"She transferred from Northport. She said that her family moves around a lot. I think she was born near Florence, maybe Muscle Shoals. I don't know very much about her family, except that they both work."

"You've never met them?"

"No, every time I pick her up or take her home, they're not there."

"Every time? Haven't you and she been out late sometimes?"

They had gotten in very late before, well after midnight. Her parent's car wasn't there. Nothing seemed very strange about that to him, but Jessica acted more provocative on those late nights. One time her top was unbuttoned enough to get a glimpse of her breast. She didn't have on a bra, and he'd spied her nipple, small and pink.

"Their car is never there," he said. "Even when I've taken her home late. She's never let me come into her house either."

"Why?"

Josh searched his memory. She'd never given him a reason why. Every time he brought up the idea, she would either completely change the subject or offer an alternative suggestion. Now that his dad brought all this up, something seemed suspicious.

"I don't know. I guess I always assumed they were poor, and she was embarrassed about her house. It's kind of rough looking on the outside. You saw it, pink walls and red shutters."

His dad's look became very serious, as if he were about to let loose some great epiphany that could tear his whole world down. "Where were you two about 6:30 tonight?"

"I was driving around, thinking. I dropped Jessica off at her house about 6:15, give or take. She hurried in without barely saying thanks or goodbye. Dad, please quit being mysterious. What's up?"

"I was called in to talk with Aunt Charlotte's doctor again tonight. They found something strange on the monitor in her room. Someone appeared and vanished." His dad made deep eye contact with him. "It was Jessica."

"She visited Aunt Charlotte, what's the big whoop?"

"Charlotte said she was visited by Connie Dearborn. One of the people killed at the massacre."

Josh shrugged. "She's accidentally called Jessica that before."

"When I say that she appeared and disappeared, I meant that literally. She didn't walk in and leave. No one reported her on the unit. It's like magic."

"Jessica is an ordinary girl. Are you calling her a witch or something?" His dad had no right to come up with far-flung theories and conspiracies about his girlfriend.

"Settle down. I don't know what I'm saying, but I needed you to know what's happened. It was not normal. If you think about it, a lot of not-normal stuff is happening."

Josh could think of nothing but Jessica and how much he wanted her. Thomas must have told his parents about his and Jessica's activities. Now his folks had made up some elaborate story to try to drive them away from each other. His parents were embarrassed that Jessica was poor. They couldn't have that.

Without saying anything else, Josh stormed out of the house. He got in his car and drove down the street. As he drove, he kept turning down streets until he sat in front of Jessica's house. Her parents' car was gone, and only one window was lit.

He parked across the street and hurried to her door. No one answered when he knocked or rang the doorbell. Even if Jessica's parents were gone, she would be there. He rang the bell again.

"Jessica, it's me Josh."

No one answered. There was no sound of movement inside. He tried the doorknob, and it turned. Without thinking about it, Josh stepped inside. The light came from a floor lamp sitting near the window of what should have been a living room. The floors were bare, as were the walls. No furniture sat around. He looked into the kitchen area. Appliances lined the walls like in any other house, but the refrigerator didn't hum. No table sat in the room. There seemed to be no evidence of food. Jessica's family was much poorer than he realized. No wonder she liked eating dinner with his family.

"Jessica?" he called.

No one answered.

Josh walked through the empty living room down the small hall. Doors lined both sides. They were all opened. Every room was empty except the bathroom, which had a sink, toilet, and shower, without a curtain. The hall ended at a door. He tried it, and it opened. Inside was a scantly furnished bedroom.

A small iron bedstead sat against the wall. A table piled with papers and other objects that were difficult to make out in the darkness sat near the window. When he switched the light on, roaches scattered across the floor. A black burn mark was at the foot of the bed. Ashes piled in the center. Josh could see the contents of the table better. There were bundles of dried flowers and other plants lying on top of a few books and scattered papers. He walked to it.

As he rummaged through the papers, he found small baggies of green herbs which smelled nothing like marijuana. They each had a different pungent aroma, but not of pot. Under a book that looked like it was written in French, he found another series of baggies that contained hair. They had names written on them in magic marker. On top of the pile was one with his name and another with Thomas's. He rummaged through them, keeping an ear out for noise. Things had started to feel a lot like one of those creepy horror movies they'd been showing on television since the start of the month. Below his and his brother's hair were baggies marked: Marcus Smithson, Jamie Morris, Bill Foreman, and Corey Aaron. Corey's bag was empty. Underneath all those he found a baggie of old hair marked Simeon McAdams/1956.

Josh dropped everything. He was getting ready to run when he noticed the library copy of *Jeffrey Presents 13 Modern Southern Ghosts*. A slip of paper stuck up from the pages. The marker held the place for the story about Hazel. Strange markings were around the margins of the book, including a Star of David and a pitchfork. They reminded him of the gang signs painted on the old Cardinal where he'd encountered Sue Browning's ghost. Josh grabbed the book and ran out of the house. Once back in his car, he noticed how his heart pounded and his mind raced. It was time to go home.

The boys from the gym gave Sim the slip. He forgot how fast teenagers drove. His grandson crept around like a granny in his sporty little car. Every time he rode with Joshua, they barely made it over forty-five miles per hour. He supposed that tricked him into thinking it was a new trend for teenage boys to poke around. In his day, they drove fast too. That was the way he, Marshall, and Johnny had caught up with Tobias, pushing their vehicle beyond the limit.

He tried not to think about that boy, but all his mind could focus on was the ghostly face still staring at him. Sim could see him as clear as day. There was no fuzziness left. Tobias wasn't even a reflection anymore. The apparition was fully formed, and if Sim wanted to be completely honest with himself, it rode beside him in the truck, staring at him with ghostly eyes.

Sim drove through the neighborhoods of Pinehurst. The numbered streets and avenues were completely empty. There didn't seem to be any movement on them, but they were festively decorated for that stupid spook holiday. The streets with tree names had a little more activity. The lights were still on in most windows. Occasionally, he could see people moving around in their living rooms. Some people didn't even have curtains to obscure the view. In those places, he would see what they watched on TV. He looked for the boys' cars, but couldn't find a trace of them. Too many houses nowadays had garages. He knew who the boys were, but he had no idea where they lived. When he finally couldn't stand his passenger staring at him any more, he headed home.

"Can you look the other way?" he asked, turning to face the phantom Tobias Abernathy. "I'm a little tired of your staring."

The face continued to gaze at him wide-eyed. Sim noticed it breathed. That unnerved him more than anything else. Hallucinations didn't breathe. His hands shook. It was unusual for him to notice the quaking while holding onto something like the steering wheel. Usually he held something to help hide the fact that his hands trembled, but tonight, nothing helped.

A car horn blared. Sim turned to see a Caprice Classic zooming through the intersection. He slammed on his brakes as the red slip of stop sign passed his vision. His tires screamed as the truck slid the rest of the way through the intersection. It jarred him hard, and his chest hit the steering wheel, knocking the breath from his lungs. Once the movement and swirling lights and sound stopped, he gasped a long draw of painful air. His vision dimmed, but recovered as someone banged on his window.

"Are you okay?"

He looked around to see a black youth staring at him through that window. For a moment, he thought it was Tobias staring at him. The kid kept banging his fist on the glass. When Sim didn't seem to acknowledge his presence, the boy started to yell. This snapped Sim back to his senses. Although the wreck had been his fault, and Sim always would fess up to his mistakes when they caused an accident, he wouldn't tolerate being yelled at by a punk nigger.

Sim opened his door before the other driver had time to react. The youth lost his balance and splayed across the pavement as Sim stepped out of his truck. His chest hurt, but he didn't flinch. He was in tough as old leather mode.

"Are you okay, sir?" the youth asked, who Sim now recognized as the Otis kid from the football team.

"None of your concern."

"Yes, it is," Neal Otis got to his feet. "You ran that stop sign. Your truck looks smashed up pretty bad. You hit the dashboard."

"Don't you worry about what I've done. You need to be worrying about yourself."

"What do you mean? Are you threatening me?" Otis stood facing Sim. "I was trying to help you."

The boy looked like some primate he'd seen on *Mutual of Omaha's Wild Kingdom*. Sim laughed and put his face right into Otis's, staring into his eyes. The smell of sweet cigar tobacco hung on the younger man's breath. Sim didn't care for it. He smiled and gave Otis a hardy shove. The boy stumbled backward but didn't lose his footing. He was the crack football player and in much better shape than Sim, probably even when he was that age.

"All right, old man, enough is enough. I'm trying to make sure you're okay. I'm going to go call the police and maybe an ambulance for you." He trotted to his car, reached into it and pulled out his keys. "You hit that steering wheel hard. Hope you ain't got osteoporosis or something."

An old feeling ran through Sim. It was bitter and brought an acidic taste up from his stomach. He'd not had the feeling for a long, long time. In many ways, he welcomed it because it gave him a clarity and youthful vivaciousness, he'd lacked for forty years. He took two large steps backwards until his thighs touched the frame of his truck's open door. Without looking, he reached behind his seat and found what he needed by touch alone. As Otis walked toward him, the older man pulled his .38 forward and fired off three shots so quickly that he thought he had an automatic instead of a revolver.

The almost giddy jingle of keys hitting the asphalt preceded Otis falling backward, clutching at his chest. Sim smelled the burnt gunpowder. An old memory pushed its way forward. Smells had a way of bringing those kind of memories back to him. He wanted to walk over to Otis and put a bullet between his eyes, but that seemed over the top for a self-defense alibi.

Feeling very good about himself, Sim turned to put the pistol away. The ghostly figure of Tobias Abernathy sat behind the wheel of his truck. The face turned toward him, showing bared teeth in a death's head grin. A spectral hand reached out for Sim. The cold fingers of the thing reached deep into his chest and squeezed his heart. The pain radiated from his chest down his arms. His vision darkened at the edges and inward. The right edge of his mouth drew down with a sharp pain. His right eyelid did the same thing. As the pain now overtook his entire body, Sim's legs collapsed from under him. He hit the pavement on his right side. A hard series of twitches cascaded down his body before the cold painful fingers pulled from his chest. He lay blind and paralyzed. Everything sounded far too loud. The worst thing of all was that warm liquid washed over his face. It was the boy's blood. The smell of it sickened him. Vomit came up his throat and into his mouth. It wouldn't exit on its own, and Sim couldn't swallow it back down. He tasted it, and it made him sicker until he vomited again. This time it forced its way out of his mouth and ran down his cheek to the pavement, mingling with Otis's blood.

His life started to flash before him, but the memories of 1956 began to play in a loop. He lay there and endured them, praying for unconsciousness.

Light shone from under his parents' bedroom door when Josh walked inside his house. He eased the front door closed and tiptoed upstairs, trying hard to avoid the one squeaky step. The last thing he wanted at that moment was a lecture from his father about storming out. He walked down the dark upstairs hallway to the small office space at the very end. The family computer was set up there, along with a few other things his dad needed to work from home.

Josh walked across the small room in the dark and sat at the computer desk. The monitor flickered on, illuminating the room like a small table lamp. The random gibberish of the startup screen scrolled through. Finally, the Windows icon popped up, as did the desktop. His dad always kept up with the latest in technology, and they had upgraded to Windows 95 not long after it had come out. He was one of the few people to have the new operating system. Josh made sure to turn off the external speakers before clicking the icon that looked like two computers connected to each other. The window for the dial-up box popped up. He clicked on the start button and watched the little connection box do its thing until it confirmed that the connection had been made. The home page opened to Excite.

The Internet remained mysterious to him. The few times Josh had used it, he typed what he wanted to find in the search engine. It would pop up. He and Thomas had mostly used it for looking up naked pictures until their folks got wise and put some kind of block on those kind of websites. Tonight's search involved no such thing. He wanted to know about Kathryn Tucker Windham, the lady who wrote the Jeffrey ghost books. Several links came up when he typed in her name. Josh looked at the first one. It listed a contact number for her through the University of Alabama and a little about her history. He jotted down the number and switched over to search for the ghost story about his town. Nothing came up. He tried the symbols Jessica had written in the book. Most of the information he found there was about a gang called the Folk.

Josh closed down the browser and logged off the net. He turned the computer off and tucked the piece of paper into his pocket. With the same clandestine maneuvers he had used to get upstairs, he sneaked back to his bedroom. Sometimes when he was in trouble or had stayed out beyond curfew, his dad would lock his bedroom door. He half expected this, but it opened easily. When the lamp came on, the bed was still in shambles from the romp he'd had earlier in the day. It made him sick to think about it. His sweet experience now felt like bestiality.

Only a few hours ago, he'd been on cloud nine about Jessica. Now a cold terror took hold of him. His stomach flip-flopped. The notion of lying in that mussed up bed was too much for him to take. He walked back across the hall and tapped on Thomas's door.

"What?" his brother's sleepy voice asked.//
"Can I come in?" Josh asked.
"What for?"

"Let me rephrase. I'm coming in."

Josh pushed into his brother's room. The streetlight outside gave him enough light to step around the random stuff Thomas kept laying in completely random places. His brother hadn't moved on his bed. He didn't even lift his head.

"What do you want, Josh? It's super late. Are you sneaking in?"

"Yeah," Josh took off his shoes and pants. "I'm sleeping in here with you."

Finally Thomas propped himself up. "What?"

"I can't sleep in my room." His shirt come off.

"Why not?" Thomas turned on the lamp. "You couldn't have changed over there?"

"I wanted to get out of there as quickly as I could. The bed is still all out of sorts from where Jessica and I did it."

"Remake it. You're not sleeping with me."

"That won't work. I think she's a witch." Josh crawled over the foot of the bed and slid between his brother and the wall.

Thomas had a double bed just big enough for the both of them. Josh slid under the comforter but on top of the sheet. That way they wouldn't be exposed to each other.

"Get out," Thomas protested.

"I'm serious. I'm scared to stay there, okay. I broke into her house after something Dad told me, and I found some weird stuff."

"Like what, her angry parents?" Thomas asked.

"Like a completely empty house except for a bed, table and some witchy stuff. It's like a hobo lived there. No one was there. I don't think she has parents."

"She's homeless and embarrassed. She's probably a prostitute too," Thomas said. "You're going to have VD or AIDS."

"She had little baggies of our hair. You remember her pulling yours out? She kept it and now it's labeled."

Thomas rolled over and looked at him. His eyes were wider, and he seemed more awake. "What?"

"Not only ours. She had hair from Marcus and his buddies, and Grandpa Sim. There was an empty baggie with Corey Aaron's name on it. I found that Jeffrey book she brought over, and it's got a bunch of weird symbols and stuff in it."

"Voodoo stuff?" Thomas asked.

"Maybe. I don't know, but don't say anything about this tomorrow. We need to act like nothing is wrong. It's going to be hard after what we did, but we can't freak out or anything."

"She's a voodoo hag," Thomas said. His voice seemed a bit frightened. He smiled. "You screwed a voodoo hag."

Josh gave his brother a punch in his shoulder, but he didn't do much else. He didn't want to go back and sleep in his room, because he may *have* slept with a voodoo hag. Deep inside him, he hoped that he was overreacting and maybe Jessica was a homeless runaway or a prostitute. Tomorrow he planned on trying to get hold of that Windham woman and see if she knew anything else about the legend of Hazel and the massacre. Thomas started to snore a little. Josh stared at the ceiling.

As he started to drift off, the phone rang. Thomas kept on sleeping, but he reached across his brother to answer it. The ringing stopped as soon as he put his hand on the receiver. His brother nudged him in the gut with his elbow. Josh settled back on his side and stared at the ceiling again. When the day had started, he would never have imagined the turns it would take. He was happy the roller coaster ride was over.

Chapter Twenty-Four

1956
Night of the Massacre

Sim, Johnny, and Marshall pulled up to the roadblock on the other side of Pinehurst. The blue lights on top of the patrol car cast a weird light on everything. They idled the Mercury Monterey on the shoulder as Bud Johnson waved for them to stop. Sim hopped out of the back seat.

"We've got him, Sheriff," he said.

Johnson chomped down on his unlit cigar. "Got who?"

"That nigger who killed those kids at the gym. He's in the trunk."

"That's his car," the sheriff said. "I've seen him driving it around town. How come Marshall Williams is driving it?"

"We caught up with him heading back to the Harrington place. We shot out the tire. We put the spare on, shoved him in the trunk, and came to find you."

The blood rushed through Sim so quickly his heart might explode. Sheriff Johnson rolled the cigar to the other side of his mouth and hitched up his pants.

"Let him go," he said.

"What do you mean 'let him go'? He's the one that killed those folks."

"Due process. He's got a right to a trial."

"Like hell he does. You know good and well I saw him driving like a demon away from that gym not long after shots were heard. By my recollection, he had enough time to kill them and jump back into his car."

"That's probably the case, and you're right that no jury in this county wouldn't say hang him, but there's the Harringtons to think about."

Sim narrowed his eyes and stared at the sheriff hard enough to punch holes through his face. A mean grin crossed his lips.

"Do you know what that spearchucker did to my sister?" he asked.

"There's rumors."

"I ain't having none of this due process. You can try and stop me to put on a good show, Sheriff Johnson, but you know what I got to do has to be done."

The sheriff nodded his head. "Yeah. I'm going to take a shot at you, but it won't be anywhere close to that car."

Sim nodded and ran back to the Monterey. He jumped into the back seat.

"What's happening?" Marshall asked.

"Get us out of here. They ain't going to do shit. It's up to us," Sim said. "Hurry before they can stop us."

Marshall hit the gas and turned the car around. They headed away from the roadblock as fast as the car would go. Sim watched through the rear window the whole time. True to his word, Sheriff Johnson shot a single bullet. The sheriff pointed his revolver at the ground.

Chapter Twenty-Five

Alan sat in the ICU waiting room. The nurses hadn't let him back to see his father yet. He wished his brother wasn't in Denver. He'd spent too much time dealing with all of this kind of stuff lately and hadn't had a good night's sleep in days. His eyelids hurt from fatigue. He could have used Mike's support, but his brother's hate for their father was stronger than his sense of familial obligation.

The hum of the overhead lights lulled him to sleep as he waited. His head hit his chin only to pop back up. When he opened his eyes, a police officer stood over him. The officer wore the look of the owl shift—no joy.

"Are you Mr. Simeon McAdams's son?" he asked.

Alan rubbed his eyes. "Yeah, I'm his son, Alan McAdams."

"Your father may be in serious trouble," the officer said.

"Don't they usually send a nurse or doctor to tell that kind of news?"

"I'm not talking about his medical condition, Mr. McAdams. Your father shot an adolescent after running a stop sign and causing a wreck."

Alan woke up like someone had given him an intravenous dose of espresso. "What?"

"I've been here trying to get a statement from your father, but he is not able to speak at this time. They have him hooked up to a breathing machine," the officer said. "Can you tell me anything?"

"No, this is the first I've heard about it. All the hospital said was that he'd had a stroke and a car accident."

"I am sorry. I know it's difficult right now, but would you be willing to answer a few questions for me?"

"I'll try." Alan rubbed his eyes and face harder to make sure he wasn't dreaming.

"Has your father ever tried to kill anyone before?"

Alan looked at the young black officer. The dark blue uniform with all the metal parts shiny like a new nickel made the officer look younger than he probably was. There was something Alan knew about him for sure: the officer was not originally from Pinehurst.

"Sit down, Officer…"

"Jackson. I'm Officer Jackson." He sat down.

"You must be from other parts if you don't know who Simeon McAdams is."

"This is my second week on the job." Officer Jackson pushed his cap back some. "Quite a way to start."

"My father is rather infamous in this town for two things. The first is, he discovered a massacre at the old gym forty years ago."

"That's him? Apparently, some kids have been planning an anniversary dance. Pretty stupid."

Alan nodded. "The second thing is that he led the lynch mob that killed the boy most of the town blamed for the massacre. He put the noose around the boy's neck."

Officer Jackson's face gave away his distaste. The truth didn't sit well with Alan either, but he'd had more time to get used it. A young black man would have his own issues with the lynching.

"Would you consider your father a racist?" Jackson asked.

"Yes, but in his defense, he's an all-round bigot. He hates everyone. He's as likely to shoot a white man if he thinks he's a communist, homosexual, or Jehovah's Witness."

"Sounds like a charming fellow," Officer Jackson mumbled under his breath. "I'm sorry if you heard that."

"You've not said anything that I don't know or haven't felt myself."

"Excuse me, are you Mr. McAdams's family?" a soft-spoken nurse interrupted.

Alan nodded his head. She beckoned for him to follow her. Officer Jackson handed him a business card with contact information. Alan told the officer he would contact him if he found out anything from his father.

He followed the nurse through the magnetically sealed doors into the beeping, buzzing wonderland of the ICU. She escorted him into the room at the other end of the hallway. His father lay in the bed. A tube was taped into his mouth. Several tubes ran from his arms to various dripping bags. Sim's face looked pale and drawn on the right side.

"My name is Lucy. I'm your dad's nurse for the night."

"What happened?" Alan asked.

"He's had a stroke. It appears to be fairly severe. Right now, we've got him on a respirator to help him breathe. His own ability is severely impaired. He hasn't been conscious since they brought him in. We found your number in his billfold."

"Is there anything that I can do tonight?" he asked.

"Probably not. If you want to go back home, we can call you if anything changes."

"I'm exhausted. I've had a rough last few nights." Alan turned to leave the room. He stopped and looked back at Lucy. "Is it true what that police officer was saying? Did he shoot a kid?"

"As I understand it from the report given from the ER, yes. They had to fly the victim to Birmingham."

Alan looked at his father, rubbed his temples, and left. He walked down the hall from the ICU to the elevator bank. Hospitals at night were empty and cavernous, creepy. He pushed the button on the elevator again, hoping it would make the carriage come faster.

"Alan."

He looked behind him. No one stood there, but from the edge of his vision, someone ran around the corner to the next hall. He looked in the direction where he'd seen the movement. A teenage girl jogged down the hall. Her hair flowed behind her as if the wind blew against it. She turned to look back. Alan stared into Jessica's eyes.

"What are you doing here?" he whispered.

She giggled and ran around another corner. The elevator bell rang, but Alan ignored it. He followed the girl. There was no reason for her to be at the hospital at that time of night, nor should she have happened upon him. Around the next corner, he found her still running midway down the hall. This wing he recognized. At the end were the large metal doors that led to the psychiatric unit.

"Alan," she seemed to say again, but the words hadn't come from her mouth.

He ran after her. His footfalls echoed down the hallway. Hers made no noise at all. He gained on her and was at the point of overtaking her. Her hair brushed his fingertips as he reached out for her shoulder. They both headed full steam toward the metal doors. He slowed down; she did not.

"Stop," he said.

Jessica looked back over her shoulder at him. "Alan."

Her lips never moved. She ran through the doors like a ghost in a movie. Alan stopped. He gasped for breath, and his pulse raced. He pushed the button to call the nurses station.

"Can I help you?"

"This is Charlotte McAdams's nephew," he said. "Did someone run in there from the main hospital?"

"No," the voice on the other side of the speaker hesitated. "It's not visitation time. You'll have to come back tomorrow."

Alan didn't bother arguing. He turned and walked back to the elevators. Jessica had to have been a hallucination conjured up by his exhausted mind. Even as tired as he was, the difference between the rational and the irrational didn't escape him.

"Go away," Thomas sounded asleep.

Josh barely registered that his brother was talking, but it brought him out of his sleep enough to notice other noises. Someone tapped on the door. It was too early to be morning. He'd just fallen asleep.

"Quit knocking on the door, Josh," Thomas said, still someplace between sleep and wakefulness. "I'm not opening up."

"It's not me," Josh worked his way to complete awareness.

The tapping became louder. It didn't come from the door but

the window. He roused himself enough to lift up and look in that direction. The room was dark except for the light from the digital alarm clock. The street lamp had gone out. A low greenish yellow light shone into the room in its place. It came from behind the curtains. The tapping now became a bang.

"All right," Thomas threw the covers off and got out of bed. "This had better be important."

He made it halfway to the door, when the banging started on the window again. Thomas stopped and looked at it and back at Josh, who had stood up on the bed.

"What was that?" Thomas asked.

"I don't know." Josh hopped down and stood beside his brother. The glass pane rattled with the next blow. "We better look before the noise wakes up the folks."

Josh reached for the curtain, but Thomas caught his wrist. His brother's hand was cold and clammy. A deep fear in Thomas's eyes stared back at him.

"Don't," he said. "Remember *The Lost Boys*?"

"There's no such thing as a vampires," Josh pulled his arm away.

"There's no such thing as ghosts and witches either," Thomas reminded him.

For a moment Josh stopped and considered that fact. Neither of them had a chance to pull the curtain back. The window exploded inward. Tiny shards of glass hit Josh's bare skin. A thousand pins pricked him. Thomas yelled and grabbed his face before falling to the floor. The curtains blew off their rods. One of them wrapped around Josh's face, causing everything to go black. He fell to the floor beside his brother. Pieces of the broken glass in the carpet dug into him.

The air in the room grew colder. Josh struggled to uncover his face. When he did, he screamed. Johnny House hung by his neck outside the window. A braid of orange extension cords held him up. His eyes and tongue bulged out of his blue face.

"What is it?" Thomas yelled. "What's happening?"

"I don't know."

"Is that Mr. House?" Thomas yelled as he finally uncovered his face.

"I think so."

The hanging man stared at them with his glazed dead eyes. He moved toward them, swinging on the cord. A wind blew into the room, colder than the coldest January. From behind the corpse, a ghostly figure appeared. It was a girl probably Josh's age. She wore old-fashioned clothes like Aunt Charlotte dressed in when her mind went. A Scottish terrier stood out on her flowing skirt. Her ghostly intestines hung from a hole above her waist.

The bedroom door slammed open. His mother stormed inside. Pulled from sleep by their screams and the commotion, her face glared with wide eyed terror.

"What's happening?" Thomas yelled again.

The ghost screamed, and the pitch grew higher and higher, until it sounded less like a human and more like a steam whistle. Josh clapped his hands over his ears to muffle the din. It did little to help. The ghost exploded into ectoplasm, leaving behind only an eerie green glow and dead Mr. House staring into the bedroom.

His mother screamed. Thomas followed suit. Josh added his own voice to the chorus without even realizing it until moments later.

Their voices faded to nothing. Josh's whole body stung from the pelting he'd received. Thomas bled from some long, shallow cuts on his face. One ran from the edge of his eye to his ear, another at an angle down his cheek. Josh looked at himself. Tiny trickles of blood ran from a few pinholes torn in his arms. Other places beaded with small droplets of blood.

"I need to call 911," their mother said. Her legs trembled so much that Josh feared she might topple down the stairs.

"What happened?" Thomas asked.

"I think Jessica figured out I broke into her house," Josh answered.

"What are we going to do?" His brother wiped his hand across his cheek, smearing blood across his face like war paint.

"I don't know."

Josh had no idea, but for some reason he was sure that Mrs. Windham would. As soon as he could, he was going to get ahold of her.

"You need to try to stop the bleeding on your face," Josh said.

"I hope I don't need stitches," Thomas said. "I don't want any gnarly face scars."

His brother left him alone in the bedroom with the hanging man. Jessica called to him like a banshee in the night. Her siren's song tempted him. His insides ached for her. He hurried to find his mother, not daring to look out of the window. If Jessica were there, he might not be able to resist her.

Chapter Twenty-Six

1956
Night of the Massacre

The stolen Mercury Monterey skidded to halt on the northern outskirts of Pinehurst. It was the farthest point from the Harrington place. As Sim and his buddies drove through town after hauling it from the roadblock, they'd jumped out at different people's houses, rousing the men and some of the women to their cause. By the time they stopped at the giant old white oak tree on County Road 13, a small caravan of pickup trucks and cars followed. Dozens of people rode in those vehicles.

Sim climbed out of the back of the car to face the mob advancing toward the Monterey. He threw up his hands and pushed the air as if shoving them back. Like the Red Sea did for Moses, the crowd stopped for him. In the beams of the headlights, they looked like a faceless mass, a mob intent on doing what he wanted them to do. He waved for Marshall and Johnny to get out of the car. They flanked him.

"We told y'all what we have in this trunk," Sim said to the crowd. "We told you that the sheriff tried to keep us from serving justice. I know that you are all here to see that it is served properly."

"That's right," a man yelled.

"Let's see the blue-gum," a woman yelled. "Get him out here."

"Give me the keys," Sim told Marshall.

He unlocked the trunk and lifted the lid. Tobias lay curled into the fetal position on the bottom of the trunk. His cheeks were wet with tears and his eyes red. Sim could make out the trembling of the black mass. It was like looking at a trapped rabbit—a trapped jungle bunny. Sim nodded for Johnny to pull Tobias from the trunk. It took Marshall and Johnny to do it because the boy resisted.

Once in view, the crowd roared outrage at Tobias. They started to surge forward, but Sim threw his hands up again. They obeyed. The power he welded at the moment filled him with an overwhelming sense of righteousness. Sim smiled.

"This is him. This is the no-good darkie that has tried to forget his place in society and become one of us. This no-good darkie defiled my sister, a raging black bull in a virgin white lily field. To cover up his wretched tracks, he killed all those kids at the gym."

"I did no such thing," Tobias yelled out. His voice was shaking but defiant.

"Shut up!" Marshall punched him in the stomach to the cheering approval of the crowd.

"No good, lying coon," someone in the crowd yelled out.

"Don't pollute us anymore with your nigger lies," another cried.

"What should we do with this boy?" Sim asked.

"Kill him!" a woman yelled.

"Hang him from that oak," a man bellowed from the faceless mass of Pinehurst townsfolk.

"I got a rope," another yelled.

"Hang him, hang him," they started to chant.

Only for a fleeting a moment, Jesus and Pontius Pilate came to mind. That crowd yelled for the death of an innocent man, so said the Bible. Sim dismissed the Sunday school fairytale from his mind and egged the crowd on. As he looked back at the black boy, Tobias's face became desperate. Fear carved it into something grimacing and grotesque like a gargoyle.

"Pass me the rope," Sim yelled.

The rope passed hand over hand from the rear of the crowd to the front. Sim walked to the closest person and took it. Whoever owned the rope had already fashioned one end into a noose. The rest would be long enough to toss over one the oak's limbs. He turned around and showed the method of execution to Tobias. The boy's expression deepened more with wide-eyed terror.

"Get him over to the tree," Sim told his buddies.

They wrangled Tobias to the oak. Sim slipped the noose over the slender dark neck and tightened the knot. He threw the other end of the rope over a limb, and nodded for Johnny to take the end.

"I don't know what to do," Johnny whispered. "I ain't ever done this before."

"Neither have I," Sim said, "but I know you have to take up the slack."

Johnny nodded and pulled the rope tight. Tobias hissed as the rope's fibers cut into his skin. The crowd surrounded them. Sim turned back to face them.

"You say hanging?" he asked.

The crowd agreed with rousing yells of yes. He smiled.

"I need some fellows to help out Marshall and Johnny. They can't lift him up alone."

Men nearly trampled over each other to take up a length of the rope with Marshall and Johnny. The town had never experienced anything like the murders. With the fresh blood of innocents still stinking in the night air, the townspeople wanted the Old Testament justice of an eye for an eye instead of the government's due process.

"Got any last words, boy?" Sim asked, mostly mocking the terrified teenager.

"I didn't kill those people. It was Sim and his buddies. I caught them. That's why they come after me." Tobias rattled the words off with the cadence of sheer horror. "I didn't do nothing to his sister either. Ask her. She'll tell you."

"They can't. She's so traumatized by what you did that she's a retard now," Sim lied. "You did that to her. You made her a retard. How can you act like you care about her?"

"You got to believe me. It was Sim that did that killing. How could I do it alone?"

Sim gave the motion for the men to pull the rope. Tobias's voice choked off as the noose first stretched his neck upward and then lifted his feet off the ground. The men behind the rope grunted with the effort of raising the boy. He gargled as the rope cut off his breath. Once his feet were high enough, his legs began to flail, and his body started to swing back and forth. The men started to lose their footing. Sim wrapped himself around Tobias's legs and pulled down with his weight. The other men pulled harder. Tobias's vertebrae popped, and the movement stopped.

Sim let go, panting for breath. "Tie the rope off around the trunk. Let them get a look at what happens to murderin' niggers in this town."

Chapter Twenty-Seven

Josh's mother woke him up at the usual time for school. The morning light that peeked into the living room burned his eyes. Thomas sat on the floor rubbing his eyes as well. They had slept a few hours in the living room.

"Can't we skip school today?" Josh asked. "We barely slept last night."

His mother walked through the living room. "I have to go to work. Your dad has to go back to the hospital." She pointed at Josh. "You have alternative school, which you can't skip."

"After what happened, I think we could all take the day off," Thomas said. "A guy crashed through our window, and a ghost hanged him."

Their mother stopped and turned to face them. "That didn't happen."

"I'm pretty sure it did," Josh said. He'd seen the ghost of Sue Browning a few days ago. The ghost that shattered the window had looked like the same sort of thing. "Why else would he hang himself off our house?"

"That's for the police to decide." His mother sounded almost frantic. "There is no such thing as ghosts."

"Dad and I saw one at school the other day," Thomas said.

"Hogwash," she said. "That old man committed suicide and for some reason decided to do it here. Period. End of discussion."

Their dad walked downstairs and into the living room. He carried an old high school yearbook. His expression was one of sheer exhaustion.

"You guys are up?" he asked.

"Momma woke us," Thomas said. "Josh has to go to school. She forgot I've been suspended."

"You still need to be up. No lollygagging because you can't go to school. We ought to have given you more punishment, but you did help your brother out."

Sleeping on the floor made Josh's face ache. He could only imagine what he looked like. His reflection in the TV screen told him. His eye puffed up large and black. A bruise ran the length of his jaw. If he had a broken swollen nose, he'd look like a prize fighter on the bad side of a contest.

"Is this the ghost from last night?" their dad asked, handing the yearbook to Thomas and pointing to a picture.

"It was Johnny House," their mother said. "I recognized him."

"Not him," their dad said. "The ghost."

Their mother balled her hands into a fist. "For the last time, there was no ghost."

"That's her." Thomas pointed at the picture and read. "Debbie Eva."

He showed the picture to Josh. The faded black and white photo looked like the ghost, except Debbie Eva's picture didn't have a hole in her torso. He nodded back at his dad. His mother fumed.

"If you all want it to have been a ghost, fine. But leave me out of this crazy *Scooby-Doo, Poltergeist* crap. I'm going to work."

"What's her problem?" Josh asked, finally standing up and stretching out.

"It is kind of far-fetched when you think about it," Alan said. "An old man hanging from a noose crashes into our teenaged son's window, and a ghost supposedly did it. That's too much for her to swallow at once."

"Do you believe us?" Josh asked.

His father looked very serious and older than he'd ever seen him before. "Absolutely. I think that the closer we get to the anniversary of that horrible massacre, something is tearing a hole in the place between us and them. I think that those dead kids want revenge."

"Why are they after us?" Thomas asked. "We weren't even alive back then."

"Is it because of Aunt Charlotte?" Josh asked. "Or Jessica?"

"I think it's a variety of things including Charlotte and her, but I think it might be your grandfather." Alan looked at his watch. "Speaking of which, I've got twenty minutes before visitation starts. I've got to go."

"Can I walk you out? I need to talk with you real quick," Josh said.

His dad nodded. They walked out in the crisp morning air. Josh wished he had on more than a T-shirt and his boxers. Chill bumps popped up all over him. They walked to Alan's car and stopped.

"What is it?" Alan asked.

"I'm sorry about blowing up about Jessica."

"You like her, and I approached that wrong."

"I think you're right. I went over to her house last night after our argument. She wasn't there. I broke in and found nothing there. No furniture and no family. All I found was a single bed and some strange stuff, like voodoo stuff."

Alan looked at his watch. "I saw her or something like her last night at the hospital. She taunted me, and I chased her down the hall only to have her disappear literally through the door at the psych unit where your aunt is. She is part of this. Now I'm positive."

"I think I'm in a lot of trouble." For some reason, Josh needed to confess to his father. His old man could help. "I had sex with her yesterday after getting sent home from school. Now that I think about it, she bewitched me. I think she knows I broke into her house. She's one that sent the ghost and killed Mr. House. I'm next."

Alan rubbed his eyes. His father let out a long sigh. "I don't know what to do about that. You should have known better, but she is an attractive girl. You didn't know she was a witch or a ghost or a zombie, or whatever she is. I've got no idea what to tell you except stay away from her, and I hope you wore a rubber."

"Don't worry," Josh said.

"I've got to go."

Josh nodded. He walked back into the house. Thomas sat on

the couch. *The Today Show* blared from the television. Elton John sang some song Josh didn't recognize, but it sounded like a love song. Apparently he was promoting it.

"Get ready," he said to his brother.

"I'm watching Elton John," Thomas said. "Plus, I don't have to go to school."

The show went to commercial. Josh poked Thomas in the back. "He's gone, and I'm not going to school either."

"They said he's going to sing 'Tiny Dancer'. If you aren't going to school, what's the hurry?"

"We're going to Selma. I'll dig out dad's cassette tape with that song on it. We can listen on the way." Josh walked toward the kitchen.

"Why Selma?"

He stopped and looked back at his brother. "That's where Kathryn Tucker Windham lives."

"Who?"

"The lady who wrote the Jeffrey books."

"Why are we going there?" Thomas asked.

"I think she might know what's going on around here."

"Because she writes about ghosts?"

"No, because she wrote about the massacre in one of her books. You remember I found a copy of the book in Jessica's house. It had a bunch of weird jotting in it. It can't hurt to ask her."

"Why not call her on the phone?" Thomas asked.

A phone call would be simpler, but Josh needed a road trip. "That way she won't know where I am."

"Who? Mom?"

"Jessica."

Sim sighed with pleasure. He opened his eyes. Connie straddled him. She moved up and down. A long time had passed since he'd known the pleasure of a woman, too long. He reached up and grabbed her hips above her ample rump. His fingers pressed into the voluptuous flesh, soft and warm. He sighed again with immense pleasure.

"Oh yeah," he said softly and almost passionately. "That's it."

"Do you like it like that?" Connie asked.

"Oh yeah."

Sim sat up to drive himself deep into her. He buried his face between her breasts and breathed in. The smell of erotic sweat filled his nostrils. He pressed himself full into her. A long groan escaped from her mouth. He moved his hand from her haunch to her face, and he pulled his finger from the edge of her lips. She took it into her mouth and sucked on it. Her tongue ran along the fingertip in a playful circle.

He opened his eyes. Connie no longer writhed on him. Instead, Jessica, his grandson's girlfriend, had allowed him into her. For a second he felt like an old man, a perverted thing enjoying such a union, but this feeling faded away as she started to press back against him, grinding as hard as he was giving. Now an explosion built up inside him. It would go at any minute. He clinched his eyes together and let out an almost painful sound as he released.

She squealed at the same time. Once the pressure released, he opened his eyes again. They still moved against each other. He remained deep inside her.

"Was that good?" she asked no longer in Connie's voice but Jessica's.

"Oh yeah, it's been too long," Sim said.

"Kiss me," she said.

Sim lifted himself toward her mouth and looked her in the face. Instead of the beautiful young woman, a festering, putrid skull stared back. Rotting skin hung off it in green and black strips. A tongue purple and swollen wormed from her mouth like a nightcrawler. Sim screamed, and Jessica laughed a high-pitched horrible cackle.

In the real world, Sim opened his eyes. His right eye didn't seem to be working very well. Everything looked blurred, like a lens with Vaseline smeared over it. He tried to swallow, but something clogged his throat. For a moment, it was the putrid tongue, and he gagged. Straps held down his arms. He couldn't move them to free the obstruction. A beeping sound changed to a buzz and something like a siren. Someone rushed into the room. He cut his eyes over to see who it was. A nurse in blue scrubs fiddled with wires. Sim tried to speak, but the thing in this throat didn't allow that either. He grunted.

"Mr. McAdams? Are you awake?" the nurse asked.

He grunted again. She tapped some buttons above his head. The siren sound stopped. She looked him in the eyes.

"Are you breathing okay?"

He grunted. She put her hand on his chest and under his nose. The monitors around him beeped. Sim smelled the odor of a hospital. The memory of Tobias's ghost reaching into his chest came back to him. The beeping increased.

"Try to stay calm, Mr. McAdams," the nurse said. "I'm going to get the doctor."

She left, and Sim tried to calm down. He focused on other things, but his mind wandered back to the ghost's attack and to the dream he'd had and back to the ghost. Finally, a doctor walked in. He asked him questions and prodded and poked Sim the way doctors typically did. After a full examination that ended short of thumping him to see if he was ripe, the doctor peeled off the tape over his mouth and pulled a long tube from his throat. Sim swallowed and coughed. His breath seemed shorter, but it felt good to have the tube removed.

"Can you talk, Mr. McAdams?" the doctor asked.

"Water."

The word slurred, and he had difficulty understanding his own words. Half his mouth didn't work when he spoke.

"You've had a severe stroke. I don't know if that's a good idea if you cannot swallow," the doctor said.

"I just did."

The doctor nodded at him as if he were a bumbling idiot. His words sounded that way, but his mind worked like it always had. He never imagined a stroke having such a result. He thought victims were not able to think straight and that caused their speech problems.

"We can try it," the doctor said.

"Alan. Get Alan."

The words sounded nothing like he wanted them too. The doctor looked very confused. He kept saying his son's name. Finally, Sim said "Son." The doctor understood. He told the nurse to see if Alan was in the waiting area since it was almost visitation. Alan walked in, and he and the doctor spoke for few minutes. Sim didn't pay much attention. It didn't matter. Nothing could be done to help him out of this state. Too many people he'd seen have strokes stayed the same way.

"Are you okay, Daddy?" Alan asked.

"Listen." Sim tried very hard to make the good side of his mouth work the best that he could make it work. "Tobias's ghost did this."

"Did he say ghost?" the doctor asked.

"I think he did," the nurse answered.

Sim would have rolled his eyes if his brain would have let him. Instead, he lay in his bed, looking up at the ceiling and hoping that the doctor didn't think the stroke made him dotty or crazy. The last thing he wanted was to end up on the nut ward with his sister.

"Doctor," Alan said, "can I talk to my father alone, for a minute?"

"Sure." The doctor and nurse stepped out.

Alan pulled the sliding glass door closed. This gave Sim some relief. He didn't have to worry about the doctor hearing what he had to say. His energy could be expended trying to speak as clearly as possible.

"Did you say Tobias's ghost made you have a stroke?"

Sim nodded as best he could. "His face was the one in the reflection. He wants to get me back."

Alan appeared to be focusing very hard on understanding him. Sim took patience and let his son process it.

"For lynching him?" Alan asked.

Sim nodded. His son didn't give him a look like he'd lost his mind. Instead, Alan looked very concerned, more concerned than Sim had ever seen.

"Would any other ghosts try to get you?" Alan asked. "Or us, me or the boys?"

Sim nodded his agreement again.

"And what about Marshall and Johnny House?"

He nodded again. It was easier.

"Johnny?" he asked.

"He's dead, Dad. Hanged himself at our house. The boys claim that a ghost pushed his body through the window. They identified her as Debbie Eva from an old yearbook picture."

He hoped that the damage done to his face would hide his guilt. Alan looked him over.

"What about Corey Aaron, Johnny's grandson? Would a ghost go after him?"

"Maybe," Sim didn't feel well now. He needed for his son to leave, but something had to be said no matter how hard it was to get out. "Connie Dearborn."

"You think her ghost did it?"

Sim shook his head in disagreement as best he could. "Everything. Witch."

Alan looked at him not with surprise but with a look something like an epiphany.

"How do you know that?"

He didn't answer. Some things had to remain secret. That one would go to the grave with him. Alan shook his head at him. His son knew that he was being obstinate. Sim closed his eyes and acted like he was asleep. The door opened, and Alan left. While he lay behind dark lids, he dreamed about Connie. He dreamed about the story of Hazel's curse and understood why Jessica looked like Connie.

Chapter Twenty-Eight

1956
The evening before Homecoming

Blood soaked everything. Sim had never seen so much of it in his life. He turned in a circle taking it in. Everything seemed unreal. As he scanned past the doors from the lobby into the basketball court, he glimpsed a face, barely visible against the darkness of the lobby. It wasn't like the one he'd seen a few nights ago while he was drinking out near the old cemetery, which he'd blamed on being drunk. This one was solid, not ghostly. This one looked nothing like a mulatto gypsy from a campfire story. It was a black face, a young black face. Tobias had seen.

Sim ran across the basketball court into the lobby. The main door closed as he made his way to it. By the time he got to the outside, the nigger's taillights lit up as he drove down from the gym to the street. Sim chomped down on the Doublemint he was using to try to stop smoking. He had to take care of that spearchucker and quickly. The boy would go back to the Harringtons first and tell them. A colored person would never go directly to the sheriff. It would be futile. Marshall and Johnny would be a welcomed help with this one. They could tail the kid and make his drive home long enough for Sim to tie up loose ends and get to the sheriff first.

Chapter Twenty-Nine

"What's the plan?" Thomas asked as he and Josh drove through a residential street in Selma.

"I'm going to go to her house, knock on the door, and tell her that I'm a reporter for our school paper," Josh turned onto a street lined with standard-looking houses.

"We don't have a school paper."

"She won't know that."

"You think this will work?"

"Mrs. Windham was a reporter for a long time. I'm sure she'll be impressed that I tracked her down to do a story." Josh slowed the car as they approached a house with a large porch with white rails around it. The copper house number shone in the sun. "This is it."

Thomas studied the house through the windshield as they pulled up the driveway. He squinted and cocked his head to the side like a dog trying to understand where a noise came from.

"Are you sure?"

"It's the address from the phone book." Josh put the car into park.

"It looks too happy."

"What did you expect, the Addams Family house?"

"Kind of. It is a haunted house." Thomas got out of the car.

Josh stepped out after him. The smell of dried leaves wafted toward him. The tinkling of wind chimes floated down from the porch. He agreed with Thomas a little bit: the place didn't match his imagination. Although he didn't expect the creepiness of something akin to Norma Bates's homestead, he had thought it might be a little more Southern Gothic. The white bannister along the porch and hanging pots full of bright yellow mums made it hard to believe the woman responsible for scaring a large number of Alabama schoolchildren lived there.

The screen door opened, and a small, gray-haired woman walked onto the porch. She wore a broad brim sunhat and large glasses. Brown cloth work gloves covered her hands. A flowered apron covered her blue dress. She looked at Josh and his brother with surprise.

"Can I help you boys?" she asked in a long slow drawl.

"Are you Mrs. Windham?" Josh asked.

"Yes." She stayed close to her door.

"The Mrs. Windham who wrote the ghost books?" Thomas asked.

"The same. I don't make autographs at my residence," she said.

"I'm sorry. We've not introduced ourselves. My name is Josh McAdams and this is my brother Thomas. We're from up in Pinehurst."

Mrs. Windham screwed up her eyes in thought. "Seems like I remember one of my books talks about that town."

"It does," Josh said. "That's why we're here. I'm a reporter on the Pinehurst High newspaper. I was hoping to interview you for the paper. It's a special Halloween feature story."

She seemed a bit skeptical and eyed them more. "Why's he here?"

"He didn't want to drive all the way down here by himself," Thomas said. "It's a long drive from Pinehurst. Look at his face, people might mistake him for Frankenstein."

"Indeed, he does look the worse for the wear, but you ain't Cary Grant for that matter," she said.

"We've had bad weather. A storm damaged our house," Josh lied.

"Windows broken, flying glass, cuts on the face, you know," Thomas added. "He got into a fight. Three guys jumped him."

"I'd believe that. I hope you got the better of them," she said.

"I held my own," Josh said. "Can I please interview you? It's important."

"I didn't anticipate entertaining anyone today," she said. "I was planning on raking my leaves."

He looked to the side of her house. A large elm had shed a yard full of yellow and brown leaves. A rake leaned against the trunk of tree, and a small pile of the leaves had already been raked. His foot was in the door, now if he could convince her to talk to him.

"If you'll talk with me, my brother will rake your leaves. It's important that I get this interview. If it's good, I plan on using it in my portfolio to try to get into the journalism school at Alabama," Josh said.

"I'm raking her leaves?" Thomas whispered. "I could have done that at home and saved the drive."

"Shut up," Josh whispered back. "Don't forget about Johnny House."

"I'd be happy to rake them," Thomas chimed in.

Mrs. Windham paused for a long moment, but she smiled and removed her work gloves.

"That sounds fine. It's backbreaking work, raking leaves. If you'll excuse the clothes I've got on, we can talk."

"Thank you." Josh walked across the driveway and onto the porch.

Thomas made his way to the rake and started piling up more leaves on the heap. Mrs. Windham sat in a white wicker chair with a large round back. Josh sat in the matching chair on the other side of round wicker table.

"So, let's get started," she said. "Where's your notebook?"

"I have an excellent memory," Josh lied.

"That's not going to cut in the professional world, son. From this point on, always bring a notebook even if you don't use it. You'll be taken more seriously."

"Yes, ma'am, you're right. I'll remember that. Can we start?"

"Of course."

The two of them sat for a while. He asked questions he thought someone who wrote feature articles might ask. The conversation came around to why she wrote ghost stories. She told him the story of Jeffrey, the ghost who supposedly haunted her house.

"How do you pick the stories that go into the books?" Josh asked.

"I went around the state and the South listening to people tell their ghost stories. I used a *notebook* to record them. After that, I narrowed them down to about twenty. Those got typed up so I could look them over with better eyes. After that, more were eliminated."

"My town is in one of your books." He took the copy he'd stolen from Jessica's house from behind his back where he'd kept it shoved in his waist band. He wiped the perspiration from it with his shirttail. "Why did you pick that one?"

"May I see the book?"

Josh gladly handed her the text. She turned right to where the marker was and smiled.

"I see you marked the story." She read for a moment. "I remember this one well. I wasn't completely honest with you. I don't pick all the stories myself. When I was writing the first book, I had all the possible stories lying in a pile on my desk when I went to bed one night. The next morning I woke up and a different story was on the top of the pile. Jeffrey had chosen it. I hadn't even planned on including that particular tale. When I wrote this book, I wasn't going to include the story about Pinehurst because I found it too, well, scary. Jeffrey put that thing on the top of the pile three times. Once even taking it out of the trash can."

"Why did you find it scary?"

Mrs. Windham smiled at him, but it wasn't a sweet old lady smile. It was more of an uncomfortable smile used to hide anxiety.

"Josh, most of the stories I put in those books are stories. There's nothing in them except a good yarn. The one about Pinehurst felt like much more than that. It was real, and evil. Looking at it right now gives me the willies. Why are those markings in the margins?"

"I don't know."

"That doesn't help my feelings at all."

"Why does the story feel real?"

"I saw things while I wrote this story, and not just in Pinehurst.

Ghosts or something seemed to follow me back here. They were angry. I think the only thing that kept them from doing something to me was Jeffrey. I think he bargained with them by agreeing to get me to print their story."

"Mrs. Windham, strange things are happening in my town. It's the fortieth anniversary of the massacre talked about in your story. People have died in horrible ways. Some of us, like me, my brother, and my dad, have seen ghosts, and possibly a witch," Josh whispered. "We're not crazy."

"I know you're not." She stared at the book, closed it, and sat it on the table. "I remember this story well. I didn't put all of the tale in there. Hazel's curse was far worse. She supposedly cast a spell to reincarnate herself to exact her revenge. The old witch's soul embodied a new human so that she could return every forty years and try to make up for the wrong committed against her. The person I talked to said that he believed she had been stopped every forty years before it could happen. She had bounded the curse for every forty years to punish at least two generations at a time, according to my source. He said that he believed when the massacre happened in the '50s that her revenge had almost been fulfilled."

"We can stop it?" Josh asked.

"McAdams was the name of the man who insisted on Hazel being hanged." Mrs. Windham stared off toward a place beyond the yonder. "That witch is after y'all, isn't she? Be honest as I've been with you. You don't write for the school paper, do you?"

"No, ma'am."

"You wanted to know what I knew." She leaned over to him and patted his knee. "You two seem like nice young men. I hope I've helped."

"You have. Thank you."

"You've got a long drive back to Pinehurst," she said. "Best get on your way."

"What about your yard?"

She looked out at the good progress Thomas had made and smiled. "He's done most of it. Not much work left, and it will be good for an old lady like me to do. The exercise will help keep me young, help clear my mind."

Josh thanked Mrs. Windham again. He took the stolen copy of her book and headed back to the car. She yelled her thanks to Thomas for raking her yard. They left with her giving them a hardy wave.

"Did you find out anything?" Thomas asked.

"I think so. I'll tell you on the ride back."

Alan looked out the window. Jessica stood on the street at the entrance to his driveway. She had been there for a while. He first noticed her not long after he'd gotten home from the hospital. During that time, he made sure to keep the doors locked, but it was getting time for his wife and sons to get home.

He let the curtains fall back into place and walked to the kitchen. His wife kept the Morton's salt in the cabinet above the stove. He took the box down and went back to the front. His wife parked as he peeked back out the window. Jessica moved enough to let the car pass but stepped back into her place. His wife got out of the car, and the girl started walking toward her. They seemed to have a conversation. The time had come. Alan stormed out the door pouring a handful of salt into his palm.

"Get away from my wife, Jessica," he said.

"What's the matter with you?" his wife asked.

He threw the salt at the girl instead of answering. She screamed and backed off. He tossed more and more until he had her backed into the street. A line of salt went onto the pavement between the street and his driveway.

"What's the problem, Jessica or Connie or whoever you are? On a low sodium diet?" he asked.

"I'll get you," she said.

"And my little dog too?" Alan asked.

Jessica's eyes flashed with anger. "And everything you care about."

"Let that girl come in," his wife said, coming up to him and trying to take the salt from him.

"She's no girl." Alan tossed another handful of salt at Jessica.

Her feet slid backward on the pavement. The power of the salt moved her back. His wife looked amazed. To both of their wonderment, Jessica cackled like some kind of Halloween character and disappeared into a wisp of black smoke.

"What was that?"

"She's a witch," Alan said. "She's trying to kill us."

"Where are the boys?"

"I don't know."

"What should we do?"

Alan threw a handful of salt in the air. "Pray."

"I'll do that." His wife pulled on his arm toward the house. "How did you know that would work?"

He smiled. *"Hocus Pocus.* You know that movie with Bette Milder."

Chapter Thirty

1956
The evening before Homecoming

Charlotte walked out of old man Shannon's store with rolls of crepe paper in her arms. She was disappointed that all he had left anywhere near the color she needed were baby blue and gray. With Homecoming a few days away, he said he'd had a run of the school colors in all products.

She fumbled with the rolls, trying to open the back door of her parent's car without dropping them. A car slid into the parking lot as she tossed the rolls into her car. Tobias jumped out of his Monterey. The engine idled. He looked like a scared animal. She stopped herself. Tobias looked like a frightened child, not an animal. Comparing him to a dumb beast was something that her brother would do. Charlotte knew she was better than that.

"What's the matter?" she asked.

"Don't go back to the gym. Don't go back."

"I have to. I've got the rest of the crepe paper," Charlotte said. "Has something happened?"

Tobias nodded his head with manic flair. "Very bad, very, very, very bad. Don't go back."

"What is it? You can tell me."

He grabbed her by the arms and pulled her into him. The pressure of his hands hurt. A squeal of pain escaped her mouth. He looked at her, and his expression told her he wanted to stop. The grip however got tighter. Sheer terror contracted his muscles. She yelled.

The door to the five-and-ten flew open. Old Man Shannon

rushed out, carrying a nicked baseball bat. Despite his frail appearance, the old owner had fire in his eyes. He advanced on Tobias and Charlotte.

"Let her go, boy." He drew the bat back ready to swing it. "Ain't going to be no trouble at my store."

"He's not doing it on purpose," Charlotte protested. "He's terrified."

"Don't care. I ain't having no colored boy hanging onto a white customer, especially a girl." He looked at Tobias. "Get on out of here, boy. Tell the Harringtons if they want something from my store to either send your daddy or Mr. Harrington himself. I won't have none of this riffraff business."

Tobias let go of Charlotte. His eyes looked wilder. He headed back to the driver's side of his car. Before sliding in, he gave Charlotte another desperate look.

"Don't go back up there," he said. "Please don't."

"I have to. Why don't you go there, too? I don't think you need to drive all the way to the Harrington Plantation in your condition."

"I can't. I've got to lose them. They're after me. He's after me."

"What are you talking about, boy? Quit wasting time and get," old man Shannon said.

"Sim. He's after me. Please don't go back."

Without saying anything else, Tobias sped away. She watched the car disappear down the street. Charlotte had an uneasy feeling in the pit of her stomach. Tobias was upset to the point of irrationality. She'd never seen him act like that, not even the day in the cafeteria when everyone had picked on him and she'd been Joan of Arc standing up for him. The idea crossed her mind not to go back to the gym—to let them make do and follow him. But if Sim was involved, she needed to get to the gym to drop off the stuff and find her brother. He always listened to her and would be happy to settle things.

She got in the family car and drove to the gymnasium. The sky grew darker as the sun set. The streetlights flickered on as she drove closer to the gym. Something bad must have happened for Tobias to plead like he had. She passed by the diner on main street. Sim and his buddies, Marshall and Johnny, sat at a booth. Charlotte whipped the car into a parking space. Her brother came out to meet her on the sidewalk.

"What is it, Charlotte?" he asked.

"Did you try to scare Tobias?" she asked.

"What are talking about?"

"I was buying crepe paper down at old man Shannon's store. Tobias drove up in a fury while I was trying to leave. He started ranting about something happening and that you were after him. What have you done, Sim?"

"Calm down." Her brother put his arm around her and walked her back toward her car. "I've not done anything. I waved at him a little while ago when I met him on the road. We were driving down the street. I had to make a U-turn because Marshall needed something from the hardware store before it closed. He must have mistaken that for me coming after him." Sim smiled. "He's your friend. I'd never do anything to hurt you or any of your friends. You know that."

Her big brother's arm and words comforted her. She smiled back and got into the car. With a hearty, love-filled wave, she set off back toward the gym. Her brother loved her. She believed it, like she believed he would never, ever hurt her or let anyone else hurt her. He had some sharp points, but all in all, she wouldn't have wanted anyone else as a brother.

Without much more thought about Tobias and how silly and excitable he had been, Charlotte worried about the crepe paper in the wrong color. She hoped no one would mind.

Chapter Thirty-One

Josh eventually called his folks. It was the last thing he'd wanted to do, but after getting lost in a detour, the time had gotten away. His parents would be worried. Fortunately, his dad answered the phone and understood why they'd skipped off to Selma. The only thing his dad made sure of was to warn him about Jessica. Well before getting back into Pinehurst, he and Thomas stopped off to eat at McDonalds. He'd gone to a grocery store near the restaurant and bought two boxes of salt, one for him and one for Thomas. His dad told him it would come in handy.

As they drove down the street that passed their grandfather's house, Thomas started rolling the tubular box of salt between his hands. He licked his lips. His brother always did that when he was nervous.

"Settle down," Josh said. "You're going to get yourself all hot and bothered."

"That's the point. I need to get fired up. If anything goes down, I'll be ready. This is how I get pumped up for a football game."

"If anything does happen, it's going to be a lot different than a football game."

"Still, I'll be ready."

As they drove past the old gym, Josh noticed lights in the high windows. Cars lined the drive up to the parking lot. He stopped his car in the middle of the street. No one was behind him, and it looked like no one was coming up the road.

"What's going on up there?" he asked.

"I don't know. It looks pretty crowded," Thomas said.

"It's not Friday, is it?"

"No."

"Did they decide to move the anniversary dance up to tonight?" Josh asked.

"I don't know. People quit talking about it around me after Corey died and a bunch of them got called into the principal's office."

Josh pulled his car into the driveway. There were no spaces in the parking lot on the hill. He parked directly in front of the doors. A few students he recognized but didn't know stood outside smoking. He and Thomas got out of the car and walked toward the door.

"What are we doing?" Thomas whispered.

"Finding out what's going on," Josh said, stopping by a pimple-faced boy with his arm draped over an ugly girl with greasy blond hair.

"What's up?" pimple face asked.

"That's what I was wondering," Josh said.

"Don't talk to them," the ugly girl said. "They're the McAdams brothers."

"Oh," pimple face said. "I don't know. I came here to smoke cigarettes and suck face."

"Be careful, sweetheart," Thomas said to the ugly girl. "You might catch what he's growing on his face."

"Hey!" Pimple face flicked his cigarette to the ground and squared off against them.

Thomas threw his arms back and pushed his chest out toward the boy, who backed off. It was apparent to Josh that even if they weren't supposed to talk to the McAdams brothers, they didn't want to fight them either.

He was reaching for the handle when the heavy metal door flew open. Harvey walked out. A joint hung from his lips. He smiled toward Josh and Thomas.

"What are you two doing here?"

"I was about to ask you the same thing," Josh said. "Are they having the massacre dance tonight?"

"Don't tell him nothing," the pimple-faced boy said.

"Shut up, Papa John's," Thomas said. "This is our friend."

Harvey stepped out and motioned for them to follow him to the side of the building. He lit his joint and pulled off of it before holding it out to them.

"No, thanks," Josh said.

Thomas reached for it. "Exactly what I need."

"No, Tommy, you need a clear head. Remember?"

"Oh yeah." Thomas shook his head and pushed the joint away.

"More for me." Harvey took another toke.

"So, is this the dance or are they having an ugly teenager contest?" Josh asked.

"It's the dance, and it's starting to thump. They got that Louie Linguine guy from Tuscaloosa to DJ. It's awesome. You ought to come inside."

"We can't," Josh said. "And you need to get out of there, too."

"Why? The fun's getting started. They haven't even played the Hokey Pokey yet," Harvey said. "Plus they've got awesome munchies food in there. Funions, dude, Funions."

"Something bad is going to happen," Thomas said. "Probably real bad."

"Why did they change the date?" Josh asked.

"To keep the man from finding out," Harvey said. "What kind of bad stuff? Are the cops coming?"

"Maybe," Thomas answered.

"I think it's going to happen again," Josh said.

"What's going to happen again?" Harvey asked.

"The massacre."

Harvey burst out laughing. It was his I'm-getting-a-bit-toasty laugh, like when he watched some Adam Sandler movie while taking bong hits. Josh shook his head and tapped Thomas on the arm. They started walking back to the car.

"Where are y'all going?" Harvey yelled. "It's thumping."

They ignored him and got back in the car. Josh turned around and headed down the driveway. He made sure to gun the gas when he passed pimple face and the ugly girl to send gravel flying at them.

As they neared the street, Josh slammed on the brakes.

Thomas jerked forward, pushing his hands into the dashboard.

"Dude?"

"Look," Josh said.

Jessica stood in the middle of the driveway, illuminated by the car's headlights. She looked more beautiful than he'd ever seen her. Light seemed to radiate from her along with primal sexual heat. He could feel it all the way from the car.

"Get out and stay for the party," she said without her mouth moving. Her voice sounded like it came from the speakers.

Josh ignored her and let his foot off the brake. The car rolled closer to her, but she didn't move. Her words kept repeating, getting sweeter and sexier every time. The car drew closer and closer.

"She's not going to move," Thomas said.

"I need to get out and check on her. She sounds like she needs something."

"She's not saying anything."

"Of course she is, can't you hear her?" Josh shifted the care into park. He reached for his door handle.

Thomas punched the button for the moon roof. It slid back as he unfastened his seat belt. Before Josh could even get his door opened, his brother stood out of the top and tossed salt toward Jessica. Bits of the stuff landed on the windshield and hood of the car as the grains sailed through the air. She vanished in a wisp of black dust. Josh came back to himself as Thomas slid back into the car.

"Thanks."

Thomas refastened his seatbelt. "Think with the big head, dude."

Josh nodded and punched the gas. They slung gravel into the air as the car turned onto the street toward home.

As soon as they'd put a few blocks between them and the gym, Jessica appeared in the middle of an intersection beckoning for them to stop. Josh kept his wits about him this time and drove through the illusion. Ghosts chased them. At one point, Sue Browning roller-skated from the sidewalk. Before Josh could stop to check if he'd hit someone, the ghost popped up at the window. By the time they pulled into their driveway, the entire phantom group that had been killed forty years ago trailed them.

They ran toward the house. The ghost of Debbie Eva, the one who'd assaulted them the night before, swooped down. Her fingernails scratched at Josh's already raw face. Thomas yelled out as Tommy Jones wrapped him in a tackle. They both got onto the front stoop. Their dad opened the door and tossed a handful of salt out over their heads as they slipped past him. He slammed the door. The ghosts banged against its wood.

"A door can stop ghosts?" Josh said.

"No, but we discovered sage could." His dad pointed to a small Ziploc bag of dried green herbs thumbtacked to the door. "We've got baggies on all the windows and outside doors. Because the windows aren't fixed in your room, Thomas, we locked your door and put some on it."

"They're having the anniversary dance tonight," Josh said.

His dad looked very concerned. "Did that lady help you out?"

"She told me that part of the legend is that the old witch Hazel cast a spell to be reincarnated," Josh said.

"Jessica is Hazel," his dad said. "Connie Dearborn was her forty years ago, but she was killed before the curse could be fulfilled."

"What about the time when the tornado came?" Thomas asked.

"The gypsy preacher man was the witch," Josh said. "I bet the tornado wasn't part of the curse but a happy coincidence. It killed him before he could get revenge."

Their mother walked into the living room carrying a cup of coffee. "It sounds like you need to get rid of Jessica."

"How?" Thomas said.

"I know," Josh said. "I've known all day. I don't like the idea."

"What is it?" his mother asked.

"I have to be the bait."

"No, certainly not. We can stay holed up here," his mother said.

"It won't stop."

"He's right," his dad said. "I don't like it any more than you do, but if we don't do something, all of those stupid kids at that dance are going to die. There's a good shot we will, too."

"Why?" his mother asked. "We haven't done anything to that crazy girl."

"It's not her," Alan said. "It was something my family did a long time ago. We're paying for their mistakes, the whole town is."

"But what about the ghosts?" Thomas asked.

"I think they've got a vendetta against us too," Alan said.

"Why?" Josh asked.

"Sim."

This didn't surprise Josh in the least. His grandfather had never been a convenient man. There was no reason for him to start being so now.

"Let's make a plan," Josh said. "I want to get this over with before I lose my nerve."

Josh and his family sat down in the living room and started planning their strategy. The sound of the ghosts hitting the windows and walls trying to get in made it feel like they were trapped in a living, beating heart.

Finally, the plan was made. "We go in an hour," Alan said.

Josh's body tensed. "I hope that's not too late."

"As long as the ghosts keep attacking the house, it's not."

Just then, the phantom attacks stopped. Everything became still and quiet.

"Maybe we go now," Thomas said.

Chapter Thirty-Two

1956
A week after the Massacre

Sim stood on the old wooden bridge that crossed Chipewanna Creek on the dirt road that ran out to an old logging camp, years abandoned. No one came down that road except to fish off the bridge or get up to no good. Most folks did the latter. He was the only person who still tried to catch crappie from the bridge. Most folks had moved their fishing over to the new county lake the state had created a few years ago. The state kept it stocked. The fishing there almost came with a guarantee to catch a mess of something.

Fishing, alone with the water, was the only thing that ever cleared Sim's mind. It was the only thing outside of drinking that calmed him down. Since the massacre and everything surrounding it, he needed some time to himself with a pole and a beer. He had both. Tranquility came as a happy free gift.

"Catching anything?"

Sim turned as a man wearing a wrinkled gray suit and straw-colored trilby with a motley blue hatband sidled up to him. A toothpick stuck out from the side of the man's mouth. He smiled. The man looked out of place, not because he wore a suit at that location as much as he was a sore thumb among pinkies.

"It's November," Sim answered. "Rarely catch crappie in November."

"Croppie," the man said, and now Sim was positive he was the detective Sheriff Johnson warned him about. Only Yankees called a crappie a croppie. "I expected you were catfishing."

"You're wrong," Sim said.

"How about nigger fishing? You're pretty good of catching those on the end of a line."

"Do I know you?" Sim asked. "You seem to think we are in acquaintance."

"I know all about you, Simeon Thomas McAdams." The man pulled a small top-bound spiral notebook from his coat pocket. He flipped it opened. "You are twenty-eight years old and live in Pinehurst, not far from the gymnasium where the massacre happened. You work for Georgia-Pacific lumber company. You are a veteran—Coast Guard."

"My eyes are green and I have two nuts," Sim said. "What's it to you?"

"I'm Jack Garth, a private detective. The Harringtons hired me to get some questions answered. You're the biggest question."

Sim almost laughed at him, but instead, he reeled in his line and flung the minnow off the hook into the water. He fastened the naked hook to one of the eyelets on the rod and leaned it on the rail of the bridge.

"What answer do you want?" he asked.

"Why did you kill Tobias Abernathy?" Garth asked.

"I didn't kill him," Sim said. "I served justice to him."

"You lynched him."

Sim picked up his rod and started across the bridge back toward the main road where his truck was parked. His place of solitude was gone, and he had nothing more to say to Mr. Garth. The detective grabbed him by the arm. Sim spun around and shoved the tip of his rod under the detective's chin.

"I don't much like being accused of murder," he said through a snarl. "I like being touched by some carpetbagging Yankee even worse."

"Touch a nerve, Johnny Reb?" Garth asked, sounding to Sim like some B-movie Humphrey Bogart wannabe. "All you cracker redneck boys down here are hopping to hang a Negro, ain't you?"

Sim pressed the tip deeper in the loose skin around the man's neck. "That boy killed my sister's friends and my fiancée.

What happened to him was better than what the courts would have done." He made the sound of meat sizzling.

Garth stepped back. "So you say, but I have reason to believe that Tobias Abernathy was innocent of those killings. The evidence points to more than a single boy being able to do that kind of carnage."

It felt like Sim's guts would explode from anger. He smiled, tucked his rod under his arm, and walked down the road, leaving the detective where he stood. The last thing he needed was to lose his cool and do something stupid. He hoped the detective would take the hint and not keep pressing.

"No so fast." The detective came up behind him. "I would like some questions answered."

Sim kept walking. "I don't have to. You're not a cop, just some dime-store private dick."

"You killed those kids and framed Tobias Abernathy."

The words chilled Sim to the core. They froze him to the spot. He turned to face Jack Garth. If he'd had a gun, he'd have shot him dead right there.

"You're crazy. Why would I kill my own fiancée?"

"According to your own mother, she jilted you. Heartbreak can make a man do some extreme things, Mr. McAdams, even multiple murder."

Before Sim could say anything, the sound of a car running wide open filled the air. It came from behind him, and he had no idea how a car could be going so fast down the rutted dirt road. Only people with beat-up old trucks even tried it, going slow. Something metallic popped on the car as it crossed a patch of road akin to a washboard. He could tell by the sound the tires made.

Sim flung his fishing gear down and himself to the side, as an early-'50s model Ford barreled past him. Jack Garth wasn't as spry. The detective didn't hit the hood of the car. It drove through him. His guts and innards sprayed out all over the road.

The car stopped. Someone got out of the driver's side. The engine idled. Sim looked at the driver. He didn't believe his own eyes. Connie stood over a quarter of the detective that contained a shoulder and a bit of upper arm.

"That was fun," she said.

Sim sat up, wanting to run but not being able to stand from sheer fear. "Who are you? What are...?"

"I'm Connie," she said. "Your fiancée, remember?"

"You're dead."

She looked at the remains of the detective. "So is this guy."

"What do you want?"

"Revenge," she said. "By my own flesh-and-blood hand."

"Do it. Kill me. Get it over with."

"I can't. I'm bound by the rules."

"The rules? Whose rules?"

"The rules I put in place eighty years ago when I first cursed this town and your wretched family. Once I put the magic in play, not even the person who put the curse out can change the rules." The ghost smiled and walked back to the car. Before climbing back in, she looked at Sim. "Look for me in about forty years. I hope that's enough time for you to stew in your own juices, Simeon McAdams."

Chapter Thirty-Three

Sim's stomach rumbled. The nurses wouldn't let him feed himself. They pushed liquid down a tube in his throat. Apparently, the rounding doctor, a gook named Kim, reported that he couldn't swallow well enough for actual food. Starving him was a much better solution. He didn't even need to be in the ICU. All the nurses talked about how remarkably he was doing. He could see the clock on the wall. A placard below that listed the visitation times in large block letters. The next one was in a few minutes. He would let Alan know about that and tell him to get him transferred either to another floor or another hospital.

"You have company," said the male nurse—something else Sim found wrong with the world.

"About time," he slurred out. Before the nurse left or his guest entered, Sim continued. "You've got to tell them to transfer me."

"Why would I do that?" Jessica walked in, sliding the door shut after the nurse stepped out. "I think you're in the right place."

Sim tried to make his right hand push the call button. It remained paralyzed, as it had since his stroke. Jessica smiled a sweet and innocent smile like a candy striper bringing around magazines or chewing gum. He saw something far more sinister in her grin. Deep in those eyes, Connie Dearborn looked back at him. Now he began to realize exactly what was going on. He wished he'd put all the pieces of his old memories together before then.

"Connie," he said.

Jessica's smile beamed larger. It looked like a shark's mouth ready to devour him. Sim lay helpless before her. She would kill him. The only thing he hoped was that it would be quick.

"You don't need this," she said, pulling the plug on the call light button from the wall.

She began looking over all his various tubes and electrical attachments. Her tongue clicked as each thing got a small exploratory tug. Finally she reached above him and gave the fluid bag attached to his IV pump a hard squeeze. It burst, and the saline spilled down on him and the machine.

"Oops," she said.

"They'll hear the monitors go off and stop you," he said, hearing his voice very slurred, but he knew she understood him because she could read his thoughts. "You aren't going to be able to get away with this."

"Oh, really?"

The entire ICU started to buzz and ring with heart monitors and other warning sirens. Even the fire alarms screamed and flashed—all of them except in Sim's room. Here, everything pulsed and beeped like it was supposed to. From the periphery of his good eye, the nurses ran around outside his room in a great flurry. The overhead speaker squawked. Someone yelled "Code Blue, ICU!" over and over again.

"Why?"

"You know perfectly well why. But maybe you mean why I am going to destroy your family. Remember that old ghost story about the witch woman named Hazel?"

The story came to him as soon as she mentioned it. His family had lynched that old woman like he had Tobias Abernathy. At that moment it clicked.

"I am Connie Dearborn," Jessica said, "and I am the Reverend Junkins killed in the tornado of 1916, and I am the old voodoo lady Hazel who Silas McAdams, your granddaddy, lynched in 1876. Now for you, I'm the angel of death. You knew all this. You were too stubborn to admit it. This time I had help, all those souls you took in the prime of life. They were more than willing to bring about your downfall, Simeon McAdams."

At that moment, she became the Connie that broke his

heart. Connie turned into a middle-aged mulatto man in old-timey clothes with a hat like parsons wore in Western shows. Finally, she was a dried up old black woman. The final version, the Hazel version, reached out and ripped all the cords of his monitors and support systems out of the wall. The old, black hand turned back to the alabaster white of a teenaged girl as it covered his mouth. The fingers felt like ice, and something not solid but not insubstantial wormed down his throat.

The icy thing in his throat wrapped around his heart and squeezed it like some kind of constricting snake. His life crushed out of him from the inside. A gasp tried to escape from his mouth but became trapped in his throat.

Chapter Thirty-Four

1956
The evening of the Massacre

Sim stood in front of the Pinehurst High School gym. A cigarette burned down, and the smoke haloed around him. Marshall and Johnny sat on the hood of the car they'd come in. They smoked as well.

"I don't know about this," Johnny said. "I've got a wife and some kids. If we get caught—"

"We ain't going to get caught." Sim flicked his cigarette to the ground. "Don't forget, I got kids too. Doing this is the only way to make sure they can live in a town free of niggers, communists, and queers."

"I get the Tobias thing," Marshall said, "but why Connie? She's your fiancée."

"I told you that she's a communist. I found the stuff in her house," Sim said. "That Tommy Jones is a queer."

"How are we not going to get caught?" Johnny asked.

"We ain't going to leave any evidence. They ain't ever going to be able to figure out who did this."

Marshall held up the shotgun that lay beside him. "These things are loud, Sim. Folks around are going to hear them."

"Let them. Only old people live around here. They ain't going to do anything."

"I don't think I can do this," Johnny said. He slid off the hood of the car and took his shotgun. "I'm going to walk home."

Sim pulled an old automatic pistol from the waistband of his pants and pointed it at Johnny. "We're going in. Unless you want to be part of the carnage, understand?"

Johnny swallowed hard and pumped his shotgun. "I don't see Tobias's car. I don't think he's here."

"Probably rode up here with Charlotte," Marshall said and giggled a little.

"I don't like how you worded that." Sim pointed the pistol at Marshall. "Are you implying something?"

"We're here because he gave it to her. You said it yourself," Marshall protested.

"I still don't like it. She's gone and will be back any minute. Let's get this done," Sim said. "You boys first."

Marshall slid off the car hood and walked to the door. Opening it, he held it for Johnny to enter. Sim followed, and the heavy door closed behind them. He pulled the slide back on the pistol to put a bullet in the chamber. His buddies were too dumb to have noticed that he didn't have one in there when he threatened them.

"Step in the doors and start shooting," Sim said.

Marshall and Johnny walked through the swinging wooden doors side by side. Both shotguns thundered out as they did. Several girls screamed, and a couple of the boys hollered out. Sim stepped in and saw Connie frozen in place. A bullet from his pistol went straight between her lying, cheating, no-good eyes and blew her slut brain out the back of her head. Brain matter splattered the wall. One of the shotgun blasts hit her gut before she fell. He whirled around and nailed Sheila Deleon in the chest. Another of his bullets lodged in Sue Browning's knee, but Marshall had already blown off her face. Johnny's shotgun ran out of ammo. He took his hunting knife and started cutting on Jerry Madison.

Sim turned around, looking for the brown skin among the white. Tobias wasn't to be seen. His friends had been right. The nigger hadn't shown up yet. Although the music from the hi-fi played loudly, the swinging doors squeaked. When he turned, he got a glimpse of Tobias slipping behind them. He gave chase, but the boy got away. Sim walked back into the gym. Johnny carved on Debbie Eva. He had always liked her sister, but never made a move.

Finally, all the high school students lay dead, bleeding everywhere. His horrible whore of a girlfriend was dead as well. He wanted to spit on her but didn't.

"Tobias got away," Sim said.

"What?" Marshall said. "We're screwed."

Sim shook his head so coolly he felt cold. "We're in a better position than we ever were. Everything that happened, he did it."

Johnny walked to Sim, tracking through Ben Miller's blood. "They'll know more than one person did this. There's more than one kind of bullet wound."

"You can't run out of ammo and need to change guns?" Sim said. "Don't worry. We're going to make sure that the folks of this town are hot and bothered to the point that they'd blame that nigger for killing Christ himself. We need to get down to the greasy spoon."

"Why?" Marshall asked.

"Alibi," Sim said. "Johnny, get your gun and take off those shoes. We don't need you tracking blood outside. Keep them with you. We'll toss them in the river after we get seen by some folks. I'll tell you how we're going to handle that Tobias. He thinks I'm after him, so he'll run scared for a little while."

"Right over to the Harringtons," Johnny said, taking off his shoes.

"No, he won't go there for a while because he'll think we'll head there first."

The three of them left with the Crew Cuts' "Sh-Boom" replaying on the record player.

Chapter Thirty-Five

Josh walked up the driveway of the old gym. It was still lined with cars. More were parked on the street at the bottom of hill. No one stood outside when he got to the parking lot. A few car windows were fogged over. The bass of the music from inside thumped hard. He took a position by the doors and waited. His pockets were full of sage. He hadn't needed it so far though. The drive over with his folks and Thomas had been uneventful.

"All right, Jessica, let's get this over with," he whispered into the night.

As far as anyone else was concerned, he could have yelled. The music from the dance was too loud for anyone to hear him. The people in the cars were too occupied to care. His family sitting in the car at the base of the hill offered little comfort. They were such a long way away, even if it was only a dozen yards or so. The tempo of the bass changed. A slow song played, which meant he'd be joined shortly by the smokers. He hoped that the ugly girl and pimple-faced kid didn't come back out.

The door opened. Josh stepped to the side to let the people by. Harvey came out with a cigarette hanging from his mouth. He smiled at Josh with glassy, bloodshot eyes. The smile looked higher than he was.

"Dude, you came back," Harvey said. "Bangin' party."

"I'm waiting for someone."

"Jessica?" Harvey asked.

"Maybe."

"Dude, she's inside."

"Are you sure?" Josh asked.

"Of course. She did some heavy grinding up against my junk to "Pony." I still got the boner if you want to feel it."

"No, thanks."

Jealousy niggled at him. Although Jessica was trying to kill him, he still didn't like the idea of her doing that with Harvey. If she was in there, he needed to find her. The plan had been to wait outside until he could run down the hill and get her into range for his dad to take care of things. Plans had to change sometimes though.

Josh headed into the old gym. The place smelled like booze and pot. Smoke hung in the air. He wasn't sure why people were going outside to smoke. The heat of the place hit him as he walked into the basketball court and understood. They were getting out for air. The place was stifling. A crappy song by Celine Dion played loudly. It hurt his teeth.

No sooner had he walked onto the hardwood floor than the speakers let out an ear-piercing squeal. It lasted longer than it should have. Everyone stopped dancing and covered their ears. Josh did the same, but kept scanning the dark room for Jessica by the flashing and pulsating lights from the DJ booth. As his teeth began to grind to counteract the sound, the speakers exploded. People screamed, but the noise stopped.

Next the fancy lights on the DJ booth flared brightly and exploded into a shower of sparks. The overhead lights did the same, and sparks showered down. Crepe paper hanging from the rafters caught fire. More people screamed and started to press toward the door. Josh became trapped in the tide of people pushing him back toward the door. From the front of the group, a girl screamed.

The crush of bodies changed directions. He was pushed farther into the room. The crepe paper fell from the ceiling in flaming streamers. The place was dark except for the emergency lights on the exit signs. The fire alarms hadn't gone off. Someone would have disabled them since they planned on smoking in the place.

The crowd shifted again back toward the main exit, only to shift the other direction. It was if the crowd was a ping pong ball. He finally got a look in the direction of the main exit. The ghost of Sue Browning had hold of one of the boys. She strangled him with her ghostly hands. Josh stood on tiptoes to look the other way. Two ghosts cut through the crowd.

"Where are you, Jessica?" he yelled, straining his voice until it hurt.

"Over here." The voice came from everywhere.

"This is between us," he said in his regular voice, knowing she could hear it.

"No, it's not. It's between us and this town," she said from above him.

Josh looked up. She stood on the rafters. Jessica clapped her hands together. Lightning ripped through the air, and thunder followed. More people screamed. They all hit the floor covering their heads, except for Josh.

"Very brave!" She clapped her hands again.

The overhead lights flickered on despite being blown out. The group of students started to look around in the light. Six ghosts made their ways through the room, killing people at random. The ghost of Debbie Eva wrapped her arms around Lee Tidwell's neck. His classmate's face turned red, then violet. After a much shorter time than strangulation should have taken, the boy's tongue fell out of this mouth, and the ghost moved on. A male ghost tore through the crowd. Nikki Hopeman's arm ripped from her body as the ghost passed. The blood spewed into the overly hot gymnasium. What the ghosts did to the drum major, Shannon Lolley, almost made Josh vomit. He couldn't watch any more.

"Come and get me," Josh yelled at Jessica.

He ran to the door, stepping on people as he went. This slowed him down as he approached the ghost of Sue Browning. She pirouetted on her roller skates and waited for him. A burning coal of evil burned in her eyes. His hand dove into his pocket. He scooped out some sage and tossed it at her as she passed by. The ghost disappeared.

Josh ran into the night air. He stopped once he was in the parking lot. Students screamed from inside as the ghosts continued their carnage. He looked around for Harvey, and found him slumped on the ground, his head facing away at an impossible angle. Neal Otis stood over him.

"Hello, Josh," Otis said.

"What did you do?" Josh asked.

"What had to be done. Now I'm going to do the same to you."

"Why?"

"Your granddaddy killed me, just like he did the others."

"I'm not him," Josh said.

"Don't matter. She said all must pay."

Otis swept toward him with speed faster than he'd used on the football field. Josh tossed a bit of sage at him. The ghost of his friend vanished in a swirl of glowing smoke. He inhaled a long breath to calm his nerves after everything he'd seen so far. Josh understood in that brief moment why Charlotte had gone crazy. No one could come out of seeing their friends slaughtered without some kind of damage.

The front doors blew open. They ripped from their hinges and hit the ground well behind Josh. Jessica walked out dragging Marcus Smithson by the hair. She laughed as she pulled him to his feet.

"Here's the boy that roughed you up," she said, and drew her fingernail across his throat.

Blood spewed out into the street lamp's light. She dropped Marcus to the ground and looked at Harvey. Another wicked smile came over her face. Josh's stomach flipped. He wanted to vomit, but he had to draw her down the hill. His dad waited with his hunting rifle. Alan could pick her off at the top of the hill. He needed her to be in the clear.

"Why?" Josh asked. "I thought you liked me."

"I wanted you to think that. It's all about revenge. I did the same with your grandfather forty years ago when I was Connie Dearborn, and eighty years ago when I was a mulatto preacher, toward an ancestor you didn't know you even had. The point isn't to kill everyone in this town. It's to make the McAdams family suffer. What's worse than betrayal by a lover?

"I hope you prove an easier kill than your granddaddy," Jessica went on. "I had to wait a long time to get him back, forty years to the day."

"I hope I'm not." Josh ran toward the exit of the parking lot.

Before he made it very many steps, Jessica appeared in his path. She grabbed him by the shirt. The look in her eyes was the evilest thing Josh had ever seen. It was like something out of his worst nightmare.

"Oh, you are," she said.

"Let my classmates in the gym go," he said. "They're innocent."

"No one in this town is innocent. Every single person here is connected. They all had something to do with my death. This town will pay for its past with the death of its future."

Josh tried to get free from her grip but couldn't. There was no way his father could see them from that point. She kept talking, but he wasn't listening. All he could do was find a way to get her to the edge of that hill. There was no other option except action. He wrapped his arms around her and pushed forward. They fell backward with him on top. Jessica began to wrestle back. Josh tried to direct their roll down toward the street. Rocks gouged and poked him in the back and knees. Jessica did the same thing to his face. A good poke at his sore eye forced him to let her go.

They stood and squared off. Josh looked behind him. They were not close enough. Apparently, the scuffle did enough of the trick for the students to get free of the gym. They stampeded into the parking lot, but stopped, staring at him and Jessica.

She looked back. "No problem. I'll finish you off and deal with the rest of them."

Jessica clapped her hands. The ghosts from the gym swirled out of the air like a glowing whirlwind. Another ghost formed beside her. It was of a young black man. It was Tobias Abernathy.

"Get him," Jessica said.

Josh dug into his pockets and brought out two handfuls of the sage. As the ghosts came for him, he tossed it at them. They all disappeared, except for Tobias. Josh went into his pockets for more of the herb. They were empty.

"Finish him, Tobias," she said.

A car horn blew from behind Josh, and headlights illuminated everything, washing out the ghost. Josh stepped aside as a blue hatchback stopped at the entrance of the parking lot. The passenger side door opened. Charlotte clambered out. She wore pajamas and had a manic look in her eyes.

"Thank you, Amanda, dear," she said into the car and closed the door. "Such a nice girl."

The car backed down the hill. Tobias reappeared out of the fading light, as did the other ghosts, the limited magic of the sage having worn off. Jessica stepped up toward Charlotte.

"What are you doing here?" she asked.

"I had to stop you," Charlotte said. "I had to stop this. I didn't do the right thing a long time ago. I need to do it now."

"How did you get here?" Jessica demanded. "I made sure they had you so doped up you couldn't walk."

Charlotte fidgeted a little. "I cheeked the meds and sneaked out during a freak hospital-wide code blue. I wonder how that happened?" She smiled at Jessica. "Lots of people will pick up an old lady in pajamas."

"It doesn't matter," Jessica said. "Kill them both."

Tobias and the other ghost swooped in on Josh. He threw up his hands to fend off the ghosts. Charlotte ran through the apparitions, positioning herself in front of her nephew.

"Stop it," she said. "Listen to me. I was your friend. My nephew isn't the one to go after. It was my brother who killed you. The only reason he did that was because of her. She broke his heart. My brother couldn't bear a woman having that much power over him."

"I tried to warn you," Tobias said. "You didn't help me."

"I couldn't," she said. "I wanted to, and it broke my heart more than it already was when I became aware of what my brother did to you. If Connie hadn't broken up with my brother, no matter how much he hated you, he'd never have plotted to kill you all. She's the problem. Believe me, Tobias. I never did anything to hurt you on purpose. I only tried to help. I loved you."

Josh watched the face of the ghost change. The hard hatred aimed toward him went away. Before his eyes, all the ghosts led by Tobias turned on Jessica. She screamed curses and orders at them. Nothing helped. They grabbed her. Bits of her flesh flew through the air as they shredded her skin. Josh vomited at the sight. When they had finished, he watched the spirit of Hazel rise up from the dismembered body. The ghosts circled it and joined with it in a swirl of green light. Jessica screamed as the whirling became tighter until they all disappeared into nothing.

"Is it over?" Charlotte asked.

Wisps of white fog came up from the ground and formed the ghost of Tobias. Josh clinched his gut waiting to watch his aunt meet the same fate as Jessica.

"It's over," Tobias said. "I have and will always love you, Charlotte McAdams."

Alan looked at the green water of the Gulf of Mexico as it washed onto the beach at Dauphin Island. Thomas and Alan played football on the hard-packed sand right at the edge of the water. They wore their shoes and sweaters with shorts. It was too cold to be on the beach, and they were the only ones there. Stupid things like the cold keeping you from having fun didn't matter anymore. He hated his new job working for Alabama Power, but his family had needed to get out of Pinehurst. The boys seemed to be okay with the move. Thomas had transferred to Murphy High School. He didn't care much for football after everything that happened. Josh had dropped out with Alan's consent. He'd passed his GED without any trouble and was taking classes at the local community college waiting for the summer semester to start at the University of South Alabama. He planned to study psychology, to his Aunt Charlotte's relief, not to be a shrink, but a paranormal expert.

Alan didn't like the idea of that, but why not? Maybe he could become a real life ghostbuster now that ghosts were real and not myths.

"Come on, Dad," Thomas yelled at him, motioning for him to join. "Josh is getting his butt whooped. He needs all the help he can get."

Alan smiled and trotted off to play touch football with his sons. They had turned out to be okay kids, and he'd turned out to be an okay dad.

About the Author

Vic Kerry lives in Alabama with his wife, four dogs, and two cats. Although he wishes writing could be his full time job, he works in the scariest place possible—junior high school—as a 7th and 8th grade Language Arts Teacher. Prior to that, he spent over a decade working as a psychotherapist on an inpatient psychiatric unit. He has published three other novels, a novella, and a short story collection. Follow him on Facebook, Twitter, and Instagram.

Curious about other Crossroad Press books?
Stop by our site:
http://store.crossroadpress.com
We offer quality writing
in digital, audio, and print formats.

CPSIA information can be obtained
at www.ICGtesting.com
Printed in the USA
LVHW011652300820
664591LV00003B/385